KILLARNEY
LAKE MASSACRE

PREVIOUS BOOKS BY THE SAME AUTHOR

Weird Crime Theater (with Mulele Jarvis)
Tanuja Ramachandran: Hunter-Seeker

KILLARNEY LAKE MASSACRE

Kumar Sivasubramanian

Copyright © 2026 by Kumar Sivasubramanian

All rights reserved. No part of this publication may be reproduced, stored or transmitted in any form or by any means, electronic, mechanical, photocopying, recording, scanning, or otherwise without written permission from the publisher. It is illegal to copy this book, post it to a website, or distribute it by any other means without permission.

Kumar Sivasubramanian asserts the moral right to be identified as the author of this work.

This novel is entirely a work of fiction. The names, characters and incidents portrayed in it are the work of the author's imagination. Any resemblance to actual persons, living or dead, events or localities is entirely coincidental. If you believe any of the incidents portrayed in this novel actually happened, please seek professional help immediately.

This book was written in accordance with the tenets of the Butlerian Jihad.

Cover art by Marc Schoenbach (https://sadistartdesigns.com/)
Proofreading by Danielle Sundby (https://daniellesundby.com/)

First edition
ISBN 978-0-9925831-4-9 (Paperback)
ISBN 978-0-9925831-5-6 (eBook)

For more information please visit KumarBooks.com

This book is dedicated to the memories of
Pakkirisamy "Siva" Sivasubramanian
and Ilango Sivasubramanian.

Some foolish men declare that a Creator made the world. The doctrine that the world was created is ill-advised and should be rejected. If God created the world, where was He before creation? ... How could God have made the world without any raw material? If you say He made this first, and then the world, you are faced with an endless regression... Know that the world is uncreated, as time itself is, without beginning and end.
—Jinasena, *The Mahapurana* ("*The Great Legend*") (ninth century)

While [Werner Heisenberg] was working on quantum theory, he went to India to lecture, and he was a guest of [Rabindranath] Tagore. He talked a lot with Tagore about Indian philosophy. Heisenberg told me that these talks had helped him a lot with his work in physics, because they showed him that all these new ideas in quantum theory were in fact not all that crazy. He realized there was, in fact, a whole culture that subscribed to very similar ideas.
—Fritjof Capra in *The Holographic Paradigm and Other Paradoxes* (1982)

How do you know that the earth isn't some other planet's hell?
—Aldous Huxley, *Point Counter Point* (1928)

Chapter 1
1990

Sally Pencilneck slammed Rick's dick in a car door, exploding it in a tsunami of gore that splattered his face and hair in a bog-thick vomit of minced-meat cock and balls. He had run out to his car from the cabin hoping to make his escape from her, exposed wiener flapping back and forth like a panicked theatergoer looking for the exits in a cinema fire, when there she was in front of him, as she always seemed to be, a hellish apparition silhouetted against the moon-glazed trees. The dick-door detonation transpired before he could even understand what was happening. Covered in his own mince, Rick wailed and wept with his entire being; the physical pain, the shame, the crushing fear of death wracking his shoulders with seismic shudders. Some corner of his persona was still present enough to suggest that he should make an excuse for his behavior, beg for forgiveness. But his conscious mind had no room for such sanity in that moment. And, anyway, in the next instant, Sally bashed him in the head with her nunchaku as many times as Elizabeth Taylor had been married, and his skull caved in like it was papier-mâché.

The best *rational* guess anyone could make about Sally was that she was some kind of a twenty-year-old survivalist, race indeterminate, with the mind of a mentally deficient eight-year-old that would pull the wings off flies. She wore a necklace of desiccated wangs, had colored pencils jabbed clear through her neck, and her face was obscured by a novelty Groucho mask with the moustache and hypno eyes, one of which was shattered and revealed an inhuman bloodshot eye behind it. And she seemed to be so fast she could just *appear* anywhere.

Rick was the sixth member of the group that Sally had annihilated that night. Dave was the first. They'd found him with his dong tied to the blade of a ceiling fan and his body doing slow, perfect circles-within-circles overhead, like amusement park teacups, until the weight and twisting became too much and his body ripped free of his cock like it was a frayed rope, and he hit the ground with a blood-curdling thud. Mike, on the other hand, had been shoved onto the pyramid-shaped World War I memorial sculpture with the point up his anus, just like the Spanish Inquisition's "Judas Chair" – a torture device that only Christians and, apparently, also Sally Pencilneck could have come up with.

Jeff Gold: stick of dynamite up his pee hole.

At first it seemed like Sally was only going after the men. Indeed, at the beginning of the evening, when Sally was still just a campfire story, they had all joked that since Sally only killed men while they were jerking off, and she could seemingly sense perverse thoughts too, the women were all safe. No: three hours later Sally had gored Megan White through the belly with an elk antler (the stump of the elk's neck still dripping blood), and nunchacked her arms off.

June Summers: railway spike through the top of the head, hammered in to the tune of Verdi's "Anvil Chorus".

Two police squad cars had shown up. Sally had the presence of mind to wait for one of the cops to radio back the all-clear ("kids pulling a prank") before she pulled off all four of their heads, spiked one onto each hubcap of one of the cars, then drove it around honking the horn for five minutes. If Sally really did die when she was eight years old like the stories said, then who had taught her to drive, one begged to ask.

Betty and Grant were alive though. Betty had run out of the cabin to stop Rick, but was too late, had seen the dick explosion, buried it in the back of her mind without processing it along with all the other horrors of the evening, and turned around and ran back into the cabin. Grant was standing there in the entryway, where he too had been about to step outside.

"What –" he started to say, but Betty's arm bolted up to his mouth, and she clasped her hand over it. She held a flashlight in her other.

"Rick's dead," she said, her voice quivering. His eyes widened. They could already hear the clink of the nunchaku chains in the distance but getting nearer to the cabin, stomp by stomp. "Grab your backpack. Out the back door," she ordered, and didn't remove her hand from his mouth until he nodded.

She slammed open the back screen door, oblivious to the noise, and they flew down the steps and down the slope into the woods.

Now it was the sea of trees, bare branches and cold bark, the crunch of leaves underfoot, forest creatures. The endless croaking of frogs. In a sense, like the animals around them, Betty and Grant were living according to a kind of law of nature now too. Sally was the hunter, and they were the prey. Nothing about Sally Pencilneck was natural though. And if it was true that she could sense thoughts… Betty let go of Grant's hand… just in case. She didn't know how little or how much it would take to make a man's mind wander, or how weird those wanderings would get. You never really knew a person. Better safe than sorry.

"Where are we going?" Grant begged.

"Shh! I don't know. Away, far away," Betty hissed as they descended the slope in short, controlled skids, making pathetic grabs at the bare tree branches as they went past them.

"Look, I realize we need to keep quiet," he said, "but I need to say stuff."

He was 6'2". Betty expected him to be braver, although, in a sense, he was brave. He wasn't having a meltdown. It was his form of bravery. He was straining against his limits though. He needed to talk it out to stay sane. She could hear that in his voice. It annoyed her that she felt like she had to be responsible for him though. She'd only just met him. It was a stupid set up, a blind date for the party at the cabin, her friends just naively assuming that they would get along based on shared ethnicity. Yet within minutes of talking together he criticized her for liking Pink Floyd, which he called "white people music". This dumbass had never heard of Sister Rosetta Tharpe or even Little Richard or even Jimi Hendrix. After that, she was put off him the rest of the night and the rest of her life as far as she was concerned, though he seemed to not have noticed. There were hardly any other Blacks at Fredericton High School, but if it was going to be like this, it was no wonder she hadn't dated the others. Grant had Scottie Pippen's haircut, plus lightning bolts on the side. She hated that too.

"Like what kind of stuff?" she said, permitting him to speak.

"Like, we should call the cops again." His voice trailed off as he said it. Maybe the cops would come again, but the cops would not save them. They had to save themselves. "Like, why'd that freak kill Megan and June? I thought she only killed men."

"How the fuck should I know?" Betty snarled. She wondered if this thought had come to Grant entirely by chance.

Trying to untangle why she had agreed to this weekend would be an indulgent mental distraction right now — a relief, but possibly also a careless invitation to death. When she saw that the video June had chosen from the Blockbuster new release shelf was *House Party* with Kid 'n Play, she knew coming to the party was a mistake. June must have been trying to impress Grant with her choice of video. It was a whole lot of drama for nothing.

No. Not nothing. The payoff was six dead. June had figured goddamn Kid 'n Play on the TV and some strangely timed and inappropriate sexy dancing around the room would turn Grant on. But it had actually set Dave off, who disappeared upstairs and was next seen hanging from the ceiling fan.

In any case, Betty didn't figure Grant for the altruistic type. She suspected that Grant wasn't concerned that Sally would kill her. Rather, it occurred to her that perhaps he felt he might have a better chance of survival since he was no longer the only target between them.

They walked without speaking for a while, their footfalls cacophonous in the dry leaves. Sally's nunchaku could not be heard.

Betty came to a sudden stop. There was a hill of rock ahead of them, and her flashlight had found a possible opening on one side into a cave a few meters up off the ground, in the rock face. From where they stood the opening had the illusion of being a kind of black obelisk, but it was perhaps large enough for them to squeeze through. "Come on," she said, and they went around to its right side, where it was easier to climb up to the breach.

From this angle, the hole revealed its true dimensions: a maw into blackness just big enough to stoop through. Betty clambered up a few more steps and shone her light in. The sucking blackness divulged nothing. "Maybe we can hide inside," she said.

"But there might be animals," Grant muttered in a quivering voice.

She looked at him in near disgust, but she held her emotions in check. He had plunged into irrationality, but she couldn't really blame him. Betty wanted the privilege of freaking out too, but Grant had freaked first. One of them needed to stay sane or both would die. Somehow, through all the gore and madness, her mind had communicated that to her.

She ran the flashlight over the opening again, smelled the loamy odor emanating from the gap, then plunged in. She hoped Grant would follow her, but she didn't encourage him or wait for him. He looked back once, beads of sweat balanced on his temple like raindrops on a leaf, then followed after her.

Inside, the opening became a tunnel, sloping down below ground level. It was wide enough to walk comfortably through. The walls were clammy. Betty swung her flashlight back and forth. It revealed nothing. They were haunted by silence. And though the ground was naturally uneven, it was drier than the walls and somehow gave Betty the impression that it had been trodden on before. It wasn't too hard to walk on. She pressed on, Grant's breathing heavy behind her.

"I can't tell if this is better or worse than being out there," he tried to joke as he felt his way through the passage.

"Better," she answered. "We need to make a stand."

"What?" he said.

"Look."

There was a glow ahead. It was so faint, for a moment Betty wondered if she was hallucinating in the darkness. She turned off the flashlight. The light was still there. It was impossible to tell how far away it was.

"Oh, no," Grant said as he began to realize what Betty had suspected within moments of entering the tunnel.

They emerged into a natural chamber lit with oil lamps and candles and decorated with pieces of soiled Barbie dolls and My Little Ponies balanced on rocks and logs that were serving as benches and shelves. There was a Strawberry Shortcake LP sleeve, three quarters of a crumpled She-Ra Princess of Power poster, an empty, bashed up Slip 'N Slide box, a ping pong ball gun, and a tattered Rainbow Brite t-shirt hammered into one wall like a tapestry. Betty picked up a Jem and the Holograms sticker book, and something possessed her to flip through it. She imagined Sally must flip through it sometimes too. It was her entertainment in those long years between killing frenzies: looking at Jem stickers, brushing Astronaut Barbie's hair before putting her shattered space helmet back on. She found what looked like a diary. None of the writing was legible – it hardly even looked like words.

There was a burlap sack big enough to sleep on in one corner.

The smell was rank.

"Oh, shit!" Grant hissed. "What the fuck were you thinking? You want to hide in her goddamn house?!"

"It's the last place she'll look."

"The others! Everyone! They're all dead! We're the last ones! She's looking for us!"

"No, listen," Betty said, shaking her head. "We need to stop her. It's up to us. I don't think daylight's going to make any difference to her. We can't have her following us into town."

Grant screwed up his face. "Who gives a fuck about that? Let them call out the SWAT team! It's none of our business!"

"You think Fredericton has a SWAT team? Jesus! Listen to yourself. Look, I don't know if she's real or... unreal or what. But she's a physical thing. And she seems to have a... a mind of some sort. Like an animal. There must be some way to kill her, or at least cripple her, even if she does seem to beam-me-up all over the place like Star Wars."

"Star Trek."

"Whatever! We're safe for a minute here as long as you... keep your thoughts clean," she said looking up at him.

Grant nodded, willing himself to understand and comply.

"Now tell me exactly what Jeff said when you were

sitting around the fire. I wasn't there. I need you to tell me everything."

"He... he said Mike was a dick for not bringing the keg like he said he would..."

"I mean about Sally! What did he say about Sally?! For fuck's sake, Grant! Get a grip!"

"O–okay, right. About Sally... Just, just let me think for a second..."

"We might not have a second, Grant! Come on!"

"Okay, okay! He, uh, he said she was eight years old, and her thing was... was cake, or... No! It was chocolate chip cookies." The story was starting to come back to Grant in detail now as he began to recite it. He tried to tell it all in the same order Jeff had. "She had certain habits. Always coloring. And her dad used to always give her cookies for dessert after dinner. And she was upset 'cause she wanted a treat and hadn't had one for days, being at camp and all. And the dude that was responsible for the kids in her cabin, he told her there was cookies in the camp kitchen, in a Dumbo cookie jar, and she ought to go over there and ask someone to get it down for her, 'cause it was up on a high shelf. Jesus," said Grant, interrupting himself, "*he* must'a been trying to get rid of her too..."

"This was Jeff's campfire ghost story?! Chocolate chips and Dumbo cookie jars? How fucking long does this go on for?!"

Grant continued. "So she went into the camp kitchen, but there was nobody there. See, according to

Jeff, the camp counselors was all dudes. And once the kids were in bed, they'd gotten into this habit… this habit of…"

Betty thought Grant was having trouble remembering what happened next, but as he continued to hesitate she saw from the way he pressed his lips together that the problem was that he was actually embarrassed. "Just say it!" she barked.

"Well, they'd… they'd go into the woods to jerk off. They just couldn't help it. Like they'd gotten into a kind of rhythm. That's how Jeff put it. You know?"

She didn't know, but she let him continue. For a second, she thought about how stupid the lightning bolts shaved into his hair looked right now.

"So she goes into the kitchen. She's got her little can of colored pencils with her still, 'cause she's eight… she never thinks to put 'em down somewhere while she's busy doing another thing. So she sees the Dumbo jar up on a high shelf, just like the counselor said, only there's no one around, so she sets down the can of pencils and starts climbing up. Up onto the counter top, then up onto one shelf, then another. Finally she can almost just reach, but it's too high, too high, and she loses her balance and goes flying backwards off the shelves right onto the can of pencils." Grant hesitated. Hearing it as a bullshit campfire ghost story was one thing. Repeating it in a cave surrounded by broken dolls and candles and the smell of piss and shit was another. And after they had actually seen her and the pencils in her neck.

"And she's dead," he said, remembering seeing her walking around "alive". Grant's voice was on permanent quiver, but he continued Jeff's story as best he could. "Was it the crack on the head? Was it the pencils in her neck? We don't know. But three years later, she came back for the first time, and anytime dudes was jerking off in the woods, or even *thinking* stuff, she, she…" He ran his index finger along his neck, miming a naively merciful manner in which Sally might kill a masturbator. "And maybe three years later wasn't the first time even. Lots of suspicious deaths around here."

Betty didn't know if those final statements were part of Jeff's original story, or if it was Grant regaining enough calm to speculate about it himself, but all she said was: "They buried her with the pencils in her neck?" As soon as the words came out of her mouth, she realized what a dumb detail it was to fixate on.

"June asked the same thing," Grant said. "Jeff said her daddy came and took the body. Nobody knows after that."

"She died, but then still grew up? None of this makes any sense…" Betty realized she was still going down the wrong alleys of the story, and they dropped into silence again. Betty replayed the story in her mind. Grant's chest rose and fell with the effort to keep himself calm. The candlelight reflected off the runnels of sweat travelling along his jawline. Her eyes scanned the chamber again, desperate for clues that could help them.

The heart of the thing was the betrayal Sally had suffered. The grown-ups (teenagers actually) were supposed to be looking after her, but they'd failed because their primary concern was jerking off in the woods, and she'd died horrifically as a result. But – beyond revenge on perverts – what did Sally want, if anything…?

Grant's gaze was darting around the shadowy nooks and crannies of the cave's ceiling. Betty read a strange look of remorse in his sad eyes and parted lips. His Adam's apple bobbed like a piston.

There was a distant tinkling sound from down the passageway. Metallic. The worst sound possible. Grant flinched at it.

"What the fuck did you do?" Betty growled. "I told you to keep your thoughts clean!"

"I did! I did!" he protested. Tears were coming down now. "I tried to think of just trees and animals and things, like all the birds and stuff we heard in the woods coming down to this hellhole… this hellhole *you* led us into! And I thought about the chickadees and wondered… wondered why they called them titmice. I mean, 'tits' and 'mice'… 'tits'… And then I got to thinking about the beavers around here too, and…"

His voice weakened to a mumble, but he didn't need to say any more. Now she was picturing hairy bushes too.

They heard the clink again, closer.

Betty's brain went into overdrive. "What's in your backpack?" she said. "Any food?"

He swung the bag off his shoulders, his hands shaking. "Maybe. I got some protein bars." He yanked the bag open.

"No! Something an eight-year-old would like!"

"Chips?"

Before he could get them out, a spear shot through him with such inhuman precision that it went in at the base of his spine and came out in a straight line through his penis, so his cock popped out of his pants and split open into petals like a red flower. Then Sally arched the spear up and slammed the point vertically into the ground. Grant, halfway up its length, began the slow grinding slide down the shaft with every sobbing groan, wail, moan, and scream his throat could muster. When he finally hit the ground, splayed-dick first, he was dead.

Sally, who had been watching the slow descent without any emotion, now turned her Groucho mask face to Betty. The pencils in her neck squirmed like trapped worms as she breathed, that hissy asthmatic way she exhaled. She took a step towards Betty.

Betty pointed an index finger at her like an angry mother. "Sally! Stop right there!" she said.

Sally actually stopped.

The contents of Grant's backpack were scattered all over the dirty ground. Betty snatched up the bag of chips he'd mentioned. Ketchup flavor. "You've been a bad girl," Betty said, "but if you're good, Sally, you can have these chips, okay?"

The chips were nunchacked out of her hands.

Betty stumbled, scrambled, and found a chocolate bar.

"How about this? It's a Pal-O-Mine. Even better than chocolate chip cookies, Sally. Even better. That's what you want, isn't it? A treat? A sweet treat?"

Sally froze again. She cocked her head to one side like a curious animal. The hypno eyes of the Groucho mask revealed nothing.

Betty lowered her voice. "Come on, Sally. Daddy says have your dessert, then go to bed." She held out the chocolate bar with trembling fingers.

Sally hesitated. Her body language, inhuman as it was, indicated confusion.

Then something strange happened. Something even weirder than everything else that had happened tonight, and something which convinced Betty that she had tipped over into madness. As Sally became more confused, Betty could swear that she saw the slasher "glitching". In brief, repeated flashes, Sally appeared not as a humanoid, but as stacks of varying two-dimensional geometric shapes, flickering and flipping over along multiple axis lines, undulating, folding, and unfolding into impossible fractal new forms blazing with kaleidoscopic colors. Gazing into these colors Betty sometimes saw Sally's internal organs, sometimes the cave wall behind her, sometimes… stars? And something like a landscape: a vast, gray tundra, sparsely populated by dead trees with noose-necked corpses hanging from their branches. The trees seemed fleshy and cancer-ridden.

Finally these otherworldly, unfixed shapes and visions that composed Sally in some way took the proffered candy bar, and the psychedelic visions ceased as abruptly as they'd started. Gingerly she opened the crinkly wrapper and turned her back to Betty to bite into it.

Betty put the weird vision she'd just seen out of her mind. She needed to focus and survive. She used the moment to cast her eyes around the cave again.

And then she saw it.

A lawn dart, obstructed from view behind a vintage Barbie motor home and some tree roots. She double-checked that Sally still had her back turned, then snatched the dart up and held it behind her back.

Sally spun at the noise, but continued chewing, chocolate now smeared around her lips. She stared at Betty through the plastic hypno eyes as she ate, then actually handed the wrapper to her when she was finished. Betty accepted it with her free hand, the hand holding the dart still behind her back. She shoved the wrapper into a pocket in her jeans.

"Okay," she said. "Good girl. Time for bed now, Sally." She pointed at the makeshift bedding in the dirt.

Again, Sally's body language said she was unconvinced, but she started to make her way towards the burlap sack.

In the back of her mind, Betty wondered if Sally took off her Groucho glasses and cock necklace when she slept.

Sally's back was turned to Betty again. Betty had one chance. She needed to generate as much force as possible. Her whole torso heaved as she paced her breathing with deep inhalations. She saw Grant's body out of the corner of her eye, and she thought of him and his stupid beavers. A low growl came out of her, then built and built to a scream as she lunged at Sally's back with the lawn dart.

But Sally whirled on her. It was Betty's thought of beavers that tipped Sally off again. Her nunchaku came down on Betty's shoulder with a simultaneous whack and clink. The agony was blinding.

Betty fell onto her back but, despite the pain in her shoulder, managed to hold the dart firm and upright. When Sally swung her nunchaku down at her, Betty rolled into Sally's legs and tripped her so that she fell face first into the dirt.

Then she plunged the dart into the creature's back again and again, shredding her organs, the candlelight throwing the shadows of her flailing rampage in every direction. Everything Betty had held back to help Grant keep it together, that she had held back all night, she let out now in a blitzkrieg that generated so much force that she was once even able to penetrate the skull of this eight-year-old mind trapped in a twenty-year-old's body.

When Sally stopped moving, Betty staggered and

stumbled back through the tunnel and passed out with a crunch, face first into the natural bed of vermillion leaves outside. A squirrel or two came close, sniffed at the air around her, then skittered off. Three hours later, the police found her, unconscious but alive.

Chapter 2
2025

It was the worst of times, it was the worst of times, Nandini thought to herself as she looked at the toaster in the break room obediently doing its job, and she wondered, as she sometimes did before she had to go back to her desk, what would happen if she yanked it out of the wall and smashed it.

Over the past fifty or a hundred years, the world had faced an increasingly ceaseless barrage of information. Over the past thirty years in particular, this information had become a tidal wave delivered faster and faster in smaller and smaller parcels by screaming voices all demanding to be heard at equal volume even if it was junk, malicious, or completely fabricated. Somehow this was turning people's brains to mush and calcifying them at the same time. It demanded their constant attention, so much so that it became hard to find any hidden pockets of brain power which could imagine how any of this might change or be resisted. Recently, the information deluge had even started eating and regurgitating itself, sucking enough power and water out of the Earth to run entire cities.

As a result of all this, governments around the world had now been taken over by degenerates and cretins. The US, Brazil, India, the United Kingdom, and Israel, among many other nations, never mind China, North Korea, and Russia, had turned to a worship of corruption in their governments so their citizens could be free to be even more cruel to those who were already being punched down on every day, even if it meant the lives of the punchers themselves were only getting worse and worse. They felt free to finally be their true selves by denying others the right to live according to that same principle. The bigoted, the abusive, the avaricious, felt validated by these walking pus bag candidates, and there were so many millions of them that, along with the assistance of some bribery and fraud, the pus bags were elected to the highest offices in the world. What used to be scandalous was now celebrated. Except in rare instances, the leaders of these countries seemingly never died and never went to jail. They were all millionaires. They advertised themselves as being just like the common voter as they shat into solid gold toilet bowls. In the past year, Canada and Australia almost fell into this abyss as well, and narrowly avoided it, but Nandini could sense it was only a matter of time. In fact, maybe it was Toronto's racist, drunk-driving, crack-smoking, prostitute-soliciting mayor that was the trigger in the first place. In any case, the same anti-immigration, or xyz-phobic rallies were happening everywhere. Wars spilled across Europe and the Middle East.

Standing on the heads of these leaders were the billionaires. This had been the way for hundreds of years, even thousands, only now these systems and structures were being pushed to the absolute extreme. These billionaires had amounts of money that could never have been attained morally by any stretch of the imagination. One only became that rich through the dehumanization of others and the violation of the Earth. These were men who were so rich that their entire solution to the planet's impending doom was to fly away on space yachts with their pneumatic brides and no one else, like reverse Supermen, even leaving their kids behind because they decided they were the wrong gender or didn't think right. The media encouraged people to revere these idiots. Thanks to worldwide media conglomeration, there was a pervasive pressure in every country and culture to think the same way about all these things, to hate the same targets, to spite even the environment, to blow their own heads off. Meanwhile, David Suzuki, a voice of comfort and intelligence through decades, had declared that the war against climate change was lost. "It's too late." Meanwhile, every facet of life on Earth was being quantified and monetized. Logos and advertising were everywhere, inescapable and suffocating.

Nandini liked to believe that she was still able to think for herself, that being thirty-two years old and not twenty, she had somehow developed a genuine identity. And yet she was a doomscroller like everyone else. Seventy percent of the world's population carried a slot machine full of lights and sounds in their pockets, and they never stopped pulling the arm, dopamine flooding their brains with every finger flick. The thing that was supposed to connect everyone in the world was instead tribalizing them, shunting them onto narrow tracks, into silos, in order to maximize ad revenue, sometimes isolating them completely. She also believed the world could be fixed, all it would take was one generation that believed in human decency, but how could such a generation ever be brought about?

Her mother, Aruna, was sixty-one years old but seemed older, and didn't care or was oblivious to all of this. When Nandini seemed to be going into a panic, her mother would say that the world had survived worse before and it would again. Also, to Nandini's exasperation, she would say that it was "none of their business". Then she went back to reading her magazines full of vampire stories. When Nandini's parents had immigrated to Canada in the 1980s, telegram was still the most reliable way to communicate with India. Organizing a phone call could take days and required screaming into the receiver to be heard. To Aruna, Facebook and WhatsApp were miracles.

Nandini didn't always fantasize about throwing the toaster. Sometimes her mind wandered into strange places. If she put two pieces of toast on a black plate, in her head, she would rewrite Ezra Pound's "In a Station of the Metro":

KILLARNEY LAKE MASSACRE

The apparition of the toast on this plate:
Petals on a wet, black bough.

Of course, Pound was a self-proclaimed fascist, so maybe her mind hadn't wandered that far. At any rate, this was the extent to which she utilized her degree in English Literature and Poetry on a day-to-day basis.

When she was at her desk and looking at her screens, sometimes, in crazed moments brought on by tedium, she felt like she could see inside the lives of the cells. This went back to something her father had told her about when he was trying to explain dimensions to her. If truly two-dimensional creatures existed in a two-dimensional world, then their beings and their existence would only consist of forward and backward, left and right, the cardinal directions, a flat plane. There would be no existence of up and down, so the creatures would not have "top" sides or "bottom" sides, and when they came face-to-face with each other they would only encounter horizontal lines, lines they could travel around the circumference of. However, if their universe only appeared to be two-dimensional to them, and was actually three-dimensional, then if a three-dimensional being like herself entered their world, she would be able to see their internal organs because they didn't have a covering or even any existence in the "up" direction, but she did so she could look down into them. She imagined these spreadsheet cells were two-dimensional beings and she could see into their guts with her naked eye, as if they were clear, flat amoebas. To them, she would appear as a series of lines, in sections, as she moved through their plane. This part was harder to grasp, but her father had explained it so wonderfully (he had been a physics professor at the university), as a child, she always wished she could experience such a thing. Would those two-dimensional creatures go insane at the sight though, at the very idea of higher dimensions?

She weighed Ezra Pound against the possibility of entire other spatial dimensions. Why did she decide to do an arts degree majoring in poetry?

She had once toyed with the idea of going into physics. She was good at everything but not good enough in anything to get past the gatekeepers of excellence. After she did her degree, she moved clear across the country to Vancouver and worked in admin for a publisher for a year. It may have been smarter to move to Toronto where most of the publishers were, but it was obvious even to herself, though she wouldn't say it out loud, that she was trying to get as far away from her parents as possible. But the rents were brutal, her car was stolen, and finally she was fired, so the decision was made for her. She came home 5,500 kilometers to Fredericton with her tail between her legs. Temporarily, she told herself. But then her father died, eight years ago now, and there were no hiring publishers in Fredericton, and before she knew it she was in a community college learning to be a database administrator. If she lived in Toronto perhaps she could have started on a path in publishing again. But, no, her mother, Aruna, wanted to stay put here in Fredericton, a place she was used to, that was full of people she was used to, and Nandini wasn't going to deny her that, now more than ever. Aruna did not ask Nandini to stay, but Nandini took it as unspoken. And, in what must surely be a sign of the apocalypse, Aruna never asked when Nandini was going to get married. On the other hand, Aruna used to yell at her husband every day like they were in a 1950s sitcom: about his clothes, the way he ate, everything he said. He went gray early, and she demanded that he dye his hair. Nandini couldn't remember her ever having complimented him. In a moment of brutal cynicism, when he died, she thought Aruna would be relieved. The sobering part was that, in fact, she had seemed less stressed ever since. Still, with her father gone, Nandini felt she had no choice but to stay close to her mother, and to try to keep the widowed woman's life as safe and normal as possible.

Her job at CrossTec was a good one. It paid well, and she worked with nice people for the most part.

She hated it.

She had her YouTube channel where she did book reviews. It was a distraction at least, a measure of joy. She tried to convince herself that somehow she was applying the creativity she'd learned at university to it, even if barely anyone watched it. She was working on a secret project too. Still, in her mind she saw herself working here forever. It was stable, and her priority was making sure her mother's life was stable, and the two things were connected, she thought. As the years went on, it was starting to feel like it was her sole function in life. To quit her job would be to enter a world of unknowns.

The week before, she'd been reprimanded for telling someone in the breakroom that she liked the smell of cow shit. "It reminds me of the times I visited India back when I was a kid," she had said. At the time, Nandini wondered if she could parlay this nostalgic sentiment into a book of poetry, win a Governor General's literary award, get a university teaching position, and pass on her knowledge to future gullible generations. Her coworker laughed, but there was someone else in the room who had reported the "incident" to her superior, possibly because she was offended by shit, but more likely by India. This was the coworker that just straight up called her "Nadine". "It's pronounced NUN-dhi-knee," she told her one time and only one time.

But there was something else, not the rage-inducing fire of the outside world, not the job, but something inside her that tempted her at times to put her fingers *into* the toaster slot. There was a pain in her mind, invisible and nebulous, and not there for the obvious reasons. It had been there so long, she couldn't even remember when it started, but it was well before all the other things that had happened. To put her fingers into the toaster would be a pain that was real and that she could understand. She wondered if her father had had similar thoughts. That would explain so much, it would be a eureka moment.

But the idea of "seeing someone" or "getting help" was so taboo, would have so shamed her mother, that she told herself it was simply *l'appel du vide*, "the call of the void," like the temptation to stick one's hand into a spinning fan. She would never really do it on purpose and subject her mother to any more than she already had to deal with.

Not today. She made it back to her desk without harming herself or the toaster. There was a personal email notification on her phone. It was from Four-Square Publishing with the subject line "Re: Love's Descent". She knew what it was going to say, but she didn't open it. She allowed herself a quantum of hope, like it was a lottery scratch ticket. She would save it until she was home and could open it on her laptop in the privacy of her room.

***

On the way home, she stopped at Willy's Winer Diner, Fredericton's grungiest eatery, a business which boasted more 1- and 2-star Yelp reviews than any other restaurant in Atlantic Canada and yet had a constant stream of customers coming through its doors. She stopped there for a burger after work and before dinner once or twice a week. It was an unhealthy habit, maybe even an addiction, but she found it comforting. She had worked the grill there herself for a summer back when she was in high school.

One of the waitresses went up to the kitchen service window with an order slip and stuck it into the order rail. "Twelve double bacon cheeseburgers, six large fries, six cokes!" she called.

Even for Willy's, that was a lot. Nandini furrowed her brow and craned her neck to peer around the dining room. There was a booth at the back crammed with six men so big they looked like they'd had enough double bacon cheeseburgers to last a lifetime already. They were all wearing baseball caps low on their heads, sunglasses, and jackets with the collars up (despite the late summer heat). The ones that didn't have their backs to her had skin so greasy she could have wiped a grill with them. There was something about the way they sat: apparently incognito, but like they owned the place, the town, the world. Nandini guessed they must be out-of-towners, up from the States. Yet there was something familiar about them too. She couldn't put her finger on it.

But then something distracted her.

Willy's was off the highway, and, past the parking lot, was surrounded on three sides by a flat grassy field that bordered the woods on one side. Out of the corner of her eye, through one of the windows, Nandini spied a deer at the edge of the trees.

Observed and observer, a hundred meters away from each other, both froze. There was something so uncanny about it that Nandini almost felt compelled to even call out to a stranger to draw attention to it, but then the deer moved off into the foliage.

Behind where the deer had been was a human figure, a barely discernible silhouette in the shadows of the trees. Nandini was mesmerized by it. At this distance it was impossible to tell, but something about it suggested to Nandini that it was a woman. It too stood unmoving, angled so it was seemingly staring at the table of incognito men as well, right through the walls of the diner. Was she smoking? No. But there was a kind of haze, a mist… a black miasma around her visible even at this distance. Then the figure turned and was gone.

Maybe it wasn't a person after all, Nandini thought. *Maybe it was another animal.* She failed to think of an Ezra Pound poem to describe it.

Chapter 3
Yorgotha Sacrifices an Alpaca

Yorgotha Axegorer (real name Heather McMillan) showed up at the parking lot of the band's gig in the basement of St. Charbel Church with an alpaca in the back of the van. The animal was cramped and clopped its feet in aimless confusion among the amps, the instruments, and the other gear.

When the other two members of the band came out to the parking lot to help her unload the gear, they already had their full makeup on – almost kabuki-like stark, black abstract shapes over shocking white. St. Charbel's Hall, the basement of the church, was right in the middle of downtown Fredericton, and was the most important venue in the little city's alternative and underground music scenes. It was five bands for five dollars, and their band was on at seven o'clock. However, the venue's capacity was only about fifty people and there were of course no changing rooms. Nemesis Decapitator (real name Gaylord Regan, drums) and Judge Judy Executioner (Judy Wright, guitar) had to put on their makeup and get dressed in their leather and spikes in the kitchenette. And yet despite all the makeup, their expressions of disbelief at this South American beast were as clear as if someone had Instagram filtered "What The Fuck" over their faces with big dog tongues hanging out.

Seeing their gaping pie-holes, Yorgotha scoffed and hopped down out of the back of the van. Even without her six-inch platforms on, she was imposing. But with the boots and the rest of her persona seemingly grafted onto her, even Nemesis Decapitator – no small man himself despite being only nineteen years old – was forced to take an unconscious step back. Yorgotha got her phone out and actually took a picture of them, laughing through her nose again.

"I don't know where to start," Judy finally said, shaking her head. "What the fuck is this?"

"It's an alpaca. Obviously," Yorgotha answered.

Nemesis Decapitator was unable to take his eyes off it. "Where... Where did it come from?"

"I stole it," Yorgotha said. "From the Brigadoon Fiber Farm."

Nemesis and Judy looked at each other.

Judy addressed Yorgotha again. "So this is why you couldn't drive us here, why we had to take the bus. You were busy robbing animals from a farm."

"One animal," Yorgotha said. "A big one." And she reached up and stroked the fur on the creature's long neck. The alpaca recoiled a step at a jab from the spikes on Yorgotha's wristband. Yorgotha's smile was positively

Satanic under the black, white, and red makeup that covered her face all the way down to the bottom of her neck. Unlike the other two, her makeup was less geometric and was designed to look like her eyes had been gouged out.

"So… are you going to retire and start a farm now, like Terminator X?" Judy asked.

For Judy to know so much about a forty-year-old rap band like Public Enemy was tantamount to blasphemy in a band aspiring to emulate the purest of Norwegian Black Metal, but if Yorgotha had corrected Judy by pointing out that retired Public Enemy DJ Terminator X raised ostriches, the finger would point right back at her like a bolt of lightning.

"This alpaca," Yorgotha said, "is to be sacrificed."

Again, their makeup did nothing to hide their shock.

"You… you're going to kill it?" Nemesis Decapitator said, his voice trembling. "But why?"

"Because the raccoon I killed out in the woods by Killarney Lake last week did nothing! It was too small a sacrifice…"

Again, Nemesis and Judy didn't know where to begin with this, and again Judy was the first to pipe up. "You killed a raccoon?! What exactly were you *expecting* it to do?" she asked.

"I was expecting it to make Funereal Devastation the biggest band of all time!" Yorgotha hissed, shaking a fist at the universe.

"Okay… Why?"

"Why?! Because isn't that what we all want?!" Yorgotha cried, grabbing Judy by the shoulders and shaking her.

"No," Judy said. "I mean, why did you expect killing a raccoon to make us the biggest band of all time?"

Judy had meant the question to be a rhetorical one to highlight Yorgotha's stupidity, but Yorgotha grinned, and even her faux gouged-out eyes twinkled. "I'll show you," she said, climbing into the back of the van. The alpaca clopped back one step in fear.

She came out carrying a tome that looked as heavy and as frightening as her, only much, much older.

"Is that… Is that a special edition of Harry Potter?" Nemesis Enforcer asked, his face lighting up.

Yorgotha sneered in disgust. "Blasphemer! This," she said, imbuing each word with import as she hefted the book aloft, "is a grimoire, ancient and worn, left to me by my uncle in his will. He was an antique book dealer in Quebec City. He had books the French settlers had brought over from Europe and that had been in their families for hundreds of years. Maybe even longer. And this one, this book of spells, was sent to me when he died last month."

Judy had to admit to herself that it was worn, but it didn't seem that authentic. In fact, it looked more like a ledger than a "tome". "So you don't talk to your family, but you were close with your uncle?" Judy asked.

"Never heard of him before I got the book in the mail!"

Judy laughed. Nemesis Enforcer was dumbfounded.

"There was a letter from a lawyer with it!" Yorgotha spat.

"So why'd he send it to *you*?" Judy asked.

Yorgotha opened the book and took a step towards her, offering it to her. The page she opened it to was marked with a very fresh 3M Post-It Note. The text in the book was in an unrecognizable script. There was also a sheet of loose leaf between the pages, though, full of random words that must have been a phonetic transcription. Judy shook her head at Yorgotha.

"*He* put that there!" Yorgotha said, pointing at the Post-It note. "Do you know what that says?"

Nemesis craned his neck over Judy's shoulder. "*Exitium Lugubre*," he read aloud. "That means… 'lugubrious destruction.'" Nemesis Decapitator was taking Latin as an elective as part of his Arts degree. Fredericton was full of his kind.

"Funereal Devastation!!" Yorgotha cried in triumph.

Judy felt the faint stirring of curiosity in her at this coincidence (at least that's what she told herself it was) but maintained her dismissive stance. "So you're telling me," she said, "that – according to what you told us when you joined this band – you've had no contact with your family for years, but your uncle the antiquities dealer in Quebec died, he decided to bequeath you this one thing, this one book, this supposed book of spells, and he knew about the band you were in, a band you've only been in for three months, and put a Post-It on a page which is titled with roughly the same name?"

Yorgotha grinned through all of this. As far as she was concerned, Judy was describing the stars coming into perfect alignment. But then Judy said, "How did he know our band name?"

"I thought of that!" Yorgotha said. She held up an index finger. "Our posters are up on telephone poles all over downtown with our faces on them. My... progenitors" (Yorgotha could not bring herself to say the word "parents") "could have seen those posters and told my uncle about them."

Judy considered this possibility. It couldn't be ruled out entirely, but the band's logo, which was completely illegible, looked like a pile of tightly packed burnt twigs and was deliberately so. She let it drop anyway. "But this book's not in French or anything European. Only the Post-It note is. Yorgotha, it doesn't add up!"

"How do you know it's not European?!"

Judy supposed that was true, but she was tired of all this preamble. She wanted to get to the heart of the thing. "And then I guess you... you caught a raccoon, and you took this book out to Killarney Lake, and you read it phonetically? And you killed the raccoon, but it didn't do anything."

"It didn't work because the raccoon wasn't big enough!"

"It didn't work because magic isn't real, you dipshit!"

Yorgotha was only listening to every other word now, but she spared Judy enough attention to snicker. She was up in the van attaching a chain and a collar – a chain and collar she had meant to use on herself on stage – to the animal. She hopped down, and then with some strained tugging, the alpaca clambered down out of the van and joined the band in the church parking lot.

"You say magic isn't real, but here is a grimoire with our band's very name in it, and it was marked out especially by my uncle – a man who must have *known things*. Ancient things. The spell lacked *ambition*. We need to *mean* it. I've rewritten the lyrics of 'Life Endurance Premiums' to match the words of the spell. During the drum solo, this animal dies on stage."

Nemesis Decapitator gasped in shock at both the threatened death of the animal *and* the interruption of his drum solo.

"I need to talk to Gaylord for a minute," Judy said, her voice smoky with anger. She grabbed his elbow to take him aside.

"No!" Yorgotha barked. "Whatever you need to say, you can say to my face!"

"All right," Judy said. "This is crazy. This is *fucking crazy*! You've only been in this band for three months –"

"This band has only existed for five months!"

"And I'll admit it, Corpsehurler was... difficult."

Corpsehurler was the band's previous and first bassist/vocalist. She had slept with both Nemesis Decapitator and Judy, and the band should have been finished right there, but somehow the guitarist and drummer had ganged up, kicked her out, and managed to hold it together. Until now anyway. "But you are way out of line, like all the time!"

"Like when?" Yorgotha answered with her arms crossed

"Like, where's the money you were supposed to pay us back from last week's gig? How come you still haven't apologized to the manager of Dolan's Pub? How come you only show up to every third practice? How come we haven't seen Gaylord's cat since the day after you joined?"

Yorgotha's body language had become defensive during this speech, but at the insinuation about the cat, she prickled. The veins stood out on her forehead, even through the makeup. Judy had seen these before, especially during the incident with the pub manager. She called them Yorgotha's "bellicose veins". "That had nothing to do with me!" Yorgotha growled. She walked right up to Judy, looming over her. "Here's a better question. How come I'm still in this band? How come you hired me in the first place when you knew you'd never see your money, I'd never apologize to anyone, I'd hardly show up to practice, and your cats would go missing? I'll tell you why," she went on, "because you want this to be the greatest band in the world too, and you knew the minute you met me, *I* was the one that was going to get you there. Now, are we here to noodle around in church basements, are we pretenders, or are we here *to live the life?*"

"I'm here to live the life," Judy said, her enhanced eyebrows a defiant V.

"You claim you believe magic isn't real," Yorgotha continued, "but I saw your face when you heard our band name in that book. You believe it, somewhere deep inside of you, and you believe in *the life*, and that's why you didn't break up over Corpsehurler, and that's why we're still here having this conversation. Now help me get this alpaca down into the bowels of that church."

There was no swelling inspirational music to accompany Yorgotha's speech, but Nemesis Decapitator took the chain from Yorgotha and began leading the animal into the venue. Judy looked at him, then at Yorgotha, and in her mind's eye could see this whole teetering tower of a relationship, this castle turret crumbling in a lightning storm, turning into a Corpsehurler situation again. She followed him anyway, and the three figures, looking like the long-decayed and flaking corpses of bats, descended, leading an alpaca into what they hoped would be an atmospheric simulation of hell through music if they played well enough.

There were two other bands on that night as well. Funereal Devastation was on second. When it was their turn, the staggering, likely drugged alpaca on stage behind the drums was a surprise to everyone in the audience. They played seven songs, all blackened dirges (tuned down as low as their instruments would allow) that melted into one long thirty-five-minute epic, a hobbling trek through a hellscape, an ash-dusted wasteland marked only by dead trees, undertaken by lost wanderers wearing only tatters over grey wounded flesh. Yorgotha had missed two-thirds of the practices, but she had written half the songs, and even Judy found herself hypnotized and transported by the performance. She was reminded of why she had hired Yorgotha in the first place and why Yorgotha was still in the band despite her unpredictability and failings. She really was living the life.

Finally it was time for "Life Endurance Premiums". The band journeyed through the intro, two verses and two choruses. Yorgotha sang from the tome in her direst Cookie Monster growl.

> *Etad-yonīni bhūtāni*
> *sarvāṇīty upadhāraya*
> *ahaṁ kṛtsnasya jagataḥ*
> *prabhavaḥ pralayas tathā!*

Then came the drum solo. As Nemesis Decapitator began to piston the double bass pedals, Yorgotha led the alpaca out to the front of the stage. The audience murmurs only augmented the drum line. Judy took deep breaths. Yorgotha held the book under one arm, and drew a kitchen knife with the other, brandishing it before the audience just as the drums swelled. She had timed the flourish with absolute precision. For a moment, Judy's admiration tempered her apprehension. The war drum tattoo intensified again with clashing disharmony. Yorgotha held the knife at the animal's neck and sneered. The audience assumed it was all a prank, some even laughed.

That is, until an RCMP Emergency Response Team burst through the door in full, clattering tactical gear. The audience, in possession of illegal substances, shocked by the guns, or both, scattered in all directions. Even Yorgotha Axegorei was stunned into silent immobility at these invaders, clad in more black and more menacing than the band themselves.

"There's the animal!" one of Fredericton's Finest cried.

The next thing Yorgotha knew, the grimoire had been snatched away from her, the handcuffs were on, and the alpaca was being led away. "I... I was only going to shear it," she pleaded, her eyebrows quivering under her ghoul makeup, "like Terminator X!"

The rest of the band was rounded up as well.

The officer that had taken the book flipped it open, and it naturally fell to the page Yorgotha had studied so often over the past many weeks. There was a Post-It note that read *Exitium Lugubre*. "What does this mean?" she asked Yorgotha just before they led her away.

"It means... your doom!" Yorgotha hissed, and then she was gone.

The officer still had no idea what that meant. The girl in panda makeup might talk under questioning, though actually the guy on the drums looked like the soft one. Or maybe someone at the station would know, or the university.

As they closed the rear doors of the police van on them out in the parking lot, Nemesis Decapitator hung his head, and Judy looked at Yorgotha with scorn. Yorgotha, meanwhile, looked longingly out the window at the alpaca. As the van pulled away, the camelid became smaller and smaller. She had almost cast the spell. All her plans ruined, Yorgotha thought, and when she was so close.

Only they hadn't been ruined. They had been a success of a sort, just not when Yorgotha thought. The spell had worked when Yorgotha had vivisected her sacrifice at Killarney Lake the week before. It had worked well enough.

Chapter 4
Aruna

Aruna Rajan could, and would, tell you about every vampire story that was serialized in *Anada Vikatan* magazine going back to the mid-seventies. In fact, she could show you all the illustrations too since her shelves were lined with all the issues.

She was not ignorant of the world, but she was happy to consider herself old-fashioned. Until she was seventeen, she lived in the kind of village that puffed up the chests of National Geographic photographers when they found them (by bus), and got some shots of the local girls in their plain green saris, standing in the dirt roads in front of goats and thatched roof homes with mud block walls and floors made with mud and cow-dung paste. Only a few houses in the village had a TV, not hers, but she went to the movies. (She liked those movies. There was no kissing in them, even to this day, only colorful songs instead. Not like the movies here. Disgusting movies.) She took the bus into town and had been on the train into the city. She had an idea what life was like outside the village. Soon enough she knew it for herself. She married Vikram when she was seventeen and he was twenty-three, moved from that tiny village outside Madras, and after a few years in Bombay, they moved to Canada for him to do his PhD. Eleven years later, after many trials, so many trials that she wondered how so much could happen in only eleven short years, came Nandini.

The marriage had been arranged. In 1982, that was perhaps beginning to change a little bit in the big cities, but not in the villages (even now), and Aruna couldn't do it any other way. She had never expected otherwise, despite having seen all the movies and read all the pulp magazines.

And, besides, the best thing in the pulps was not the melodramas but the vampire stories. These stories were from even before her time, and they weren't exactly vampires per se, but her mother had read them, and later in life after her mother passed away, Aruna had developed the habit of scouring the internet looking for back issues and getting them shipped all the way to Fredericton. She accepted that a component of this was about nostalgia and a memory of her mother, but in recent years her interest had intensified, and one time a particularly blunt acquaintance suggested that she had only really become interested in these kinds of stories after Vikram passed away, but this was so brazenly incorrect that it made her clench her teeth. The chronology couldn't be more wrong. It was plain as day.

Aruna avoided speaking to that person again if she could help it.

The magazines were well organized, but stacked two-deep on the shelves, which irritated her. She needed more shelves. She complained about this to everyone with a genuine scowl on her face. It wasn't just conversation. She asked her daughter to buy her some more shelves and help put them up, but she refused. Nandini found the books to be a waste of time. She thought they were "bad art". She could be an ingrate sometimes. Her own mother was of a generation that did not remember their children's birthdays or what time of day those children had been born. Aruna, on the other hand, did everything for her daughter. But the girl lacked filial piety. And so the shelves were double-packed, in her tidy living room, in a tidy house in the suburbs of Fredericton, this house that was too big for her now, a universe away from that village in South India. Here, life was still nothing like the movies, and sadly – though she would never admit it as such – nothing like the pulps either.

These vampires were not Draculas or post-modern Draculas. They were flesh-eaters birthed of Brahma's fury, or were temple prostitutes, sorcerers, or *vetala* (emaciated corpses with bat wings), demons that sought out pregnant females, *jigarkhwar* (a witch-vampire and thief of livers), or poor souls improperly buried and damned to seek revenge.

Sometimes, like now, after her shift at the library,

she would stand and peruse the shelves for a while, though her legs got so tired these days, especially if she'd been to curling as well. She would pull out a few issues at a time and flip through them before deciding which ones she would reread that night. In the back of her mind, she wondered if she'd been too hard on that woman who made the comment about Vikram's passing.

She heard the front door open around the corner and Nandini come in. "I'm home!" she called out.

"Hello, baby," Aruna called back.

Then Nandini came into the room and paused. She saw her mother perusing her shelves, and the look of disapproval on her face was obvious. The magazines were the lowest of the low as far as art went. She thought the pulp monster stories were completely imbecilic. As a kid she had watched reruns of *The Hilarious House of Frightenstein* every day after school, and that was some low-budget Canadian kids' show weirdness, but she valued even that more highly than her mother's trash taste. Her mother could be gullible too, as was her father. One time someone in one of their social media groups shared an obviously photoshopped picture of a three-headed cobra, and they believed it was real. Even her father, a university professor! It drove her crazy.

Still, she came over and hugged her mother, and tried to kiss her on the cheek, but her mother dodged her head this way and that, trying to avoid it.

"*Aiyo*! *Chee*!" Aruna cried. "Disgusting! You smell like a *vada* fresh from the frying pan! Did you go to that diner again?" She pinched Nandini's cheek somewhat meanly, like she was still eight.

"What's for dinner?"

"No dinner here. Put your clothes straight in the laundry. Go take a shower. We've got Dr. Jayakrishnan's retirement party at the temple tonight."

"I forgot all about that."

"You can't just squirm out of it," Aruna said. She swished her arm like a water snake, and her bangles jangled. "It's important. He's a good friend. To the whole community." Aruna herself sounded annoyed saying it though.

"I didn't want to squirm out of it. I wouldn't miss it." Nandini was already in the laundry. "Mother," she called.

"Mm?" Aruna had slipped on her glasses to look at an illustration of a gray-skinned fiend with fangs the size of tusks riding a tiger in the deepest jungle. This one always demanded her attention.

"I think you'll be interested in this. I stopped at the Westmoreland Books on the way home, and they had a poster in the window saying that writer, Katherine F. F. Jordan, was going to be there on Wednesday night. Book signing."

"Who's that?" Aruna said looking up from her book.

"I bought you one of her books!" Nandini poked

her head out of the laundry room. Her shoulders were bare.

"I don't know," Aruna answered looking over her glasses. "Just tell me!"

"I thought you liked it! It was about vampires."

"Ah! The one about the vampires that need to drink the blood of virgins but can't find them anymore because comic books are popular now, so the vampires starve. Why should I care about this! Rubbish!" She heard the sound of the washing machine coming on.

"Not your cup of tea, Mother. Not garish enough for you." Nandini sometimes tried to understand her mother's interest in that junk she read and engage in conversation with her about it. But it was from another world. Being in another language, Nandini couldn't even actually read it herself. She could only hear her mother try to describe them and then look down on them with cultural superiority and disdain. Rationally she knew she shouldn't care. And yet the magazines drove her crazy for some reason. She sewed it up tight inside her.

"Did you see any books of poetry on the shelves while you were in there? Any poetry by Indian ladies?" The sarcasm was as lethal as cyanide.

Nandini said nothing in response to this.

"Don't walk around in your underwear!" Aruna cried. Nandini had emerged with a fresh towel to take upstairs to the shower. "Did you remember to buy bananas?"

"Oh. Sorry. I forgot."

"*Chee*! I only asked you to do one thing! Why can't you do it? Wait. What's that on your arm?"

"I bumped it on a coffee pot." That was true. It was an accident.

Aruna looked at the burn sadly and sat Nandini down at the kitchen table with her first aid kit and treated it with tender care. This was another reason Nandini would never burn herself on purpose.

After Nandini's shower, it was revealed to her that she was obliged to massage her mother's aching feet before the older woman got dressed in her sari and jewelry. Nandini suggested this could have been done before her shower, or not at all if Aruna had spent less time standing up looking at her shelves after working at the library all day. This was met with a scrunched brow, lips jutted out in abhorrence at her disrespect, and a dismissive swoosh of the hand that meant: "Begone! But also stay and do your duty!"

Actually, though Aruna would not even admit it to herself, she was glad her daughter had defied her even in this small way. She hoped she was sticking up for herself at work too or she would end up working there forever. Disappointment – this was an emotion many an Indian parent felt towards their children. It was the fuel that kept them plodding along, like a wind-up sparking Godzilla toy. But pity, well, that was a different matter. That was an emotion Aruna felt for her daughter but didn't like experiencing. She suspected that Nandini really did want to skip the party tonight, and yet she deferred to her mother. She almost always deferred to her mother, something she had done since Vikram had passed away, and the only thing she could do to make life easier for her mother was to be a good girl and try to do what her mother wanted. But she failed so often! Like Aruna had failed her own mother by moving 13,000 kilometers away, forever. Aruna feared that Nandini had sublimated her personality and might become a non-entity. Parroted knowledge about poetry doesn't constitute a person. Although... would that make her *less* marriageable or more so? Who could tell these days? Better to be less marriageable anyway. Down the path to marriage came its own secret unhappiness...

As Nandini massaged her heels – dark, cracked skin like the hide of a Tamil vampire, Aruna thought – it occurred to her that if her husband was there with all these same feelings too, their combined strength would amplify them in a feedback loop. Such feelings of disappointment, coming from *both* parents, with no siblings to absorb any of the blast, would deluge Nandini like a tidal wave. In that sense it was better he was gone. Even Aruna could see that. Yet if he were there to massage her legs instead, she thought... what a relief that would be to Nandini.

But, of course, Aruna said none of these things. It was not in her nature. And that nature had imprinted onto her daughter, who, in her own silent way, was trying to ensure that if her mother was going to live out a lonesome widowhood, she would at least be as fulfilled as possible within it with her vampire stories, foot massages, and retirement parties.

***

It was slow going getting to the temple because there was a dead body in the road next to the woods. Aruna had complained loudly about the slow traffic until she found out the body was the reason.

The police had cordoned off the left lane, and it was clogged with emergency vehicles and swirling police lights. The cops were guiding cars through the other lane at a crawl.

As they pulled up to the scene in Nandini's Volvo, Aruna entreated her daughter to drive even slower than necessary. Nandini obeyed but snickered on seeing the veins on her mother's neck bulge as she strained it to get a good look out the driver's side window. These were bulging veins of glee, Nandini knew, despite her mother's glower.

They had arrived nice and early, it seemed. The body was still in the road, covered by a blanket. There was a car too, and a woman sitting in the road, with a blanket around her shoulders, being consoled by emergency workers. "Poor thing," Aruna said. "She must be in shock."

"The driver? What about the person under the blanket?!"

Aruna shook her head. "I don't think she's responsible."

"How do you know? Mother! You're right in my lap! How can I drive?!"

"I am your own mother! You can still drive!" Aruna cried, as if this made any logical sense. But she returned to her seat. A police officer waved them through, and Nandini started to accelerate, but then Aruna cried, "Hey! Hey! Roll down your window!"

Nandini saw what had caught her mother's attention and stopped the car and put the window down with a sigh.

"Michelle! Michelle Chow!" Aruna called out, waving at one of the police officers. She was right in Nandini's lap again and even had one hand on the window frame.

Michelle was confused for a moment, then saw who was calling her and came and leaned into the window. Her smile was polite.

"Hey, Nandini. Hello, Mrs. R."

"Hello, Michelle," Aruna said. "How are you? How's your mother? How come you haven't been around for *gulab jamun* in so long?"

Michelle raised her eyebrows. Nandini snuck her an apologetic look. Michelle hadn't been "around for *gulab jamun*" since she and Nandini were about seventeen. "My mother is fine. I'm keeping busy, as you can see."

"What happened, dear?"

"Now, Mrs. R, you know I can't tell you that."

"You know what I have right here in my purse?" Aruna pulled out a plastic take-out food container from her bag.

"Oh, for crying out loud, Mother!"

"*Mysore pak*. We're on our way to the temple. I was going to take it, but you have it, Michelle. I know how you used to love it…"

"Oh, jeez. Mrs. R, I really can't…"

Aruna attempted to make sad doe eyes at Michelle.

"There's not much to tell," Michelle said. "Adult male came stumbling out of the woods. Seemed to have been mauled by an animal. Driver managed to stop before hitting him, but he fell over dead in the road anyway."

"That's it?"

"Mother, she's a cop. She's not supposed to go around telling people the details of open cases. One-minute-old cases!"

"Trust me, Mrs. R. You don't want to know any more. It's far worse than anything in your magazines."

This statement made Aruna's eyes light up. Nandini sighed at the sight.

Aruna rattled the box of cube-shaped ghee sweets. "Go on! Take it!" Aruna insisted, reaching across Nandini.

Michelle pressed her lips together looking at the clear box. She deliberated for another second before she accepted it, looking around to check that nobody else saw her do it. "That's an extra three hours of cardio right there," she said, cradling the box. "Well," she said, "I suppose you're going to read about it in the paper tomorrow. Some creep from The Daily Gleaner was already lurking around a minute ago." She sighed. "How can I put this?" she wondered aloud, as she pondered how to deliver the lurid details to the mother of a friend. "Do you know who RevDev is?"

"Trust me, she doesn't know who RevDev is," Nandini said.

"Who's RevDev?"

"RevDev's this rapper from Toronto."

"I see."

"Well, he's got, like, three million followers on Instagram or something, and last week he posted that he believes in 'getting back to nature' and so he only, uh… 'pleasures himself' in the woods."

"Okay," Nandini said. "That's enough. Mother, do you really need to hear any more of this?"

Aruna was staring too intently at Michelle, seeking the rest of the story, to respond to her daughter.

"So," Michelle continued, "there's been a whole rash of men lately… in the woods. Long story short, our victim came out of the woods with no pants on and his junk all messed up before he fell over dead in the road. Probably a bear. Every few years it seems, some animal on the rampage. Bear or a lynx or something."

The two women in the car were wide-eyed at this. To Michelle, Aruna said, "Not a great way to go."

"No, Mrs. R. Not a great way to go."

"Are you satisfied now, Mother? Stirred up an appetite?"

Aruna glared at her daughter for her disrespectful sarcasm.

"Sounds just like Sally Pencilneck, though," Nandini said to Michelle. Michelle nodded back.

"Who's Sally Pencilneck?" Aruna asked.

"Never mind, Mother. It's nothing."

"You know, I heard a Sally story just a few weeks back," said Michelle. "My daughter came home from camp and told me her friend's cousin knew somebody that *let* Sally have her boyfriend, and then like a week later that person got some job she always wanted."

"I heard those stories too."

Michelle and Nandini chuckled. "Anyway. Thanks for the treats, Mrs. R," Michelle said as she backed away from the car.

After they drove off, there was a minute of silence before Aruna said, "How come she stopped coming around for treats and things?"

"I don't know, Mother. We just kind of stopped hanging out."

They drove in silence for another eight seconds.

"Did she get married?" Aruna asked, but the dissemblance in her voice was obvious.

Nandini wasn't going to play into it. "No," she said.

"Why not? Pretty girl."

"She's thirty-two."

"That's the same age as you."

Nandini sighed and shook her head.

"Is she... a gay?" Aruna's whole face contorted around the word.

Nandini kept her eyes on the road.

"I'm a modern woman, you know. I know all about these things. The Indian government made it all allowed in 2018. Gays can do as they please now. We have to do whatever they say." The speech was meant to prove Aruna's liberal attitude, but she sounded incensed through every word of it. In fact, unknown to Nandini, Aruna's brain was on the verge of short-circuiting as she tried to avoid any further speculation about why Michelle and her daughter had stopped "hanging out" and the train of thought that led down. "Why can't people just be normal!" she spat.

Nandini sometimes wondered what her mother thought about the *Hijra*, those gender non-conforming communities that had been documented and talked about in India for thousands of years. Aruna must have heard about them, but Nandini was sure her mother would deny any such thing existed. "Sadly, none of this information is relevant to me," Nandini said, but Aruna had almost forgotten what they were talking about.

"Who's Sally Pencilneck?"

"It's just a dumb kid thing, Mother. It's not the sort of topic I really feel like discussing with my mother."

"Kid thing?"

"When Michelle and I went camping in Girl Guides, they used to tell this story around the fire about some crazy screwed-up woman that lived in the woods and could read men's thoughts and then… messed them up." She remembered the rhyme: *If you see Sally Pencilneck, you had better run like heck!*

"Bad thoughts?"

"Uh huh."

"I see. An urban legend."

Nandini looked up in thought. "No. I'd say more like a ghost story."

Aruna sunk into thought for a few moments before she spoke again. "How come I never heard about this Sally Pencilneck business before?"

"'Cause you're not a ten-year-old Girl Guide."

"What an ugly business. Do you think she'll be okay?"

"Michelle? Oh, yeah. I wouldn't worry about her." Nandini looked over at her mother and saw, predictably, that the expression on her face was not so much one of concern for Michelle as it was one of suppressed excitement. She even had a hand over her mouth. "Besides," Nandini said, "she's packing heat."

After a moment, Aruna asked, "Did you know a *bootham* can grant wishes, like a genie?"

"Are you wishing you could get a picture of Sally for your Facebook group?"

Aruna frowned. "I'm just making conversation."

"I'm sorry. That was mean of me to say." Nandini

sighed. "I don't remember anything about them granting wishes. The thing I do remember from the stories I heard or read was that they were all really fat. They were kinda human but had ugly demon faces and crazy moustaches or braids."

"They can take all sorts of shapes. And they can go where they please. Actually," Aruna went on, "the Kuki people have many types of demons that can grant wishes. The Kashmiri ones too sometimes. Do you know the Kuki people? They're from the very, very northeast corner, near Bangladesh, Burma, that area."

She didn't say any more about it. This was the random way many conversations went with her mother.

Chapter 5
The French Horse-Butt Sniper

Aldous Chretien, the prime minister of Canada, hesitated for only a moment before pressing the button on his desk's intercom panel and leaning into it to say: "Christine, please send in the French horse-butt sniper."

Chretien was young, impossibly handsome, and heir to the political legacy of his father, Jean Chretien, who had served as prime minister from 1993 to 2003. In fact, that inheritance was a weight on his shoulders driving him into the ground with every step of his career. The pundits were constantly comparing him to his father, or saying he was too liberal, or not liberal enough, that he was a milquetoast unable to take decisive action on any issue. He'd tried to please everybody: he'd done black face, brown face, yellow face, and none of it had worked. In fact, if anything, it had all backfired.

His advisors had been warning him for years now that his career needed a landmark, something that would carve him into history, his own giant phallic monolith, like the CN Tower, metaphorically speaking. Without it, he had little chance of surviving the right-wing tsunami that now seemed to be clamoring in opposition at every election. However, after the phone call he'd just received, he knew that perhaps the moment was finally here. To prove himself, he'd have to think outside the box, to find a nonlinear solution to the crisis he'd been called about. And yet, knowing this, he wondered why he had hesitated before pressing the intercom button. Why had he made the sniper wait in the outer office at all? It poisoned his spirits to think that his detractors might be right. Nevertheless, he brushed his perfectly coiffed hair with his hands, then sat up straight in his chair with his hands clasped on the mahogany desk and waited for the door to open.

Aldous's secretary, Christine, opened the door and showed the sniper in. The sniper stood in silence as the door closed behind him with a quiet click. He wasn't at all what the PM had imagined a sniper would look like. The man was surprisingly… rotund. He looked like he was dressed for a day at the races circa 1982 in an angular jacket with shoulders padded for the apocalypse and the creases of his shorts (shorts!) ironed so sharp they could cut metal. He carried a helmet with a spike on top under one arm. Contrasting or complimenting the outfit (the PM couldn't say), his blonde hair was oddly shaggy. The man had a jocular smile. That made the prime minister hopeful, but he tried not to betray any emotion one way or the other.

"Claude Boudreau, I presume," he said. "Please sit down." He gestured to a chair across from him. The chair, like the desk, was 250 years old. "I appreciate you coming over here on such short notice."

"Never been in here before," said Boudreau as he flopped into the seat. He acted casual but there was something keen and mechanical about him, like he was following step-by-step instructions to strip a machine gun. The man was a professional. He put his helmet in his lap and stared silently at Chretien, waiting for him to speak.

Chretien cleared his throat. "You're, uh, you're the horse-butt sniper? You come highly recommended. Mayor of Toronto said you were the best he's ever hired."

The sniper flicked the tip of his nose with a finger. For an instant, the PM thought it seemed an odd gesture, but the very next moment the sniper pointed at him with the same finger and said, "You've got some cocaine on your nose."

"Oh, oh, shit." The PM wiped the nose with his palm, snorted, wiped his hands on his pants, then returned them to their clasped-together position on his desk. Having settled himself, he again looked at the sniper expecting him to speak. He continued to stare at him.

"All right," Chretien said, "I'll get right to the point. We have a situation in Fredericton. There is a... a killer there. An unstoppable killer. An unstoppable serial killer. Worse than that pig farmer out in BC. I got the call only moments ago."

Now Boudreau's eyes narrowed with interest.

Chretien continued. "She seems to turn up every five or six years, kills a bunch of people in the woods. We hush it up, say it was a bear or bobcats. The pulp mill in the city of Saint John pours so much gunk into the river, it's mutated the beavers out there into carnivores too. Lots of easy scapegoats. Every time, we send our own people to Fredericton to clean it up. Even the local authorities don't know what's really going on out there."

"Why hush it up at all?" Despite being known as a "French" sniper, the man had the strong nasally accent of Newmarket, Ontario.

"This woman, the killer… She's been taken down before. In the end someone always got her."

"Always got her?"

"Killed her, but she…" He looked away, up at a corner of the ceiling. "She always… came back."

Boudreau rolled his eyes, stood up, and put on his helmet, chuckling. "Call an exorcist," he said, and began to walk away.

"Wait, wait, wait!" Chretien pleaded. "I'm not saying she's some sort of boogeyman. Just that she… defies the laws of science in ways we don't understand yet. And, actually, we did call an exorcist. They found him with his testicles in his eye sockets and his penis jammed in where his nose should be. Okay, maybe she *is* some sort of boogeyman."

Boudreau sat back down, this time almost in slow motion.

"Ever since we found out about her, the military has been desperate to capture her dead or alive. They want to dissect her, find out how she's doing it. You have to understand, the military applications are beyond imagining. We have the makings of an army of unkillable soldiers out there. As long as we've known about her, the policy has been to keep the whole thing quiet so no one else ends up trying to get their hands on her. We want her for ourselves, but… it can't be done. We've sent Joint Task Force teams out there. She wiped them out. Wiped them out so badly… it was almost like she was *more* drawn to *them* than to anyone *else*! Like they were magnets. At any rate, normally that just means sending a bigger team, but…"

"But that would be linear thinking."

"Yes!" he cried, wagging his index finger. "That's what they always do, send in a team. But what if I did the opposite and sent in just *one* person, one person that could do the job?"

"One person who could secure your political footing."

He froze. In that thick Newmarket accent the words were somehow even more acidic exactly *because* the man sounded so friendly about it. "A body came out of the woods there just moments ago," the PM continued. "Real bad shape. They're saying bear attack, but being Fredericton it's gotta be *her* again."

"If you catch her and hand her over to the army, that will win you their favor but not votes."

Chretien hesitated an instant too long before responding, and they both recognized it. He cleared his throat. "I've got a line on a major online retailer that wants to open a bunch of warehouses across the country. Forget the super soldiers. Imagine fulfillment officers that you couldn't work to death even if you tried."

Boudreau shook his head. "Bears, even serial killers, can be worked to death." He put up his palms. "But let's say it's true. You wouldn't be creating jobs for voters at these warehouses. Let me guess. The owner of this online retailer would become your financial friend. That's the angle."

Chretien found a reservoir of defensive bravado in himself. "Well," he countered. "Can you do it?"

"Mister, that there is an insult to me and my family," Boudreau said, and though he claimed to be insulted, there was still a half smirk on his face. He stood up and glared down at him. "In World War I, my great-great-grandfather was the French lieutenant who came up with the brilliant plan to build hollow papier-mâché horse rears to create the illusion of fallen steeds on the battlefield from which the French could snipe at the enemy. The Germans had no idea what hit 'em. He passed that wisdom down through the ages, down all the way to me, as I now teach it to my daughter. Of course I can do it! You're a sniveling turd,

Chretien. If I had my papier-mâché with me, I'd be tempted to build a horse butt and snipe you right here in this office! But I like a challenge, see? And this boogeywoman is certainly enticing. Mark my words, though. She won't be anything spooky. You oughta be ashamed of yourself for allowing yourself to believe in ghosts and goblins. She may be tough, devious, but she's gotta be flesh and blood, and flesh can be sniped. Sniped from a horse butt! Now, can I assume you have a charter flight ready and waiting to take me to Fredericton?"

"One moment," Chretien stammered, picking up the telephone receiver on his desk and making a clumsy effort to dial.

Boudreau chuckled and stood up to leave again.

By the time he got down the stairs and walked out the front door of the Office of the Prime Minister and Privy Council building, there was a limousine waiting to take him to get his things and go to the airport. The whole time in the vehicle, he couldn't help but visualize everyone they passed as being in the center of a targeting reticle, and him pointing at them through the hole punched in the ass end of a papier-mâché horse.

Chapter 6
Love's Descent

On the outside, Fredericton's Hindu temple could have passed for a one-room school house from the 1930s. It was a simple, white, weatherboard building – inconspicuous. Inside, though, the function room was done up like every Hollywood comedy about Christmas lights rolled into one. The illustrations of the gods in the actual puja room were garlanded in white and yellow flowers and looked like they'd been sent off to a sixteenth century monastery for even more blinding illumination with silver and gold gilding.

By the time Nandini and her mother got there, the noise in the function room was deafening, and that was the swish of saris alone, never mind the cutlery, the music, the children, the booming voices conditioned to be heard over the noise of a nation of one billion people. Mother and daughter mingled in tandem for a while, Nandini pretending to be more than mildly interested in news about childhood friends she hadn't seen in ten years or more. When Aruna went away to deposit her contributions to the potluck at the buffet table, Nandini was stuck with an old couple, both a little taller than hobbits, whom she couldn't remember the names of and didn't have the tact to *not* ask her about her career plans once they were reminded that she was thirty-two years old and had an arts degree. Her mother was gone for a very long time. In fact, Nandini guessed she'd become distracted and had no intention of coming back. Nandini finally extricated herself from the elderly pair with the claim that she was starving, then went and heaped a paper plate at the buffet.

She was approached by a retired professor, an old colleague of her father's, who she could barely remember. "Hello, Nandini. Your father would have hated this, wouldn't he!"

"Hello, Dr. Vishwanathan."

Dr. Vishwanathan was so skinny he was almost skeletal. He wagged a bony finger at her. "He was a very closed-minded man, you know. He said there was no proof of God in the world. I said, but you are a professor of physics, you yourself explained to me about other dimensions. God could be in some other dimension."

Nandini couldn't tell if he was being rude or just Indian.

"Excuse me," the interloper said. "I'd better go indulge in my vices." He pulled a pack of cigarettes from his shirt pocket and shook it.

"Okay."

She watched him leave the temple. That's all he had wanted to say to her.

There was a brief respite from the noise for a few minutes of speeches, then the clamor broke through the levies again.

On her second trip to the buffet table, she ran into someone she used to play with as a child but hadn't seen in more than twenty years. His family had moved back to India, then to Canada again. He asked her for her phone number. She couldn't see the point but couldn't think of a polite excuse not to give it to him either. She suspected she would get a text from him the next day that said: "Show bob's and vagine."

She found a seat at one of the dining tables where she could eat by herself. It was unlikely she would be disturbed since really she hardly knew anybody there.

However, there was soon a slap on the back and an exclamation of, "Hey, beanpole!"

"Oh! Dr. Jayakrishnan!" she said, covering her mouth and swallowing her food.

"I'm glad you came," he said, sitting down next to her and angling his chair towards her. Dr. Jayakrishnan was not a physician, but another professor at the university like her father had been. And, like all Indian men of a certain age, he wore a striped dress shirt tucked into slacks held up with a brown belt and had little more than a horseshoe of grey hair on his head. His smile was warm and genuine, and so was hers.

"Why wouldn't I come?" she asked. "It's your retirement!"

"I know, but I know how much you dislike all this temple business."

"This is hardly a religious event," she said.

"Your father... might not have come!" he said laughing.

"Dr. Vishwanathan just said almost the same thing to me," she answered. "No, he would have come. But he'd be unhappy about it, and he'd make sure everybody knew about it. He'd try to hold it in, but then after an hour of having to socialize in the temple, he'd explode and say all the human effort spent on religion was the ultimate waste. Maybe I'm just more diplomatic."

"Yes, you're exactly right!" Jayakrishnan said with a snap of his fingers. "I'll tell you what. You remember when you were starting in Girl Guides and they made you swear that oath?"

"'To be true to my faith.'"

"And you refused to do it! At eleven years old! Ha! He was so proud of you for that. He always talked about it."

"They called Dad in to talk about it and everything."

"So did you quit?"

She shrugged. "In the end I told them my faith was in science, and they let me join. They bought it."

"Do you know the story about the temple in Jayankondam? For more than ten years, your mother couldn't get pregnant. Then they went to that temple to pray for a child. After that," he snapped his fingers, "she became pregnant!"

"Yes, I've heard this story many times. The part she leaves out is that she went to three or four temples on every visit to India after her marriage to pray to fall pregnant. Ten or twelve temples total. So, actually, it was coincidence. He would bring that up too if she told the story and he'd had a few drinks."

Jayakrishnan shook his head. "Funny, though. Whenever new students appeared on campus fresh off the plane from Chennai, your father made sure to invite them over for a warm meal. He used to tell me he remembered how hard it was for him when he came over. He was so congenial you'd never believe it. The opposite of how he was when he talked about religion or politics."

"No, I believe it. They were constantly streaming through the house like it was a soup kitchen."

Jayakrishnan laughed again. "They would borrow from your mother's 'library' too. It was those students that started calling her 'Eerie Aruna,' you know? Because of her *taste* in literature."

The way he said the word "taste", like he was trying to get a hair off his tongue, made her chuckle.

"Did you see that accident on the road?" Dr. Jayakrishnan continued. "It wasn't far from your house. Did she make you pull over?"

"Ha!"

"Okay. Anyway. How's life? I bet you're sick of talking about it already. I saw you over there with Mr. and Mrs. Gopal before. They must have given you the third degree."

Nandini rolled her eyes.

"Don't let it bother you," he said. "They're just making chit chat. And our generation, you know, in our mindset, the only reason to *be* in this country at all is for education. You can't blame them. Dr. Khanna once told me something. In the 1950s, as new medications for schizophrenia were developed, patients would be treated and released. And it was found that individuals in families or communities with high criticism, hostility, or emotional over-involvement were more likely to relapse. Studies then found that in all cultures criticism was related to hostility. *Except one.*" They both laughed. "So you can't blame them."

Their conversation was interrupted by some people leaving the party who wanted to pay their respects to the doctor. Nandini knew them only from other such functions and didn't even know their names. They politely nodded to her. Dr. Jayakrishnan gave them a "thanks", a head wobble, and a beaming smile, and they were off, jewelry jangling and saris swishing, leaving the scent of jasmine perfume behind them.

When they were gone, Nandini said, resuming, "I don't blame them. Life's fine. I'm still working at CrossTec."

He frowned. "Really? You don't sound fine. Perhaps you're regretting your educational choices. Well, I say, who cares? It's not like the old days. Do people have 'careers' anymore? My own kids have changed jobs two, three times. You'll land on your feet.

You've got the brains. And keep writing your poems."

"Thanks, uncle." She swirled her food again.

He looked at her moving the food without eating it, and after a pause, he said, "Nandini… are you *really* okay? I mean, *really*?"

She looked at him and pressed her lips together but struggled to come up with an answer.

"Maybe you should talk to someone," he said. "Dr. Khanna or Dr. Bhairav. No – forget I said it. What stupid advice – to see doctors you know personally. But maybe I can find someone to recommend."

"I'll be okay, uncle, really," she said with a thin smile.

He nodded, but with a certain reluctance. "Okay," he said. "You'll have some dessert, right? I can't eat all that *gulab jamun* by myself!"

"I'll have some dessert," she said.

He seemed about ready to leave, but they were interrupted again, this time by Professor Elizabeth Clover. Professor Clover was one of the few non-Indians at the function, and, like most of the other non-Indians there, had worked with Nandini's father in the physics department at the university.

"Congratulations, Akshay," she said to Dr. Jayakrishnan. "Please don't get up."

Thankfully, she herself sat down in one of the plastic chairs too. She was already a tall woman. With her piled braids, she seemed even taller and towered over people. It was a relief to the other two when she sat down.

"Thank you. I'm glad you could make it, Liz."

"I was late. There was an accident of some kind on the road."

"Nandini and I were just talking about it."

"It wasn't really an accident," Nandini said. "Someone was mauled by a bear, they think."

"Really?" said the Professor.

"Sadly, such things are not unusual around here over the years," Dr. Jayakrishnan said. "My daughter even used to say it was some kind of monster."

"Sally Pencilneck," Nandini offered. "My friend's a cop and even she mentioned her. Professor Clover, you grew up in Fredericton. You must have heard those stories too."

"Oh, yes. And my daughter used to talk about her too. A killer in the woods. A story to scare Girl Guides."

Professor Clover's daughter was younger than Nandini, but she hadn't seen her in years anyway. Professor Clover's husband had left her, and the daughter had gone with him. The details were unclear, but Aruna would recount what gossipy details she knew in disapproving tones.

"Is it true she can grant wishes?"

This was Aruna, who had joined the group and was standing behind Nandini's chair.

Nandini sighed. Professor Clover tried to be polite. "Mrs. Rajan, since the character is fictional, anything you say about her is 'true' in the context of her being made up. Is it true that vampires drink blood?"

"Yes!"

"I could write a story that says vampires are allergic to Wi-Fi, and it would be 'true' because vampires aren't real, so anything you say about them can apply. You can just make up whatever you like. Like with the idea of gods." She waved an arm over head to indicate the whole temple.

"But what about with real vampires?"

"Mother!"

Dr. Jayakrishnan was laughing.

"I mean vampires from stories!"

"They're made up from square one by someone at a typewriter. If Le Fanu had just typed the words 'Carmilla was allergic to Wi-Fi', then that would be 'true' in our concept of vampires."

"Mmm, but these stories always have some earlier roots, you know? Real things that happened."

"Those roots, or the explanations for them, are made up too, just not with a typewriter. Mrs. Rajan, vampires aren't real, and neither is Sally Pencilneck. Nandini, you can't let your mother go on believing this. I know she likes those magazines." The Professor started to get up, taking her purse off the back of the chair. "I'm sorry, but I have to get going," she said.

"Already?" Dr. Jayakrishnan said with genuine surprise. He got up as well.

"Yes. I wasn't planning on staying long, but I wasn't going to miss the occasion completely and not pay my respects. Congratulations again, Akshay." They shook hands, and she left.

"I'd better go and mingle too," said Dr. Jayakrishnan. He slapped Nandini on the back again. "It was good to see you again, Nandini." He gave an amiable head wobble good-bye to Aruna and she wobbled back. He left.

"What's up, Mother?"

"You know, the texture of Padmini's *barfi* is always so slimy. Every function, the same thing! Why doesn't anyone say anything to her?!"

"Uh huh."

"Anyway, I'm ready to go."

"What? But you're having such a good time."

This was more disrespectful sarcasm, but Aruna didn't pick up on it. "Yeah, sure, okay, I'm having a good time, but let's get a good night's rest."

An odd thing to say. Aruna was beating around the bush. She wanted to say something else, but Nandini could guess what it was. It was written all over her face.

"Is it about curling tomorrow? I told you I'd pick you up myself after work tomorrow, Mother."

"Yes, thank you, *chinna kutti*. That's it."

"No, Mother, that's not it."

Aruna exposed her teeth in a pained grimace. "It's just so silly," she said.

Something came over Nandini, and she said, "Dad would want you to not be silly and just say it." As soon as she said it, she couldn't believe the words had come out of her mouth. Her dad was on her mind.

Aruna's eyes widened too, then softened and she

nodded. "I want to go into the woods by Killarney Lake tomorrow," she said, "and look for Sally Pencilneck."

"That's demented."

"Why do you have to be so rude?!" She clapped herself on the forehead with the heel of a palm. "If we had raised you in India, you wouldn't be so disobedient! Why can't you just be a good daughter?!"

You're being a bad mother, she wanted to say. "You can go by yourself, Mother. Nothing's stopping you."

"The lake will be cordoned off by the police."

Aruna would be the toast of her cryptid Facebook group, Nandini knew. "So somehow it's okay if I'm there with you?"

"I don't know. Let's just go there. What will you be doing? Just wasting your time making YouTube videos."

"Why not go look for the Loch Ness Monster while you're at it?" she scoffed.

***

Nandini had written "Love's Descent" in desperation when she returned from Vancouver with her tail between her legs. As a child she had dreamed about becoming a poet or a novelist. By her teens she realized that was unrealistic, and she thought she should at least become a university professor like her father, but in poetry. When it became clear she didn't have the right academic mindset for that, she thought she would at least become an editor. Then Vancouver happened, where she only ever worked in admin. Then her father died, and she was back in school at a community college learning to be a database administrator. Here, at a dead-end, those old dreams withered and almost forgotten, she mustered the will to produce an epic, a last attempt to at least have something, however small, to show for that little girl's fantasies.

The main character was a gender-swapped version of herself. It was so lazy it was embarrassing. Shameful, even. Mortifying. *Insufferable*. It was supposed to be a romance, and the love interest was the one ex-boyfriend she still thought about, now a woman for narrative purposes. She had dated Robert in university, only for less than half a year. She had soured on him because he cried. Not at, say, something like movies or certain songs, which would be forgivable, but when they got into an argument. It was so unmanly that it unnerved her. And yet eventually it was him, who, sensing that something wasn't clicking, broke it off. Looking back, especially after her father passed, she was horrified at her own behavior. Ever since, he was the one she fantasized about, even though she had dated other men since, and others for longer. She replayed their conversations over and over, rewriting them in her mind so she said the right things. She treated him much better in these replays, but he would also conveniently give her whatever it was she needed. He too would say exactly the right thing. She shaped him, easily. So they were still together when they were eighty years old and barely able to walk. In reality, if she saw him from a distance somewhere in town, she would go out of her way to make sure he didn't see her. She avoided walking past the York Regional Museum downtown where he worked.

But it all worked out for the couple in the book, maybe a bit too well. Maybe that's why nobody wanted it so far. Her favorite novel had been rejected twenty-three times. So she set herself a limit of twenty-four. After the first fifteen rejections or non-replies, for the next five submissions she changed the name of the main character to "Ryan McKenzie" and her own name to "Alice M. Woodside," but it was still rejected. She tried a few more, then finally, for the twenty-fourth, she submitted the original version to Four-Square Publishing, a Canadian literary publisher that was supposedly seeking "diverse Canadian voices". This was the last shot.

Aruna came up to Nandini's room with a grocery list written on the back of an envelope for Nandini to go pick up the next day. When she looked in, Nandini was sitting at her desk with her laptop open.

"What's wrong, baby?" Aruna said. "Why are you crying?"

Nandini didn't know what to say.

"Did your book get rejected again?"

Again, Nandini said no words.

Aruna came over to her and rubbed her hunched back. "It doesn't matter," she said. "You have a proper job. You shouldn't waste your time with such silly things."

Nandini's body froze like a marble statue. One floor below them, there were shelves and shelves or utter pulp junk, right below her feet. Nandini could feel their trashiness radiating up through the floor, through her feet, and suffusing her whole body, threatening to turn her into a human inferno. Thousands and thousands of published pages, every one of them full of absolutely moronic monster stories, badly written, and worse, objectively worse, than the worst page of her own book. Her mother's titanic hypocrisy made her want to fly through the roof, smashing it apart, and blast through the universe screaming at the top of her lungs. She wanted to teach her a lesson, to put her in her place, and show her once and for all how stupid she and her idiotic stories were.

She looked up at her with puffy eyes. "Okay, Mother," she said, "I'll take you to Killarney Lake tomorrow."

***

Outside the temple, it was a clear night, the last of the day's sun seeping quickly away. Unlike the cacophony inside the temple, out here there were only the sounds of birds and crickets, and the frogs, seemingly louder than ever this year. Here, so far from the light pollution of the city, the stars were out in full force. There were woods not far away, the line of the trees a jagged black silhouette against the last, dying edges of purple light.

Dr. Vishwanathan stepped away from the harshly lit steps of the front entrance so he could enjoy the sparks and crackling sound of his cigarette each time he inhaled it. It was his third cigarette break of the evening.

He thought about Nandini. He remembered she used to be so skinny. She wasn't anymore. She had grown up into a fine young woman. She had… filled out. Why, if he was thirty years younger…

There was a sound from behind him. Something that sounded like an exhale and a hiss at the same time. His brain translated it as the sound of something living. He spun to look at it, but there was nothing there. As far back as the tree line, nothing. But there was a vague motion in the trees – more than a wind. More like a pushing through, trampling, but near invisible in the woods, which were a purely negative space against the universe.

Dr. Vishwanathan didn't like it.

He put out his cigarette early and went back inside.

Chapter 7
Show Bob's

The tears were streaming down Vijay's face. That woman – that thing – had cut a huge gash in his leg through his jeans. He was so afraid. He was sobbing like a child, his shoulders heaving, snot running over his lips, his throat dry but somehow gurgling at the same time and closing shut as if to suffocate him. The sweat dripping over his eyebrows blinded him. His whole body had turned against him. Cloaked in darkness, the flashlight of his cell phone provided very little light, with his hands quivering too much to point it in any useful direction, and the light serving as a beacon to his location anyway. Trees everywhere, but the fear and the imposed blindness had reduced the entire forest to a black box little bigger than a coffin. Sometimes, his chest quaking as it heaved, he could just reach out a trembling arm and feel his way from trunk to trunk, but the pace was glacial. It was like the terror had struck him at the base of his spine, and now a tingling chill radiated out from that point in constant but unpredictable waves, sometimes only on his left side, sometimes in his esophagus, sometimes reaching the back of his neck and his shoulders. The sensation was almost paralyzing. He didn't even have enough collectedness to do up his pants. His brain allowed no room for a strategy out of this, only emotion-choked lament. And why wouldn't those fucking birds and frogs and crickets shut up?! Couldn't he have any peace?! Why was this happening to him? What had he done to deserve this?! Why was that freak after him?!

When Vijay had first left Dr. Jayakrishnan's retirement party at the temple and stepped out into the woods, he was on a high. He couldn't believe his luck. It had been so easy to get Nandini's phone number. He understood women, he really did. One look at her and he could tell two things. One: that from her high-and-mighty Canadian throne she would look down on him as an Indian village yokel with his poor English and take pity on him. Two: that she would lack the assertiveness to simply refuse to give him her phone number. Whether he was right or wrong, she had given the number.

The last time he had seen her, they might have been six years old, and she had grown up, that was for sure. Not so much filled out per se, but she was a woman, tall, kind of skinny for his tastes, but he liked the way the Maritime air made her hair so frizzy. When she went and sat by herself, picking sadly at her food with a plastic fork, he stared at her from across the room and felt his juices start to rise.

He wanted to see her bob's and vagine.

It had only been fifteen minutes since he got her number, and he knew she had given it to him because she didn't know how to say "No". But what if, just what if, it was something more than that? She probably didn't get many boyfriends because of her frizzy hair, he thought. So, in fact, in his mind *he* was the one being noble by showing an interest in her. She would be grateful, and maybe more.

He needed to send her a dick pic.

Actually, this was all spurious logic. The reality was that since about the age of twelve or thirteen, the chemicals coursing through his nervous system had turned his penis into his body's most focal and most pleasurable organ. The fact that the entire culture found it an object of disgust crushed him, and he needed someone, anyone, to validate what his body had programmed him to believe was the most precious part of his being. Deep down he knew this, but to admit it to himself would have destroyed him. Instead, he thought about all the inspirational memes in his Facebook feed. "Dream big and believe in yourself." "Don't let anyone tell you you're not worth it." "You are brightening someone's day more than you know." Etcetera, etcetera.

He got out his phone and unlocked it.

Where to do it? The bathroom? No, the temple bathroom was too antiseptic, he felt. She looked like an artsy-type. She said she had studied painting or something. Out of habit, he looked at the screen of his phone. He had left it open on Instagram. It was a post by the rapper RevDev – a picture of him wearing an 8-ball jacket in the woods and grabbing his crotch, and the words: "When I jack it, I jack it in the woods. Keepin' it real yo. I gots mad respec 4 Mutha Earth."

Yes, the woods. He would go out there, take his time, and do it right. Vijay decided to leave.

His mother caught his elbow and asked, "Where are you going?"

"I, uh, I just got this party invitation, Mummy."

"What? *Now*?"

"Yes, I'll take an Uber over."

"This is Dr. Jayakrishnan's retirement function!"

"I know, Mummy, but we agreed I should try to settle back in here as best I could. Going to this party is important." It really was important, he thought, but it wasn't a party.

She would let him go. He knew she would. Since they had moved back to Canada she had found his behavior disobedient, even shameful – drinking, leaving the house at night. She had lost control of him. However, she wanted him to settle in. She felt some guilt for uprooting him. Whenever that look appeared in her eyes, he caught hold of it, clutched it, and twisted it.

"Okay," she sighed. "You're an adult. I can't stop you."

He kissed her on the cheek then dashed out of the building, across the lawn, and into the woods.

Immediately, he realized his error. It was too dark.

But, no: he wasn't going to let himself get disheartened. He had half an erection, and he couldn't risk it abandoning him, feeble as it was. It would feel like failure. Plus the flash on his phone was decent – he could make this work, he was convinced of it.

Actually, the bigger distraction was all the rustling going in the foliage. Squirrels, birds, who knew what else? But as he went deeper into the woods, trying to find a location that would put him on the same level as an Influencer like RevDev, the commotion of the forest creatures seemed to die down.

After a few minutes of pushing through the leaves and bushes he found a good spot, but it was pretty deep into the woods. There was just enough room to stand, but it was flat. Vijay shone the narrow beam of his cell phone flash light around the area. It looked enough like the place where RevDev took his selfie. It was inspiring.

This was it. He filled his lungs, then exhaled with a sharp "Hooh!"

He undid his belt buckle, the button on his jeans, zipped down his fly, froze. How far to drop his pants? To his knees, he decided. His own decisiveness in that moment also inspired him. He lay his dick on his palm, like a maître d' displaying the label on a wine bottle to a discerning diner, then squared his shoulders, and took the shot.

In the same instant the flash went off, something

clambered through the bushes behind him, but he didn't even hear it. He was so single-minded of purpose in that moment.

He looked at the photo. The flash had made his dick and pubes look like a rare tuber found by a nocturnal botanist. He thought about taking a better photo, but he hesitated for a second. What if he sent Nandini the tuber photo? If she responded with even marginal warmth to a photo that bad, that would mean she was *really* up for it. Still, he decided he couldn't risk it. Best foot forward, and all that. He needed a better photo with a better dick.

He looked from the screen back to his dick, still in his other hand. What to think about? He thought about Nandini and her frizzy hair. He thought about doing things to her that would be considered revolting by most of the population.

There was more rustling in the bushes behind him. This time he heard it but pushed it out of his mind. There was a faintly bad smell too.

After thinking about Nandini, there was a little bit of activity downstairs, but then he imagined doing the same things to Kate Middleton and there was great improvement.

There was a cacophony of leaves behind him. This time he spun to look, automatically, and his phone light fell upon a horror that turned his dick back into an artichoke heart.

It was a dark-skinned woman, maybe middle-aged but

her face was obscured by a Groucho nose and moustache and hypno glasses (in one eye, the right "lens" had been knocked out). Her hair was a nappy mess that looked like an eagle's nest. There were pencils coming out of her neck. She wore a t-shirt (original color unknowable), jeans, and a necklace of... artichoke hearts.

Vijay stumbled back a step. The "woman" wasn't moving. She was just staring at him, just waiting it seemed, for... what? Should he panic? Something made him think... He dared to glance away from her and down to his shriveled penis. When he looked up again, there was the clink of a chain, and his head was clobbered by what felt like a heavy stick of wood.

It sent him flying back a few feet. He staggered up. She hadn't moved from her spot. It was obvious she was toying with him. "What the shit?!" he cried. She took a step forward. He turned with blinding speed and shot off into the woods, still holding his phone and clumsily trying to pull up his pants with his other hand and failing.

But... she didn't seem to be chasing him. She wasn't chasing him. Why wasn't she chasing him?! Had she done all she wanted? Whack him upside the head with a stick? Was that the end of it? Or, worse: was the game she was playing with him going to go on and on?

The more important question, though, was: why was he running deeper *into* the woods? He dared to stop in his tracks. The woods were soundless except for the creatures. Which way was it back to the temple? And he couldn't have been that far from the road – where was it? Where was the noise of traffic?

There was a noise, just a rustle of leaves, but it screeched through his being. Then it stopped. It had passed, like a mortar shell, and he swelled with relief, his forehead a map drawn with sweat and veins. It was in this waiting silence, this vacuum, that she slashed his leg. Had he had more awareness in that moment, he might have wondered about the weapon or where she had suddenly appeared from. Instead, all he did was shriek and hobble away, cursing his own stupidity for ever having stopped in the first place.

Now he knew his life was in danger. And worse: he had been standing still, but the slash was non-lethal. It was deliberate: she was toying with him. Even his addled mind was able to realize this. His fear drove the pain into a corner of his awareness, compartmentalized it to use for fuel, and forced him to pick up the pace. It was pushing him to survive, but Vijay was no survivor. He was an IT support technician that had fucked a prostitute but never kissed a girl. His conscious mind knew this and recognized that this was his death despite all his hormones and physiology were doing to keep him alive. The tears came, the snot came, the chills came.

What was the point of running anyway? Both times he had seen her, she had seemed to just *appear* where he was, like she could read his thoughts and knew where he would be before he got there. He stopped again, panting. The cone of light from his phone revealed a vague microcosm of roots, dirt, and flora, isolated from the rest of the black universe. Such a warm summer night, but he was so cold, and his wiener was still poking out over the top of his underwear through the open button and fly of his pants saying, "Kilroy was here." His leg was throbbing and stiff. He needed to know. With trembling hands and against all better judgment he maneuvered his light around to the gash. It was on the back of his left thigh. The wound looked like a fleshy portal to hell.

A footstep sounded in front of him. Another concussive blow to the head came. His phone had fallen on the ground face up, giving the space the light of a secret ritual. He staggered backwards, was stopped by a trunk tree. It was too instantaneous to process. Her fingers wrapped around his penis and scrotum like octopus tentacles.

She snapped her arm up like a whip with such speed that it tore the penis from the body along with an inch-wide strip of flesh that went all the way up to his bottom lip, where she snapped again and that end ripped free, leaving Vijay with a red racing stripe up his trunk to his chin, screaming.

The despair and pain was too much. He fell to his knees, wailing for his mother. He wanted this woman to get it over with, to kill him. He wanted relief. But again his body betrayed him, and, facing the threat of death, would not even relieve him of consciousness.

In the vapory light, through his tears, he watched her. She had flipped the flesh strip around so she was holding it by the "forehead" end and whapping the penis against her other hand like a school teacher with a flaccid ruler, pacing while she did it. Finally, she stopped in front of him. Somehow, he suppressed his screaming until it became a pathetic wet noise. The red stripe pulsed a clanging agony through his whole body. A pocket of his mind noticed that she must be at least a C-cup, and if circumstances were different…

The penis whip struck him. She backed up and swung it around like a gymnastics ribbon, running at him with spins and twirls, and struck him again, pummeling his cheek with his own scrotum and sending the testicles flying in different directions. He succumbed with a moan and slumped to the ground.

Sally stood over him and whipped him again and again like an Indian washerwoman slapping clothes against a rock in a river bank. Her movements seemed to shift through space in a weird way, like she had ten arms or five heads. Finally, she coiled the flesh whip around his neck, swung it over a branch, and hauled him up. As she held the free end, he kicked and kicked. But he did not actually want to resist. It was a mechanical action. He was ready to give up consciousness, to abandon life. And yet somehow, as he was suspended there, kicking and looking down at Sally, for a moment the very space itself which she occupied seemed to be folding on itself in a strange, rapidly reconfiguring origami. Through the shapes he saw not the forest floor, but a strange gray world full of monolithic islands of fused bone, plains on which walked the skeletons of strange lumbering creatures, vast ruins overgrown with flesh, and teeming with man-sized eyeless insects on four legs. These visions were worse than his physical pain. He looked up and caught sight of the stars, as he never would again. And a thick, inevitable dark began to murder the light of his being.

Chapter 8
Cheese Cruds

The six men in their black "disguises" lumbered out of the SUVs, and as each stepped down onto the ground, the vehicle's shocks rocked, then eased up a quarter inch with a creaking sigh.

They'd pulled up in front of the "executive lodge" at Killarney Lake, tires crunching over the rough ground. It was a three-story mansion really, that was rented out for elite prices. It was theirs for three days: a retreat where they could have their "summit" without any distractions, where they could be anonymous, without all the press and the left-wing witch-hunting media, where they could be themselves and say what they felt without fear of censure, far from the cities, not even in their own country (though they could have recruited local "talent" easily enough too), in this backwater Canadian town. Here, for a weekend, they could be free again. And yet none of them dared to take off their hats or sunglasses before they got in the lodge. As each alighted from the van, they surveyed their surroundings, not as nature lovers, but as men looking for accusers and photographers waiting to jump out from behind every pine cone and maple leaf.

In turns they filed into the house, and inside it was palatial. They finally doffed their ball caps and jackets and tossed them to waiting staff. This small but thoughtful detail helped to relieve the tension for some of them. It was a hint of the kind of courtesy they were used to in their old lives. They were here seeking salvation, and perhaps things would turn out okay after all. However, many of them disliked each other, and seeing the luxurious inside of the lodge some of them became enraged that last night they had been forced to stay at what passed for a five-star hotel in town instead of here. But they were not allowed to arrive here before their host. That had been made clear. He had made them come early and wait an extra day *deliberately*.

First in was Al Garfield. He'd started out in stand-up comedy and kids' shows way back in the seventies. He was known for his material being so clean he would even call up other comedians and give them hell for cursing in their sets. In the eighties, he turned his wholesomeness into an industry, launching what was to become the biggest TV sitcom of all time, and also signing multimillion dollar commercial and advertising deals shilling kids fruit juices and stereos. He had it all. He had single-handedly made white America no longer afraid of Black people if they were rich Black people. Now white America was only resentful of them. He had hundreds of millions of dollars, fame, a wife, eight kids, cars, mansions, willing women as far as the eye could see… Well. There was the problem. Sometimes, it was better when they were *unwilling*. He had a little concoction that he called his "barbecue sauce" that made women go all "huggy buggy". Actually, it knocked them out, and then he rolled his sweaty mass on top of them and made whoopy to their inert corpse-like bodies to the best of his ability. And now, now these women had the gall *years later* to complain about it! They'd all been asleep – what did they care anyway? Here was a man who had transformed race relations in America and made it safe for rich Black men, who had brought joy to millions of families and children around the world, and suddenly these money-hungry little vixens were coming out of the woodwork, scurrying around, rolling their eyes, looking for a cut. If anything, they should have been worshipping him and begging him to drug them again. So now here he was, by this obscure Canadian lake, not having smiled in years, and with sagging jowls like Droopy Dog.

Coming in next, so mousy and diminutive in stature he was almost completely obscured by Garfield's bulk, was Oscar-winning pedophile Corky Phillips. When Corky was thirteen, he had loved thirteen-year-old girls. When he was fifteen, he had loved fifteen-year-old girls. When he was seventeen, he had loved seventeen-year-old girls. When he was forty, he still loved seventeen-year-old girls. When he was sixty, he married his girlfriend's twenty-year-old daughter, in a sense his own adopted daughter. ("Alleged daughter!" he would always protest.) "I, I really love you, you know?" he would tell them with his meek, stuttering voice. Almost all of his movies starred himself as a man with so many anxieties and insecurities that he could barely speak and yet would desire – and successfully bed – beautiful women sometimes a third of his age. For this his art was heaped with accolades, though even the awards committees were forced to wince at the details of his private life. Indeed, without his work, American cinema would have been so much the poorer. Who wouldn't concede that? And wasn't it vital that the gem-encrusted canon of American cinema be protected and held aloft – wasn't that the greater good that outweighed the cost to a few? Besides the women had all – almost all – consented. He was a millionaire with Hollywood power, and they were mostly dependent on their parents for allowance money, but they weren't unwilling. In fact, Corky was disgusted by the behavior of Al Garfield, the sitcom star who had to drug the women he wanted to have sex with. At any rate, despite the undeniable value of his art, Corky's transgressions were seen as so distasteful at the very least that he was forced to flee the country to France. In Paris, his proclivities were met with a shrug and a smirking amusement that a country could be so puritanical that he would be forced to flee it for such a thing in the first place. Well, now he had snuck back into North America for this summit and a promise that something would be done.

Third in, flipping off his hat and shades, was Jeffrey Woes, former chairman of Dingo Media Enterprises, and a man who looked like a pig that had been genetically spliced with a human by a mad scientist. With every step he took, a bead of sweat erupted on his temples. Woes had offered raises and promotions to women at Dingo Media in exchange for sex. Sometimes he tried to kiss them or made comments about how sexy they were. He had done far worse, but none of those women had come forward. Some of them never would. The conglomerate rewarded him with a $40 million exit package. However, Woes saw this as a punishment. He could have paid for all the prostitutes in the world with all his wealth. Some gold-diggers might have even tried to marry him – he could have strung them along one by one, never marrying any. However, he was loath to spend his own money as that would make him a whoremonger, and he was above that. That was for the lower classes. And that's where he was stuck now, never able to take his Lamborghini out on Sundays for fear of being recognized, forced to buy shirts from Armani instead of Burberry. He knew he was fat and repulsive. Did that mean he did not deserve love? And yet here he was, being punished for seeking what was merely one of his basic rights as a living human being.

Fourth: Larry Biermug, Hollywood movie mogul, and king of the casting couch. Though younger than Woes, Larry was just as fat, slobbery, sweaty, and jowly as the former Dingo boss. Also, he had produced and financed some of Corky's movies. And yet the resentment he felt coming from them and the other men who'd come out of the SUVs was as obvious as his cocaine-reddened eyes: because Larry had been the first to fall. He had been the domino that knocked down all these other men. The worst thing about it was that he had done nothing wrong. He didn't invent the system. He was just another one of the cogs and so were all those actresses. They knew a hundred percent what working in Hollywood meant: trading sexual favors for tens of thousands or even hundreds of thousands of dollars for a few months of work on a movie and the launching of careers. Did anyone really not know that this was how it worked? Well, that's how they were all acting. He'd requested that one woman watch him jerk off into a potted plant. Afterwards, he paid her bags of money and turned her into a movie star. Now, years – years! – later the incident was prime fodder for every slavering media outlet, and his career was over. (He was still worth millions and millions of dollars, but he'd probably never make a movie again, and the threat of prison time loomed over his head.) And why? Was his dick really that awful to look at? What was worse, now this rapper (MagLev or whatever his name was) had made jerking off into plants – into entire trees! – all the rage. Where was the Tweetstorm destroying *his* career? Where were the tree-huggers racing in to defend the dignity of the poplars? The poplars weren't even getting paid! Despite his disapprobation of the rapper, however, Larry had to admit to himself that this train of thought was making him horny to go jerk off in the woods himself. He looked forward to the opportunity to sneak off on his own. He was sure none of these amateurs would miss him.

Behind Biermug came Cardinal Geoff Mell, Catholic serial fucker of young boys. And not only did Mell fuck eight-, nine-, and ten-year-old boys himself, he also saw to it that dozens of other Christian priests fucked as many boys as they pleased, some much younger – even four or five years old. He enabled, facilitated, sometimes even provided. Of all the men on this "retreat", Mell was the most philosophical about his so-called crimes. To be a man of the cloth, he realized, was to contemplate free will (did it, or did it not exist?) almost every minute of every day. Often, as one pored over the Bible hour after hour, one felt that the battle was lost – that free will did *not* exist. Cardinal Mell postulated that to compensate for that lack of control, the priests needed to feel some form of control, right now here on Earth, and that need for control manifested itself as complete and utter sexual control over children. Of course, Mell also realized all his philosophizing and psychologizing was beside the point. The fact of the matter was that God watches everything, and God had watched every child "molestation" in history and never intervened. Since Mell and his ilk were men of God, what this meant was: God wanted His priests to fuck those children. It was the very will of God. How to reconcile this with the tale of Sodom and Gomorrah, the Cardinal wasn't quite sure. Sometimes he allowed himself to wonder if there weren't some lost books of the Bible out there. And did it not say in John 13:23, "Now there was leaning on Jesus' bosom one of his disciples, whom Jesus loved"? Yes, Mell too loved all those little boys and their sweet little mouths and thighs, and he loved that *control* he had over them. At any rate, the ridiculous uproar about this complete non-issue was just further proof that modern society had strayed too far from the good book and traditional religious values. The Vatican was doing all it could to ensure that Mell and the priests, being good, ordained men, could keep on fucking tiny children as they had been, but under the increasing influence of Satan, the pressure of these draconian modern laws was finally tightening the noose around Mell's neck. He could feel it. Normally he would never associate with these other men, men who represented the ultimate depths of modern man's decadence and depravity, but the invitation to this summit suggested the hope of a solution. As desperation loomed in the back of his mind, he snapped at the opportunity. Besides, he had checked ahead and found out there was a Boy Scout troop camping in the area.

The last man to enter the house was Alfred Albert Christian Edward, a genuine English prince. He loved showing off his wealth and carried with him an heirloom rifle strapped to his back, and he carried a bejeweled scepter, proof of his royal lineage. He also wore a crown, which he shouldn't have been. Given his status, he believed he stood apart from the laws of man. He was entitled to *droit du seigneur* and *jus primae noctis*. He interpreted it to mean it was his honor-bound duty to have sexual relations with women ages seventeen and under. Even that dirty colony India had its own version, *Dola Pratha*, so why shouldn't he?! Yet somehow in England they disagreed and his titles were at risk. And his net worth now was maybe five million pounds. Not like the old days. What's more, he'd had to pay that girl twelve million pounds. Actually Mummy had paid for that. Effectively, that was the cost to sex traffic a seventeen-year-old girl. If he'd had his old fortune, that glorious tax-free fortune, he could do it again and again. It was worth it. The other option was to somehow bring the cost per infringement down... But here he was. He found it distasteful to have to come to North America (he sneered at the very words) for a helping hand, but here he did have one ally left – an ally in the highest office in the land, so he wasn't about to turn down this invitation from him even if it meant having to spend the weekend with that pervert Mell and the colored fellow from the telly. *Where is our host anyway?* he wondered.

There had been another man with them in this first group. Hart Clansman was a Supreme Court judge who had raped several women in college and then cried when he was accused of it at his nomination hearing, and so they swore him in. That wasn't entirely shocking since a precedent had been set by another Supreme Court judge nominee who had attempted to turn women on with talk about pubes on Coke cans and was then confirmed. The culture snowballed from there. However, Clansman got carsick easily and had gone for a walk as soon as they pulled up to the lodge, and he hadn't returned.

After coming in the front entrance, the men were guided into one of the large entertaining areas. There was a dining table there which would have been ideal for a family playing Scrabble, but in this instance there were three chairs on each side, and the names of the six men were on name plates in front of each seat. Al Garfield, the former sitcom star, picked up his name plate and frowned at it. Or rather, since he was always frowning, it would be more accurate to say that he pointed his frowning face at it. This meeting was supposed to be top-secret, and yet these plates had been professionally printed. Some of the other men had similar doubts, but some were oblivious. Cardinal Mell in particular took the name plate as a sign of respect towards his office and his religious leadership and sat down in his seat with a delighted grin. The other men, suspicious or not, followed suit. Even Garfield.

The instant after the last man sat down, the French doors at the rear of the parlor burst open. Four secret service men filed in and marched two to a side in perfect formation like they were in an Esther Williams synchronized swimming routine.

KILLARNEY LAKE MASSACRE

The soundtrack from the 1988 Jean-Claude Van Damme film *Bloodsport* blared out from a strategically-placed Bluetooth speaker, dry ice machines hissed gas into the doorway, and Donald Ruby, the President of the United States, leader of the free world, lumbered into the room like an amorphous mass of slow-spreading orange sludge in a black suit and red tie, his hair standing up in feeble wisps like distant, dead orange trees on top of a volcano. He was the human equivalent of three hundred pounds of vomit, diarrhea, snot, smegma, earwax, and jizz scraped out of a dumpster, vaguely shaped into a person, and taught the vocabulary of an ape that spoke in sign language. Mell, Biermug, and Woes applauded with unbridled enthusiasm. They were the kind of men who appreciated the pomp that was earned through wealth.

The secret service men closed the doors, and the President waited a moment for the dry ice smoke to dissipate, bobbing his head (really just the neckless extension of his giant slug-like body) to the music. He gritted his teeth. This appreciation of his glory was somehow both pleasurable and painful to him. This pain had been lurking in the background of his life like a slinking shadow for over seventy years, even through all his years as a real estate mogul. He refused to acknowledge its existence, but it was there in the head bobbing and teeth gritting. He wasn't some pansy that was going to lie on a therapist's couch to untangle it though. There was nothing to untangle anyway.

As the smoke cleared, the music faded out in

perfect sync. "Bring out the girl," the President said into the air. He had not deigned to notice the other men in the room yet.

A somewhat dark-skinned woman with an expensive perm was escorted into the room from a side door. The music started up again: this time it was a waltz conducted by Andre Rieu. The woman was wearing only stiletto heels, G-string underwear, and sparkling faux-diamond earrings. The President tried to clap in time to the music, but it was a real struggle for him. He sang as much of the national anthem as he could remember over the unrelated Andre Rieu music, opening and closing his mouth like a fish when the words escaped him. It's possible he did not know the Rieu tune was *not* the national anthem. The woman came and stood beside him and held his arm. "This is Rocky Hush," the President said. "Not ten minutes ago she gave me the most amazing blowjob, like you wouldn't believe." Biermug and Woes grinned in awe at this. However, Garfield and Phillips, the two "artists" of the group, found it tacky. Cardinal Mell was offended on religious grounds but said nothing. This was the point of money and power, they all thought.

But actually there had been no blowjob. And the woman's name was actually Rokeya Hossain. If the President had known that, his brain would probably spurt out his ass. Over the course of the past few days, she had considered telling him just to see what would happen. She had been hired by a third party for a huge amount of money and was surprised to find that her client was actually the President of the United States. She happily signed the NDA. It had been a weird weekend though. No sex. Just his bad breath and the smell of shit coming from his diaper until his handlers came to take him away and clean him up. And now they'd come all the way to Canada.

The President tried to snap his fingers, and again in perfect synch, two secret service men brought out a throne which they set down at the head of the table. The President poured his bulk into it. Rocky was escorted out of the room. This was the moment in which he finally looked around the table at the six men and acknowledged their existence. He had doubts about Corky Phillips. Phillips wasn't as rich as the others, but the President had to concede that he had as much right to a place at the table as them. He didn't like Garfield the sitcom star either because he didn't like Black people. That Garfield was Black *and* rich only made it worse – it made him uppity. The President certainly wasn't going to say anything about it though.

"You know," he began, "some of my best friends are Negros," he said looking right at Garfield. Garfield's eyebrows went up. "That's all right though," the President continued, "you're as welcome here as anyone, I suppose. Even though there was a time when you were all slaves. Doesn't show good business sense really. If the Negros had read my book, my book that

I wrote about business, slavery would never have happened." The realization of this truth, one that had hit him that very moment, put a huge grin of pride on the President's face.

Garfield sighed. He wanted to get up and leave, but if he did he knew the only road left to him would be straight to jail. He only came to this summit hoping for the glimmer of an out, and now he was forced to sit here listening to this immoral dope.

The President started again. "Anyway, gentlemen, you all know why we're here. Where's Hart? I guess we'll start without him. We're here because of a conspiracy of libtards and snowflakes," (words the President had picked up from the internet,) "who are trying to convince the bullshit media that we're guilty of some sort of wrongdoing. Well, let me tell you gentlemen. We've done nothing wrong. And even though we did, they've got nothing. Absolutely fucking nothing."

The men clapped. One called out, "Hear, hear!" But, in fact, even if the men did not believe that the things they did were wrong, they knew that the media definitely knew what they had done. The men tried to deny their deeds to the skies, but it seemed like people couldn't talk about anything else these days. And so they wanted what the President had said to be true. They wanted it to all go away so they could get back to the business of making deals and entertainment and fucking children and drugged and/or unwilling women.

Garfield wasn't happy about the President's stream

of foul language, but again he checked himself from saying anything.

The President's hands flailed wildly as he spoke. "Now, everyone in this room – we've all been falsely accused by the so-called media. They're not media. I mean, what does that even mean? Do *they* even know what that means? I don't think so. These comedy shows? They're not funny. These news programs. You'll notice they're all run by women. Women are buzzing all over them like zebras. Zebra women. Did you know that zebras have 'smart' vaginas that can flush out the semen of men they don't like? Well, the media has been taken over by these women because of political correctness. And these women, I mean, what's their problem? We know what their problem is. They're all so ugly with faces like," he contorted his face as much as he could. The effect was indeed grotesque. "They're wondering, 'How come I'm not getting that kind of attention? The kind of attention these men are giving to their false accusers?' That girl that was in here before – she wanted to be here. Why wouldn't she? They always want it. By the way, these accusers always fall out of windows or helicopters. Have you noticed that? Very clumsy. Larry, have you tried the poutine since you got here?"

Larry shook his head. He was still thinking about RevDev, and after also hearing about the President's blowjob, he'd been a little bit distracted and wanted to go jerk off on a tree even more than he had before. He wondered if he could somehow get a hold of the girl with the perm to go with him, but she seemed to be presidential property. He also didn't want to have to sit next to Cardinal Mell much longer because the man was a degenerate homo.

"You should try it," the President continued. "They make it with real cheese cruds here."

"I think you mean 'cheese curds,'" said Corky Phillips, ever the writer. Unlike Biermug, Corky hadn't been distracted by the girl since she was too old for his tastes and also hardly related to him in any way.

"That's what I said. Cheese turds. So these women get into these media positions, and they just want to lord it over us. It's reverse sexism. Forzine!" He barked this last, meaningless word at the top of his voice. He was having a mini-stroke. They hit him about once a week, the result of tour-rider levels of cocaine and Adderall consumption and seven hours of flickering TV a day. None of the men were alarmed by this, but Mell did hope the man didn't die and take all his hopes of a resurrection to the grave with him.

The President recovered, showing no awareness whatsoever of his own nonsensical outburst. "Well, let me tell you what, folks. Everyone in this room right here, we're the real Illuminati. We're the lizard people. I bet Cardinal Mell over here knows a thing or two about lizards." The President smiled at his own penis joke. No one else got it. Mell himself guessed at his meaning. Yet since Mell was not a homosexual, he didn't take offence. He was fucking those boys because the Lord willed it. In fact, he thought the President's comment might even be some sort of joke about dinosaurs and evolution.

"Everyone here has influence in the media, in the arts, religion, and politics," the President went on. "All of you still have connections. If you combine strings and pull those forces, you can get back on top and get these buzzing zebras out of my face so I can get back to the business of running the country. I've got nothing against queers, by the way," he said to Mell. "By the way, as a special gift for your attendance here today, you will each be receiving a special gift of 1000 NFTs of Madonna's vagina.

"That's it, gentlemen. Start networking, coming up with ideas. You can help each other. I want a proposal on my desk by the end of the weekend. Dinner's in half an hour."

The men looked at each other. There was a round of glares and sighs. Some of them, they could bear to deal with, others they wouldn't touch with a ten-foot pole if they could avoid it. But there *was* no avoiding it. Every one of them had their neck in a noose. In slow drips they started to murmur to each other.

"Well, folks," the President began, but he was interrupted by a stirring amongst the secret service men. Their hands went to their earpieces. One of them came up and whispered in the President's ear. The President's eyebrows crinkled in annoyance. "Why are you telling me this?" he barked at the agent, spittle spurting off his lips. "Who gives a shit?!"

"What is it?" Corky asked.

The President shook his head and huffed. "Nothing," he said. "One of our drivers has apparently decided to go get lost in the woods somewhere." The President laughed. "The rest of the evening is yours, gents. My men will show you to your rooms. Let's reconvene in the morning. I can't wait to hear what you come up with."

"Just a second," Al Garfield cut in as the men at the table started to get up. The President sighed. He wanted to go do his cocaine, not listen to this Negro, but he let him go on. "There was a rumor going around that we weren't going to be the only ones here."

The President smirked. "That's right, Al TeeVee. You can expect big peoples here, yuge numbers. Yuge. I've invited fifty more. Including… The Master. They'll all be arriving later tonight."

There were murmurs around the table. The fifty was impressive enough, but the Master was the greatest child fucker of them all, and a billionaire to boot with his own island where he and his friends could fuck as many children as he pleased. He'd even tried to get Stephen Hawking in on the child fucking game. He hadn't been successful, of course, but everyone at this table had to admire the attempt. After the stir died down, all six men stood up to be shown to their rooms.

Biermug piped up. "I might, uh, I might go for a walk actually. Catch some fresh air."

"Don't go too far, Larry," the President said laughing. "We wouldn't want to lose you too. Cordjfar!"

Chapter 9
Hog-to-Hog

At her regular Saturday afternoon curling match, Eerie Aruna scored well for her team, but they didn't win. The ice was keen, and the hog-to-hog time was good, but she was preoccupied, missed two hit-and-roll takeout shots, and nearly pulled a hamstring not even delivering but sweeping when she slipped, burned a stone, and nearly derailed the game. At the end of it, her teammates – three white ladies of a similar age to her – asked her what was wrong, but she brushed it off. "Just distracted," she said. A long time ago, Aruna used to play mixed doubles with her husband, who himself had been introduced to curling by a colleague at the university. The good thing about it was that it wasn't hard on her hips. In fact, curling was the one sport you could play with a donut in one hand the whole time, making it the most Canadian sport of all. Aruna and Vikram had both believed in keeping fit. However, they were outraged by female bodybuilders because "They can't have babies!"

"About that bear attack, I bet," said one of the women.

"It's like something out of one of those magazines you read, Aruna. Only it was on the front page of The Gleaner!"

"I saw it," Aruna nodded.

They looked at her with questioning brows.

"I mean, we were driving past where it happened last night. I saw the body," Aruna said.

"You saw it?!" the others gasped.

"Well. I saw the blanket on the body."

The Caucasian three were aghast, but one named Beatrice was determined to one-up Aruna, and said, "I actually heard he was jerking off in the woods when it happened. Craig knows somebody on the force."

The other two white women scrunched their faces in disbelief and disgust. Aruna was fully aware that Beatrice was trying to steal her glory and couldn't hide it in her expression. She saw Nandini waiting for her at the top of the steps, and called out, "Just give me ten secs!"

"What is wrong with people?!" one of the women said.

"Not people. Certain male animals," Beatrice said. "It's some internet thing, like eating Tide Pods or unscrewing a bottle cap by kicking it."

"What's the kicking thing?" Linda said.

"It's on Facebook," Beatrice answered.

"Oh."

"I have to go," Aruna said. "Nandini is here."

They waved goodbye to her, she wobbled her head at them in return. Then she left the ice and picked up her kit bag from the stands where she'd left it and changed her shoes, then met her daughter.

After Nandini had agreed to take her mother to Killarney Lake the previous evening, she said, "Let's talk about it tomorrow." And then she had avoided mentioning it again that evening, or this whole day so far. She had some excuses: some work-from-home that needed doing, meeting a friend for lunch. Then, in the afternoon, Nandini drove her mother to her curling match, dropped her off, and went to the mall for an hour before coming back to the ice rink. She had left her purse at home but stuffed her pockets with necessities. She didn't think they would be out long.

Saturday had a routine, and these routines were indeed boring, but Nandini used that boredom strategically, allowing as much of it in as possible to distract her from her anxiety. What bothered her about her mother's request to go to Killarney Lake was not just the maddening, childish stupidity of it, but also that it was a break from routine. It threatened to upset her precariously balanced equilibrium. And her mother got upset so easily, Nandini worried her mother's balance was even more tenuous than her own. Nandini actually hated driving her mother everywhere, but any time Nandini reached breaking point and ventured to suggest the woman start driving again, Aruna would be incensed. It was better not to mention it and instead just allow the irritation and boredom to take up her space in her psyche and balance there like a boulder on a cliff.

As her mother came up the steps in her team uniform – hair rinse blue with white piping – Nandini steeled herself. "I suppose we're going to go for that walk in the woods now, right?" she asked her mother when she reached the top of the steps.

Aruna did an impressive job of pretending Nandini's passive aggressive question was nothing of the kind. She went in an entirely different direction. "Did you talk to Vijay last night at Dr. Jayakrishnan's retirement party?"

Nandini was surprised. "Yes. Why?"

"His mother called me an hour ago. He went to some other party and didn't come back. Did he say anything to you about it?"

"No." Nandini shook her head.

Aruna gave a head wobble to say, "Forget about it." She followed with, "Apparently he does it all the time."

"He's not adjusting well," Nandini offered.

Aruna got back on track. "It's a nice night," she said. "Yes, we should go for a walk. But first let's get some dinner, hm?"

Nandini was surprised her mother wasn't raring to go straight to Killarney Lake. She wasn't interested in going home and getting changed first, but they went out for Chinese buffet anyway and hardly said anything to each other. Aruna asked her about work, wanted to know if anything interesting had happened at the mall. Of course not. And, in fact, they'd already had this conversation. She asked about who was still working at CrossTec, who had quit, etcetera. Nandini talked about it for a couple of minutes. Aruna's eyes glazed over.

***

Finally, they drove out to the lake. There were no other cars in the parking lot, not even police cars. When Nandini brought the car to a stop, she was laughing.

"What's so funny?" Aruna asked.

"I can't believe we're really here."

Aruna was crestfallen. "I thought you were interested too. Isn't that why you agreed?"

"I… I don't know why I agreed, Mother. I mean, what do you think is going to happen out here?"

Aruna opened her door, and it creaked loudly. "This door is so annoying!" she said for the third time that day. She pushed her annoyance aside. "Let's just go for a walk around, okay?"

She got out, and Nandini followed her, staying silent in anticipation of her mother's answer to her question, but none came. Aruna ambled down to the walking path that led into the woods that circled the lake. There was police tape up, tied across a series of trees that stretched not just across the walking path, but from the lake all the way up to the road. Aruna lifted it and ducked under. Nandini trailed behind her. Now she *really* couldn't believe they were here. She couldn't hold it in any more. "Well, Mother? We're here? Is it all you imagined?"

"Aren't you at least curious?" her mother asked.

Nandini wanted to explode, but she checked herself. Her mother had been raised religious and superstitious, and she tried to act like that was all in her past and that she only read her magazines for cheap pulp thrills, but it was a clever veil. Nandini struggled to understand how her father, a man of science, had put up with her. Perhaps she wasn't as bad when he was alive. "No," Nandini said. "It's a literal campfire story. We just crossed police tape!"

"Do you really believe that person was killed by a bear?"

That was hard to argue with. "No, but it could have been a lot of things. At the most extreme end, it could have been someone pretending to be Sally. That's extreme, but it's rational."

The evening birds were starting to sing, but the frogs were just as loud with all their weird trilling and chirps. Michelle, Nandini's police friend, used to be able to name all the frog species and match them to their calls. Nandini herself learned a few when she was in Girl Guides, but she'd forgotten all about them now. After another minute of walking, the trail was surrounded by trees on both sides. On their right, through the branches of the sloping bank, in the dim light, the water sparkled. Creatures rustled in the foliage. Nandini began to understand why her mother had lingered so long over dinner. She had been stalling, waiting for it to get darker. *Sneaky.*

"Where should we go?" Aruna asked.

Home, Nandini wanted to say. But she suppressed that thought. She suppressed even the fact that she had agreed to come here because she was being vindictive. She told herself she was being altruistic. What else did her mother have in life? *Let her have these things. Give her whatever she wants.* This was far beyond driving her to curling, but still... "The path forks up ahead," Nandini said. "That one time I went snowshoeing, it was here. We'll take the branch that cuts away from the lake and goes deeper into the woods." It was actually sort of creepy out here and getting worse every moment as the light faded. She'd have to use her phone as a light eventually. Nandini thought her mother would have second thoughts and want to turn back, but instead she wobbled her head and marched on ahead of her, still in her curling team uniform.

They came to the fork, took the branch, and strolled along the path for a few more minutes. Aruna looked all around.

"Well, in the stories," she said, "how would Sally appear?"

"Oh, that's easy," Nandini said. "I'll just think of something sexual, and then she'll come kill me." The forest animals stopped, and the woods became quiet.

Aruna's face was a disapproving grimace. "*Chee*!" she snarled. "My own daughter thinking such things! I can't stand it! I'll do it!"

Nandini's face took on horse-like proportions. "*You'll* do it?"

"You don't think I can do it? I'm a modern woman! I can do it!"

"*Chee*! My own mother thinking such things!"

Aruna didn't laugh.

"All right, Mother. Close your eyes and think the most disgusting thing you can think of."

Aruna bristled and straightened her back to its full height. "All right, I will!" she declared. "But first tell me something. Why do you think the existence of this Sally is so impossible?"

The question was so exasperating, Nandini was speechless. Her mouth opened and closed like a fish. She tiptoed around her mother's feelings, but whenever this argument came up, she cracked. It took her a few seconds before she managed to get out: "How can you think it's remotely *possible*?!"

"I know what this is. I know the real reason. You're just like your father. If you admit that one supernatural thing exists, then you must admit that other supernatural things may exist. Maybe God."

"Oh, for –"

"We humans don't know *everything*!"

"So what?! That doesn't mean you can just assume *anything*."

"It's not just anything. Why do so many people believe it? Why can't you? Can you prove God doesn't exist?"

"Which god? Where did the information about this god come from in the first place? Anyway, it's like if I declared there's a teapot in orbit around the sun too small to be seen by telescopes," Nandini said, quoting Bertrand Russell's teapot analogy. "Just because you can't prove it's not true doesn't mean it's there."

It was a mistake to say this though because Aruna didn't understand it, and it killed the discussion. In fact, she hesitated, and there was a look on her face that Nandini recognized, and somehow she knew: Aruna was thinking something about her late husband. Her sudden reluctance was so pronounced that Nandini wondered if the religious business was all somehow actually about something else. But *what* was she thinking? Nandini didn't pry.

"I can do it," Aruna repeated, wagging her finger. However, this time she meant that not only could she think a filthy enough thought, but also that she could also summon Sally. When they'd first entered the woods, she didn't really herself believe that Sally was real. Now she willed herself to.

At another fork in the path, they stopped walking. Aruna closed her eyes and squeezed them together like a five-year-old playing hide-and-seek. She strained so hard, the veins stood out on her neck.

Nandini did have to admit there was a… menace in the way leaves paused and watched them in between breezes, black darts against the hot purple void of the sky. *No.* That was actually just her imagination getting carried away with her. Even she was susceptible to such thoughts, but she had enough composure to push them out. *To anthropomorphize the woods is irrational. Don't do it*, she told herself. *It's only natural to be wary of the forest.* She knew that. Still, if you inhaled hard enough though, you could detect the faintest bad smell coming from somewhere. Not natural. Like pus and infections. Sickly. That was discomforting.

Nandini wondered what her mother could possibly be thinking. Even if Sally were real (*Don't even think it*, she told herself), and no matter how much her jugular threatened to burst, could her mother possibly allow herself to think up something vulgar enough to summon her? At first blush it was unimaginable, but then again they had actually come all the way to this point, Aruna hadn't even once complained about her aching legs even after curling. Actually, she was in good shape. So here they were, standing in the woods trying to summon Sally as if she were real. Maybe Aruna *would* cross that bridge. Unbidden, as Nandini tried to imagine what her mother was visualizing, an image invaded Nandini's mind – the only image she could imagine her mother mustering up – of her father climbing onto Aruna in the dark.

Nothing happened. "Let's just keep walking," Aruna said. She was obviously disappointed that it hadn't worked so easily, but she wasn't frustrated yet.

"Mother, it's going to get dark."

Aruna wobbled her head. "It's okay. There's still lots of time." She walked on without waiting for an answer. Nandini followed her. *Just let her do her thing,* she told herself. *Try to at least enjoy the summer air. You're at Killarney Lake!* The shimmering water glimpsed through the trees was indeed beautiful.

But then she began to slow down. There were some sounds in the woods, a shuffling movement that seemed larger than the birds. There was the smell again too, stronger now. Her mother noticed that Nandini had lagged behind, and turned to ask her, "What's wrong?"

"I don't know," she said, and in the very same instant she was slimed from above, as if she had said the secret words on *You Can't Do That on Television*.

"What the fuck?!" she cried, looking at the goop on her hands, feeling it dripping down off her hair. She looked up, and heavy clumps of flesh fell from the tree above her. She screamed. Now came the entrails, the organs. She screamed. Her mother stood horrified, wanting to grab her and pull her out of the way, but too shaken to get near her. Nandini tried to wipe off the chunky gore. Some had gotten in her mouth, she was spitting and gagging. Another lump fell on her head and she flicked it off and it hit the ground, and it was a face.

Her next thought would have been to call the police, but something shot out of the woods with a swishing sound, and Nandini crumpled to the ground choking on a shriek. Aruna looked in the direction it had come from. On a slight hill maybe about fifty meters away, there was a strange object. It looked like the rear end of a dead horse. Too late, she saw the rifle barrel poking out of the creature's anus, for in less than a second she too was hit and unconscious, as still as the bodiless face between them.

Chapter 10
Killing Two Birds in the Hand with One Stone in the Bush

Woes, the former head of Dingo Media, and Biermug, the former movie producer, had an embarrassing encounter in one of the lodge's darkened hallways. Both men had waited until it was closer to dusk, then crept out of their rooms and accosted separate secret servicemen to find out what room the woman that had serviced the President was in. As it happened, Woes tiptoed into the hallway her room was in from one end at the same time Biermug crept in from the other. Woes had been planning to tell her how sexy she was before threatening to report her to the police for prostitution if she didn't have sex with him. Biermug's plan was much more elaborate. It involved offering her a movie role and required that there be a potted plant in the room. When they saw each other in their bathrobes, poised like overweight luchadores ready to pounce, they both had to chuckle in embarrassment. There was no confusion about what either of them was here for. Neither of them intended to back down though. They straightened up and marched to the middle.

"Jeffrey," Biermug whispered.

"Larry."

"Fancy meeting you here."

"Not as fancy as that bathrobe, Jeff," Larry hissed, spittle flying from his lips even as he whispered. "Is that Burberry?"

Woes frowned. "Fucking Armani. Might as well be goddamn K-Mart."

"Don't I know it. But that's why we're here, isn't it?"

"Don't try to distract me, Larry. What about why we're right here in this hallway right now? I was here first. Better luck next time. Enjoy your evening."

Even in the dim light Woes could see Biermug's furrowed brow. "You were here first? Mm. No. I don't think so. Besides, you owe me, Jeff, remember? We had a handshake deal on TV rights for that Tarantino movie, and you screwed me."

"The one where Hitler gets killed in a movie theater? Made no sense. Hitler did not die in a movie theater, for fuck's sake. Nobody wanted to see that crap, Larry. The syndicates wouldn't shut up about it."

"Look, I'll just come right out and say it. She's out of your league, Jeff. You can just tell with her type. She needs glitz, excitement. Not some boardroom, CEO type." (Woes's hands clenched into fists at his side, but Biermug kept talking.) "Jesus, Jeff. Look at the state of you. What do you weigh now? You'd probably kill her as soon as you rolled onto her."

"You think... I don't deserve love because I'm fat?"

"What?"

Woes's fist smacked into Biermug's head. It was a pathetic blow, like getting hit with a roll of toilet paper, but it caught the former movie mogul off guard, and he stumbled backwards into a table with a vase on it, knocking it all over. Within an instant came the sound of secret servicemen on the move coming up the stairs from the side Biermug had come in from.

"Come on!" Woes hissed, and he ran back the way he came.

Biermug picked himself up and followed in a panic.

When they got to the bottom of the staircase opposite the one the secret servicemen were charging up, there was no question about them going quietly back to their rooms. Biermug's boner had deflated like a toy balloon stretched for fart noises, but he could get it back despite the fact that he'd already been out to the woods once already to jerk off. Woes had taken a Viagra, and his boner was still down there somewhere.

"Outside?" Woes asked, pointing with his thumb back over his shoulder to the back patio door behind him.

Biermug nodded.

The men almost raced to the door, opened and closed it as quietly as they could, and went down the slope to the middle of the lawn. But some lights came on in the lodge, and secret servicemen could be seen in the windows with their guns drawn, heads darting around like they were pigeons, looking for danger.

"Come on," Biermug said, and he grabbed Woes's bathrobe sleeve and pulled him along. At the edge of the backyard, where the lawn met the woods, to their right there was a poor excuse for a path that led through the trees to a groundskeeper's shed. In the heat of the moment, Biermug figured if the secret servicemen followed them out here, that's where they would go first. So he didn't go that way. He pulled Woes to the left, past the edge of the lawn and into the trees.

They pressed deeper, looking for a good spot, stepping over tree roots, and ducking branches. Finally they came to a place that seemed level and clear enough. The constant sound of crickets and birds and toads was distracting, but there was still plenty of light. Larry took up a low stance. He'd been in some street fights in his youth. Woes, on the other hand, stood tall and put his chest out and pedaled his fists like a cartoon boxer. "Put up your dukes!" he cried.

Larry wanted that girl to watch him jerk off and validate him so bad. Out here surrounded by all these trees he thought about that rapper again, and he could feel his boner coming back. He considered just jerking off out here, but then he thought, why shouldn't she want to watch him jerk off and be rewarded with fame and bags of money? He concentrated all these thoughts of rage and frustration into his right fist and lunged at Woes.

Woes easily stepped out of the way.

Woes's erection was limiting his movement a little bit, but he was able to make it look like a confident swagger. He threw a punch and missed. It was slow, almost like Woes had been reaching out to pat Biermug on the shoulder. Out here in the fading light, Biermug could see the punch coming this time. It wasn't easy to land one like it was in that dim hallway.

Biermug clasped his hands together to deliver a heroic-looking clobber to Woes's gut, but it was like punching a sofa cushion and had little effect. Woes planted his palm on Biermug's face and shoved him out of the way to make some distance. It worked, Biermug staggered back two steps. Biermug was sweating now. The old guy had more in him than Larry had imagined. Biermug felt the edges of panic start to creep into his awareness. If only he had some sulfur and potassium nitrate, he could mix some gunpowder, fashion a weapon.

Woes tried to kick Larry, but the attempt turned into something like a sumo move: he lifted his leg, flailed it out, and was then forced to plant it again when it didn't meet any target other than air. It landed at an unnatural distance from his other leg. He lost his balance and fell onto his rear end with a painful thud. Biermug tried to take advantage of the situation and kick him in the face but also stumbled and ended up falling gut-first onto Woes's crotch, wrenching Woes's erection to a painful angle under Larry's pasta-reinforced paunch. Both men grunted.

As Biermug struggled to his feet, he saw a dark silhouette further in the trees. It was a person, seemingly standing there watching them. It was just a black figure with hair like a bird's nest and something weird about the eyes, but the outline had a feminine quality about it somehow. Squinting in the dark, he could tell she was holding something in her right hand, but he couldn't tell what. For a second he wondered if it was the President's woman.

"Hello?" he said.

By now Woes was back on his feet and had seen her too. "It's her!" he yelped. He immediately started to dash towards her, out of the clearing, leaping over roots as he went. Biermug gave chase.

Sally started running towards them, arms pumping like a sprinter. Within a few meters of Woes, she leaped into the air, did a mid-air pirouette, and brought her nunchaku down onto Woes's head so hard that it split in two down the middle like a karate chop demonstration done on a block of cheese instead of bricks. Woes's brains, nasal organs, and teeth went flying out in all directions.

Biermug got splattered, was momentarily elated that Woes was dead, then realized in the very next split second that he was next. The girl snapped her nunchaku to flick the gore off the shaft. Larry used the instant to turn in insensate horror and huff it through the woods. He'd produced over twenty movies where just this sort of thing happened all the time, but all he could do was flap his lips and lift his knees.

After several stumbling meters, he dared to look back over his shoulder. She wasn't there, but he kept moving. Or at least he tried. He couldn't really keep up the pace anymore. He was already exhausted from that two-fisted blow he'd delivered to Woes's gut. He had to stop. He rested a hand on a tree, bent over, huffed and puffed, leaned his whole body against the tree, then heard the wraith crunching at speed through the pines and maples not that far behind him. He got moving again.

Within a few paces, the groundskeeper's shed came into view. It was the size of a barn. There'd be tools in there, he thought. Things he could use as weapons. Something better than nunchaku. If he could get to them fast enough.

He came out of the trees and got to the door. It wasn't locked, thank god, but as he lifted the latch he dared a moment to look back and check. No, she wasn't out of the woods yet. He had time.

He groped around on the inside wall for a light switch and found it. The illumination revealed a big shed for a big property. The ceiling was a high steeple. There was a huge workbench in the middle of the room as well as benches along all the walls and tools of every variety on every surface. There could've been a whole team working away in here. There was a buzzsaw nearby. He picked it up, but it was too awkward to handle with ease, and he dropped it back on the bench with a noisy clank. He looked back at the door. She wasn't there. He looked around some more, found a chainsaw, but it was so heavy that when he picked it up, he lost his balance and fell over, the blade almost hitting his foot. The buzzsaw he dropped before fell off the table and hit his foot instead, hacking through his bath slippers and taking off two of his toes.

"Aw, fuck!" he cried as blood gushed and spurted from the wounds.

The shed door slammed open.

It was her. He could hardly understand what the fuck he was looking at. As he thought before, there was something weird about the eyes. He still didn't know how to describe it. She had a mustache. There were... pencils (?) sticking out of her neck from every angle. There was a putrescent smell. Her movements created strange after images, making it look like she had extra limbs. And was she... was she wearing a chain of desiccated dicks?

She shoved the nunchaku into her belt and grabbed a hefty power drill that had been sitting on a bench right by the door. If he'd had the presence of mind to curse himself for not seeing it himself, he would have. She pulled the trigger. It emitted a whir like an oversexed hornet.

Larry Biermug started dragging himself backwards across the floor in a pathetic effort to escape, his foot trailing a Jackson Pollock of blood in his wake, two toes left behind on the floor like Vladimir and Estragon, as the *whir whir whir* of the drill approached...

***

Cardinal Mell's plan had almost been ruined.

The president's secret service men had, of course, scouted (hah!) the area before they settled in, and through some clever, innocent sounding banter with one of them, the cardinal was able to ferret out the location of the Boy Scout camp.

However, after dinner, as he was on his way downstairs from his room to sneak out of the lodge, he'd almost been spotted by Biermug, the Hollywood man who produced all that sinful trash, trash that was the very antithesis of decent Christian values. In less than a century, Hollywood movies had corrupted the divine morality that had been dictated and held together by the scriptures for thousands of years. The mere sight of Biermug filled Mell with rage. *"I will strew your flesh upon the mountains and fill the valleys with your carcass. I will drench the land even to the mountains with your flowing blood,"* he thought. Ezekiel 32:5. Yes, he wished he could do that to all the Hollywood people. Why were there so many of them here anyway? There was that Black fellow too – Garfield. Just think: if it weren't for slavery, the Negroes would not have been brought to America to be washed by the blood of Christ and be saved. But he was probably an ingrate like all the others of his kind, Mell thought. Of course even Cardinal Mell had to admit that, yes, maybe the church had gone a little bit far in the past. Between the seventeenth and eighteenth centuries the church castrated 5,000 boys a year to sing in the Sistine Chapel Choir. It was for the glory of God, so it was understandable, but the idea of little boys with their precious little bits mutilated almost brought a tear to Mell's eye. He didn't like the idea of circumcision either, but… Anyway, this was all reminding him that he needed to sneak out and find that Boy Scout camp. Good God, he might even have three or four in one night. His record was two. They were altar boys, absolutely pure and untainted, their snow-white buttocks like scoops of ice cream. He wondered if, unlike the altar boys, the Scouts might even be willing though. That might not be as good actually. He put the thought out of his mind. They might be younger and more numerous, that would make up for it. He almost wished the archbishops were here with him so they could share. Sometimes, when they only had one boy to share between them, by the end of the night the child was like a lifeless ragdoll and didn't bother even to squirm or moan anymore. Then there was Father Ryan who threatened to ruin it all when he said he wanted a girl. What was the point? Besides, you could only use them once: "If the tokens of virginity were not found in the young woman, then you shall bring out the young woman to the door of her father's house, and the men of her city shall stone her to death with stones." Deuteronomy 22:20. Besides: "A woman should learn in quietness and full submission. I do not permit a woman to teach or to assume authority over a man; she must be quiet."

Timothy 2:11. He was getting distracted again, Mell realized. Yet how divine to be distracted by the glory of the Lord's teachings! Never mind those Hollywood people – what was *he* himself doing here?! A man of the cloth!

Suddenly a realization struck him, and he felt ashamed of himself for his lack of faith: of course, the Lord had guided him here specifically because the Boy Scout camp was nearby! Well, it was a momentary lapse. Even the Lord, whose memory was infallible, had a memory which was fallible and needed to invent the rainbow to remind Himself of His covenant with all life on Earth. Genesis 9:16.

Well, he evaded Biermug only to almost run into Woes who was tiptoeing around too and then was barred by two secret servicemen patrolling around the French doors that opened onto the back yard. Curses! But the hand of the Lord moved again. There was a commotion upstairs and the servicemen went to investigate. Cardinal Mell managed to slip out the back doors and cross the lawn to reach the woods.

His sense of direction wasn't the best, but he basically understood what the secret serviceman had told him, and he followed his hints to the best of his ability.

Miracle piled upon miracle. Within minutes he had found the camp, but that wasn't the only thing. They were actually nubile little *Cub* Scouts. And the well-behaved little darlings were already asleep, and under lean-tos, not even tents!

Mell approached an angelic lad sleeping right at the edge of the circle, the cardinal's fingers squirming like tendrils as he closed in for the snatch. There was always a split second of hesitation at this moment. Would the Lord intercede and protect – no, *prevent* him from interfering with the child? There never was, but Mell always paused.

Mell grabbed the boy and held him close. The child did not wake. Which meant the Lord approved. Mell bolted. Even as he ran, giddily skipping over tree roots, the child slept soundly.

But… where could they perform the acts? Not out here in the woods like some "rapper" on Instagram. Mell stopped running to think. The child was beginning to feel heavy in his arms, and Mell was over seventy. It hit him. There was a big shed for the groundskeeper. It had a peaked roof, which was not a steeple, but it would do to put him in the right mindset. He set off again, but again his sense of direction hindered him until the Lord placed the shed in front of him. There was even heavenly light coming from within. Mell beamed, tears of glorious faith welling up in his eyes. The shed door was even unlocked, but Mell had to shakily maneuver it open with his foot, cradling the boy like Mary cradling Jesus in Michelangelo's Pieta.

But once inside, he wasn't prepared for the sight that awaited him, nor the sudden realization that the Lord had finally abandoned him.

In one corner of the large room was Biermug, dead on the ground, partially propped up against the wall, but his entire crotch area was a red, squishy mess. Standing in front of the corpse was a creature unlike any described in the Bible. Her back was turned to him. She seemed to be occupied with something in her hands that was making gory noises, but at the sound of the door opening, she turned. In one hand she held a power drill. Biermug's penis was shoved over the drill bit, blood trickling down over the drill chuck and handle. Looking at Cardinal Mell, the creature pulled the trigger and Biermug's penis spun at 300 RPM.

Sally abandoned her previous work, as if drawn compulsively to Mell's much more kinetic aura of perversion and began walking towards him.

Mell threw the child to the ground. "Blessed is he who seizes your infants and dashes them against the rocks." Psalm 137:9. The Cub Scout emitted a grunt but remained asleep. The Cardinal turned and fled. Sally Pencilneck started to follow him out of the shed at a brisk walking pace, but something caught her attention on the work benches and she paused.

For Mell, this meant the advantage of a decent head start on her, though he didn't know why. But now he floundered. Left or right? He huffed and puffed. What was she? He felt older than ever before, as if the Lord was finally calling him home. For the first time that night, he regretted wearing his full episcopal vestments out into the woods.

He stopped to catch his breath, braced his hand against a large tree in front of him. What followed happened too quickly for him to process. A crunch in the leaves behind him (her footstep), his head started to swivel at the sound, but before it could fully turn: a hand on the back of his head, twisting it back forward, then smashing his forehead into the tree trunk. He was in a daze, blood flowing down his nose and over his mouth. He slumped to his knees. She grabbed his right arm, yanked it up against a high branch, putting an agonizing strain on his shoulder and lifting him off his knees. He mustered the energy to look at it. It was then he saw the hammer and stake-sized nail in her hands. He cried out in fear before pain as the nail went into the back of his hand with a single hammer blow that seemed to resound through the entire forest, sending birds from trees. He wept and wept. He was still facing the tree. Now with immense strength, she pulled his other arm up, held his hand up against a branch on the other side. Another nail went through the flesh and bone of his hand like they were butter. His head lolled back. He could try to pull his hands free, but the pain was too great. He was even trying to stay on his feet to prevent pulling his hands on the nails. Then he heard the whir of the power drill. Now, somewhere in his mind, he truly rued wearing his cassock. Biermug's penis went into Mell's anus at maximum RPMs. For a split second, he thought about Sodom. "Where are the men who came to you tonight? Bring them out to us so that we can have sex with them." Genesis 19:5. But then it went through his intestines, his stomach, shredded his diaphragm, drilled through his chest ripping his lungs to bits, his esophagus, his neck, entered the base of his skull, sending bone fragments flying, turned his brain to mush, and then exited the top of his head. Sally's arm had ripped his back open as she went, and his cadaver fell apart into two halves, each dangling from a branch of the tree where it was nailed by the hand. Sally let go of the trigger and the sound of it slowed like a bug landing on a leaf. Nothing of Biermug was left on the end of it. She gave a cursory look at the ground to see if the penis had fallen off somewhere, but she didn't find it and walked away.

Chapter 11
Dulce et Decorum est

What spooked him was a reflection in a plate of glass that — for a split second — looked like his long-deceased grandmother.

Robert Vanier was a night watchman at the Fredericton Region Museum. It should have been an old man's job, but he was only thirty-two. Also, more importantly, the museum did not need a security guard day or night. It was well-positioned right in the middle of downtown Fredericton, and it was in a handsome historic building that had once been officers' quarters. However, inside the exhibits were a random mishmash of military paraphernalia, antiques, crafts, and, worst of all: the Coleman Frog.

The Coleman Frog was a taxidermied 20-kilogram frog that was supposedly captured as a normal-sized frog around Killarney Lake in 1889 by a man named Fred Coleman. Coleman fed it whiskey and baked beans, causing it to grow to the size of a bulldog, and he claimed it would answer to a dinner bell and entertain guests. The frog was supposedly killed in a dynamite accident, but

Coleman then had it taxidermied, and now it resided in the museum in its own glass showcase on a pedestal on the ground floor, where anyone could see that it was so obviously made of papier-mâché, wax, and paint that it was embarrassing for the visitors and the museum alike. The museum's visitors tended to be school groups from around the province, in which the kids only cared about the Frog, or visitors from out of town who had been duped into thinking the museum would be interesting by a guidebook or its historic exterior.

Nobody was going to steal anything, not even the Frog, from the museum.

But there was a security guard on during the day, and then Robert would come in at closing time to take over for the night. When the changeover happened, they barely spoke to each other. There was never anything to report.

Most of the night, he would sit and read. Eventually, the museum would be almost dark except for a few pilot lights. And there was a desk lamp that he kept on to read by. He had become a voracious reader in the last few years for some reason he didn't know. No. He knew why. He had once dated a girl who was a real reader, they broke up, and after the fact he decided it was an aspect of himself he could work on or even improve, if only to stop doomscrolling even, and he found himself hooked. He sometimes wondered if it was too late to go back to university.

He was obligated to do a round of the museum

once an hour. It was completely unnecessary, but he didn't begrudge it. He liked stretching his legs at least. Sometimes he even read standing up. So at 8:00 on the button, he put down his copy of *Crime and Punishment* face down on his page, and he set off. For some reason, he was having trouble focusing on it tonight anyway.

There was a certain section of the museum on the second floor, a kind of short hallway made to resemble a dark World War I trench, where army and nurses' uniforms were on display in large floor-to-ceiling glass showcases, some of them depicting whole scenes inside. Even during the day, this hallway was dark, and the showcases were lit from inside, individually. As a little kid here on a school field trip, this hallway scared Robert because of the display with the mannequin in it clad in a World War I gasmask and uniform.

It was on one of these showcases that tonight he saw his grandmother reflected back at him.

And she said, "Wear."

He jumped.

Actually, it was a trick of the light from his flashlight hitting the glass, and his foot creaking on a floorboard at precisely the same instant.

Robert Vanier was not a superstitious type, but he had to constantly prove it to himself. He worked out and wore a shirt one size too small. He had a handsome face to go with his handsome name. He had molded himself into a tough guy. Why would he be scared of a reflection? Even so, he had to close his eyes and breathe deliberately, and, as he did so, he could feel his heart – *bam, bam, bam, bam*.

He hadn't liked this dark mock trench with the gasmask since he was nine years old. There was something at the back of his mind that he had to overcome every time he inspected it, either consciously or unconsciously.

The last of the daylight was coming in through the windows in the main room, which he forced himself to consider may have been a factor in the illusion, but when he flashed his light at the glass again he was unable to recreate it. It was an effect he had never seen before. Of course, the light from the windows didn't reach around the corner to this area anyway. No matter how hard he stepped on the floor, he couldn't get it to say "wear" again – it only creaked.

There seemed to be a weird energy in the air tonight, something going through him and all around the museum, but he dismissed that as well. He knew he was just spooked. He tried to convince himself of this even though he had been feeling it since he started his shift and even when he was downstairs reading.

The problem was exacerbated by it being *his grandmother*. People in the family had sometimes said that she was a seer or could tell the future. What it actually was, was that she had sometimes had dreams that came true. For example, as the stories went, she would dream of a relative she hadn't spoken to in ten years, and then that morning they would get word that that relative had died. As a kid he believed it, but in his teens he learned that Grandma had seen Aunt Elaine much more recently, they'd been talking about her the night before, and she actually died more like a month later. More importantly, everyone has five to six dreams every night, whether they remember any of them or not. That's over 1,500 dreams a year. It would be stranger if *none* of those coincidentally related to subsequent events. And if you happened to remember them, then, *voila!*, you can tell the future. Even as a fourteen-year-old, he knew this, he was becoming pragmatic already. That was the same year she passed away. Her mind had been going for years, and in her final months everything she said was either complete gibberish or something from her childhood, her words reduced to miserable gurgles. He was not close to her, but he was asked to be there by her bedside. He resented it. She didn't even recognize him, so he couldn't see the point. She was so wrinkled. Tiny reservoirs of saliva gathered at the corners of her mouth. He was sadder about his mother's impending grief than he was about the old woman. There was a particular moment when he was the only one in the room with her. *Why me of all people?* he wondered. Later, older, he would always regret that lack of empathy. In that moment, though, she held his hand to pull him close and mumbled into his ear with her gross mouth, "Wear a frock." Then she died. He had never even seen a dead body before. Now he was holding one's hand.

Robert pressed his foot into the floor again. It would not say "wear" again no matter how hard he tried. He shone his light at the glass, avoiding the display cabinet with the gasmask in it.

But then he did hear a sound, something thin cracking, peeling, like an eggshell, coming from downstairs. After working here three years, he knew the sounds this place made: the pipes, the floorboards, the wind. This was a new sound.

He went to the top of the stairwell and shone his light down. There was no more daylight. The cracking sound stopped. So he had imagined it. Or it was a rodent, something which could damage the exhibits and was within his purview to report. Reframing the noise as a component of his nightly duties had a somewhat soothing effect on him. But then it started again. Now there was a tinkle of glass as well.

He forced himself down the stairs. He had to confirm it was a mouse, that's all. His body wanted to halt on every step, but he summoned up his tough guy persona and tried to take the stairs at a normal pace. The noises stopped again but there was that weird energy in the atmosphere. He froze on the steps. The light from his flashlight was jittering on the wall, the handrail, the steps. He started his descent again, like the engine of a lumbering machine slowly starting up, just to keep the light from doing its witchy dance.

On the ground floor, with extreme hesitation, he shone his light around the exhibits – medals, documents, photographs – in glass cases, but nothing was out of the ordinary. He wanted it to be a thief after the medals. That would explain the sound of glass he'd heard. He moved into another room. Still nothing. But, as he went from room to room, the feeling going through him, that feeling he'd had all night, was getting worse, not better. He felt like he might even vomit if it kept intensifying like this.

He was in the reception area. He shone his flashlight around, then turned his head for a cursory look in the room with the Coleman Frog and froze. He could not move his hand holding the flashlight to light the scene. But he saw the silhouette of it there, vaguely frosted in the moonlight coming in through the window.

The shattered glass on the floor.

Flakes of the paper-thin, dry epidermis scattered around the platform of the pedestal.

The *thing* still there, the twenty-kilo beast, poised, breathing in the dark, its great clammy chest heaving with malevolent patience, its damp skin all green and new hesitantly limned by the moon, this thing summoned back to life by the dark energies swirling around Killarney Lake, calling to it to join them there.

"Robby, wear a frock," Robert heard his grandmother mumble, and then the thing leapt at his throat and tore the flesh from his body like he was being ripped apart by a revenant grenade.

Chapter 12
Quid Pro Quo

Nandini started to wake up first, someone's thumbs prodding open her eyelids, but Aruna started to come to only seconds later when someone kicked her feet. Their minds were still muddy, but the dim light of an oil lantern revealed they were in a large army tent, big enough to stand up upright in, the details of which were becoming more defined as their heads cleared. They were side-by-side, tied to chairs, their arms behind their backs. A few meters in front of them was a man dressed in an immaculate military uniform that looked straight out of World War I, one foot up on a stool, leaning an elbow against his raised knee: Boudreau, the horse-butt sniper.

He allowed himself a half-smirk of satisfaction at the exquisite precision of his tranquilizer doses. "Ain't that just the greatest!" he exclaimed. "To be able to adjust the doses to account for your different weights with such precision that you still wake up in the same instant. Yes, I sure am the very best there is, if I don't say so myself."

As the women began to murmur, he watched them with childlike anticipation. He liked this part. Realization, distress, the fruitless struggling against the ropes.

Nandini was the first to cry out. "What is this?!" Her mind went immediately to panic. Even the man's uniform filled her with terror. She knew without having to think it that this man was "Sally". That Sally wasn't real, but the stories were, and this was the man responsible for the bodies out there. It was him and not an animal that killed the man whose body lay by the side of the road. And the other one… The memory started to make her nauseous again, but she fought it down. His guts were still on her. She tried with all conscious force to calm herself, to think of a way to talk her way out of this, but her breathing was becoming faster and faster. She could hear her mother beside her praying in Tamil through gasps and tears. She didn't want to turn to look at her. She was too frightened.

Boudreau straightened himself. "Whoa, whoa, take it easy, ladies," he chuckled. "I'm not here to hurt ya. Not necessarily. Ha ha. But let me ask you this."

There was a table beside him covered with paraphernalia, and, more importantly: an array of firearms. Aruna's purse was there too, and its contents spread out. Their phones were placed next to each other, like they themselves were.

Boudreau picked up a sniper rifle from the table, a glistening black insectoid piece of hardware. Nandini gasped, her mother sobbed louder.

He walked over and stood in front of Nandini. "Murdered anyone lately, hm? Chopped anyone to bits? Wandering around in these woods like that. There's nobody supposed to be in here, ya know. But they say a criminal always returns to the scene of the crime. Now, I saw that poor fella up there, I thought to myself, I'll bet this is as good a place as any to wait and see who shows up. And what do you know? Two for the price of one!" He looked back and forth between them and laughed, then went back to inspecting the barrel of his rifle as if he were checking his testicles for cancer lumps.

Now Nandini was starting to wonder if this man was *not* the one who killed that person they saw under a blanket by the side of the road the night before, or the one that spilled all over her just earlier. Or maybe it was some sort of game. Now she didn't know what to think, but the threat of him was ever-present.

Boudreau moved a few steps over to Aruna. He looked at her for a moment, but she was blubbering. He sighed and returned to Nandini.

"You don't really look the type, I guess," he said, "but sometimes it's who you least expect." He looked at her and grimaced. "Look at you. Red-handed, red-faced, red-haired even. What a mess. Not very careful, are you? Let me guess. As a young girl, you tortured and vivisected animals in the woods behind your house, inspected their insides. Sad story. It happens."

He backed up so he could take in both of them. "Well? Is it one of you, or not? I must admit, there was a small part of me, the tiniest part, that sorta wished it were true that it were some supernatural thing. But that would have been ridiculous," Boudreau droned on. "A child's fantasy. One doesn't reach my levels of expertise in the taking of life by indulging in realms in which life and death are but figments of the imagination, if ya know what I mean."

"You're... you're talking about Sally Pencilneck?" It was Aruna who spoke, still sniffling but perking up as she put the pieces together.

Boudreau swung towards her. "What do you know?"

Aruna's head did an Indian head wobble. "My daughter knows *all* about her," she said.

"Mother!"

He pivoted towards Nandini, pointed the muzzle of the rifle in the general area of her chest as an almost casual afterthought. "Tell me everything."

The terror of the rifle muzzle paralyzed her. It was a real gun, real steel, the texture of it was palpable without even having to touch it.

Nandini finally found some words, and gulping said, "You're breaking the law! You can't just tie us up and threaten us! You can't own that gun! I don't think you're even allowed to put up a tent in these woods. Who the hell are you?"

He nodded. "I understand. Even a cold-blooded

killer like you can become distressed when they sense the fingers of law and order closing in on them. You want to call for help. Call the police even, irony of ironies. Here, why don't I call them for ya?"

Boudreau went back to the table and picked up the phone on the left, Nandini's position. He tweaked it between his fingers in her direction, as if to ask, "Is this the one?" She didn't know what was happening but managed a trembling nod in response. He positioned his fingers over the screen. "Code?" he asked.

"Three..." she stuttered, "one... four... one..."

"Police?" he asked.

Again, she just managed to nod.

He dialed 911 and put the phone up to her ear.

"911. What's your emergency?" asked the voice on the other end of the line.

She worried it was a trick, and he would snatch the phone away before she could ask for help. The words poured out of her like hot lava, but she tried to keep them orderly. "My name is Nandini Rajan!" (It was one of those moments where she wished her name really was "Nadine".) "I've been abducted and my mother! We're being held at gun point!"

Boudreau smiled at her approvingly.

"Where are you, Nandeenee?" the 911 voice asked.

"In the woods outside Killarney Lake, but I'm not sure where exactly!"

"That's okay. We can find you. I'm going to send some cars out there now. Stay on the line."

A beep followed by a buzzing noise came from one of Boudreau's pockets. He reached into it and pulled out his own phone, swiped the screen with his thumb, then showed it to Nandini. It was a text message that read: "Civilian incident call in from Killarney Lake. Google coordinates: 46.014512, -66.619142."

"Nandeenee, are you there?" asked the voice on the phone. Nandini was dumbstruck, mouth agape, looking up at Boudreau with watery eyes.

"You see?" he said. "Unfortunately for you, I am here under the auspices of the federal government. Every incident report in this area goes straight to the top, and now to me. The government believes this campfire story is true, and they sent me here to catch the killer. I am Claude Boudreau, great-great-grandson of the horse butt-sniper."

"What's a horse butt-sniper?" Aruna asked, and Nandini could hear the edge of a thrill in her voice trying to shoulder the mania out of the way.

Boudreau heard the hint of excitement there and turned to her like a viper. He had an in with this woman. "Did you see that papier-mâché butt of a fallen horse on the hill? The butt from which I hit you with my tranquilizer darts? No, of course you didn't. Because I'm just that good."

Aruna was riveted. "But how…" she started to ask.

"Now, now," Boudreau said. "I'll tell you everything you want to know. Gladly," he added with an avuncular smile. It was strange how jolly this fellow was. "But you need to tell me something too. That's only fair, isn't it, Mrs…"

"Aruna Rajan," she muttered.

"Mother!"

"Good," Boudreau nodded. "Now, as I said, Mrs. Rajan, you tell me something, I tell you something. Quid pro quo. Tit-for-tat."

At the word "tit", a gust of wind tore through the tent, rippled the flame in the oil lamp. Outside the tent, the sound of twigs snapping under a footfall too heavy to be one of the usual creatures in this region.

The sound shot through all of them in the tent. "What was that?" he said. Boudreau straightened and his every sense became alert. He returned to the table, swapped the rifle for a pistol, cocked it, and headed for the flap. He looked back at them one last time, then lifted the flap and went out into the hot night.

For a moment, there was no more noise. Then they heard him cry out. The women tensed like iron. Then came the pistol's report. Again. Again. Three cracks. Boudreau shouting. A sound like a head of lettuce being ripped apart. Continued cries and sounds of struggle. Aruna and Nandini started screaming too. They were shouting and pulling at their bonds in futility.

They shot desperate glances at each other. Nandini craned her neck, looking around the tent for anything they could use, but she only did it because that was what she was supposed to do. She knew it was ridiculous. They were still tied up. Her mother was muttering to herself in Tamil, her head bowed and trembling.

The chairs were folding, lightweight, and somewhat flimsy. She attempted a sitting hop. She tried again, shouting, "Haah!" and slamming the chair legs into the ground with as much force as she could muster. There was a faint crack. One of the legs was wobbling a few millimeters more than it had been. This could work, she hoped.

***

Outside the tent, more than a hundred meters away on a hill that had a perspective down on it, a woman covered head-to-toe in a hooded ghillie suit lay flat on her stomach in the dirt and was watching through binoculars when Boudreau erupted from the tent, muscles alert, swinging his pistol in a wide arc. *Another clown*, she thought, *just like every other clown they've sent over the years*. There was enough moonlight to make out what was going on, and yet Sally Pencilneck seemed to appear out of nowhere, plummeting onto Boudreau from out of midair, like a jaguar, her nunchaku spinning like a helicopter propeller. She must have been up in a tree. The woman on the hill recoiled at the sight. It was something she could never get used to. Unconsciously, she hunched further back under her hood. In the back of her mind, she recited a litany: *vomit, rotten eggs, zit pus...* Surprisingly, though, Boudreau had turned his gun on Sally in time and was putting up a fight, a decent fight. The nunchaku didn't connect. That meant he had a chance. He got off three shots, shouted in frustration, then started to back away further into the woods. The woman on the hill lost sight of him.

Now there was the matter of the two bundles the man had carried into the tent that looked suspiciously like body bags. They hadn't emerged. The faux-leaf-covered woman moved her binoculars away from her face and rubbed her chin. She could risk going down there, but how long would that trigger-happy sap actually be able to keep Sally occupied? The safer way, if her mind was set on going down there, might be the forest's underground tunnels. Gingerly, still avoiding an excess of motion, still worried that Sally might appear at any second, she pulled out a folded map from one of the pockets of the ghillie suit. Quietly, slowly, she turned it the right way around, unfolded it, and studied its lines, lines she'd drawn on it herself. One dot followed by two dashes were the legend for the underground tunnels.

She looked up at the tent again. The tent seemed to be in the right place, and she knew where there was a tunnel entrance nearby. The problem was Sally appeared in the tunnels sometimes too. After all, Sally was the one that had dug them out in the first place. They were hidden all over the place, like spider webs, so one would normally think the chances she'd be down there in the same spot as you at the same time would be low, but that was almost never the case with Sally Pencilneck. The ghillie woman thought for another second, scanned the area through the binoculars again. Perhaps she could steal a trick from Sally herself and go through the trees from branch to branch…

The ground was hard and lumpy against her thighs and torso, even through the ghillie suit. She wasn't cramping yet, probably wouldn't for a long while given all the training she'd done, but she convinced herself that she might start cramping any minute now – a distinct disadvantage if she had to face Sally – and it was another reason it was better to be on the move. So she made up her mind. Mentally, she recited her litany (*shit on the seat of a public toilet, a tapeworm ripped in half, a bile-filled goiter…*) and then abandoned her position and sought out the nearest climbable tree.

***

Nandini was still trying desperately to smash her chair legs against the ground, shouting as she did so. Aruna was sobbing and mumbling incoherent prayers in Tamil. There was the gunfire from outside the tent, further away now but still audible. And, maybe worse, somehow through all this, at the edge of her awareness Nandini could hear sounds from *above* the tent as well. It could just be an animal. She focused her energies on shouting and hopping in the chair, not allowing herself to go so far as to think the thought that: *It could be Sally*. But it could be, and so she jumped harder.

The back left leg on the chair half snapped, hurling her face first into the dirt and twisting her left ankle with an ugly crunch and an uglier groan from the victim. Worse, despite her effort and partial success, she was still tied to the chair. She was also aware of a new kind of zipping sound from overhead, and when she turned her face up from the dirt, she saw a knife blade slashing open the canvas.

Some kind of leaf monster swooped through the hole and landed on the ground in front of them. The prisoners shrieked.

"You?!" growled the leaf monster, throwing back her hood.

"Professor Clover?!" Aruna and Nandini exclaimed at once. It was her, instantly recognizable, despite the weird outfit, her hair being tied down, and the camouflage paint all over her face.

"Why are you here? Why are you dressed like that?" they asked.

"Shut up!" she barked. The authority in her voice was undeniable. They immediately complied.

Professor Clover's eyes were darting all over the tent, scanning every corner, nook, and cranny. The weapons on the table mesmerized her. "My god," she muttered. "Never seen that kind of hardware before." She edged closer to the array, ran her fingers over the harsh metal grip of a pistol. "Could actually do some damage with this stuff." Her voice trailed off. A voice interrupted her reverie.

"Professor Clover?"

Clover spun to face them. "Why are *you* here? There've been… animal attacks. You told me about it yourself last night. You even saw a body –" She stopped herself short. What was the point of berating them? Lying to them? She was wasting time. "Never mind," Clover said. "I'm going to cut you free. Say nothing, think nothing." Clover set Nandini upright, the chair unstable but standing again for the moment.

Then she pulled a frighteningly large Bowie knife from under her leaf covered garb like it was a magic trick. Nandini suppressed a gasp. The sight of the knife and the way she had fondled the gun a moment earlier, more than the camouflage paint and the outfit, made Nandini somehow uncertain about their rescue. Nandini was stunned that Clover owned, carried, and needed such a knife.

Clover started on Nandini's feet first. As she was working the knife, she said, "Whatever happens, you can't think about…" She paused from cutting Nandini's ropes and checked over her shoulder. The sounds of fighting were too far away to be heard. Or, worse, the fighting had stopped completely. She looked up at the hole in the canvas she herself had made above them and held her gaze for a moment. There was no movement up there. Finally, she started speaking again, but in a low, almost fearful whisper. The authoritative sharpness was softened. "You can't think or say anything about… S-E-X. You understand me?"

Something about the way Professor Clover said it made Nandini realize that, amazingly, the woman was able to spell the word without thinking it. *How much mental training does that take?* But this was all a distraction. The implication of what she said was madness. Nandini fought, fought to think rationally. "You're a scientist. You can't mean to say –"

Aruna cut in, her voice suddenly clear. "You mean she's real?"

"Now's not the time, Mother."

"It's all real," Clover said through a cold grimace.

Nandini expected some kind of girlish, giddy reaction from her mother, but the older woman looked away from Clover in an introverted kind of way.

"Who was that man?" Clover asked as she worked.

Nandini shook her head. "He said he was from the government. There was a body, in the woods, in a tree."

Clover nodded, knowingly. "And he waited for you. I've seen that move before. Amateur hour." She looked at Aruna and felt especially sorry for her. Unlike Nandini she was not covered in gore, but she was trembling.

"He," Nandini continued, "he thought we did it, I think, or that's what he seemed to be saying. I'm not sure."

"This one's MO is a new level of incompetent," Clover said to herself. "Now, listen to me. Both of you," she said. "What's the grossest thing you can think of? Something you can visualize to make sure you don't have any… S-E-X thoughts."

"What do you mean?" Nandini asked.

Clover gave her a hard stare that said: *Don't make me repeat myself.* Nandini still didn't answer. "Let's move this along. How about barf?" Clover said.

"No…" Nandini said, her voice croaking. "One time there was this guy, and I tried to… Well, whenever I think of barf…"

Whatever had happened was completely beyond the possibility of Aruna even imagining, or admitting she could imagine at least, but she was apoplectic with disgust anyway. "*Chee*! *Chee*! Ptoo!"

"Come on, think of something," Clover said.

"Divine eating fresh dogshit."

"I didn't know you were a film buff too," the Professor said, and almost smiled. She started working on cutting loose Nandini's hands. "What about her?"

"Don't worry about her," Nandini said. "She hates anything to do with you-know-what." She pictured a zit oozing pus.

Her hands came free and she rubbed the wrists. Professor Clover came around in front of Nandini to face her and shook her head. "That's almost worse. That means she thinks about it all the time, even constantly. I've dealt with her kind before. She's obsessed. Sometimes it's all they think about. She'll be like a beacon. Remember when Richard Gere kissed Shilpa Shetty on the cheek…"

"Disgusting!" Aruna spat.

"... and there were calls for her to be beheaded," Clover continued, ignoring the outburst. "*Those* are the ones you have to be worried about."

Clover started working on cutting the bonds around Aruna's feet. "Mrs. Rajan," she started, her voice as soft as she could make it, "what are you going to think about?"

"I'll think only about Sally," Aruna said, giving a little head wobble. In seconds she was free too. As she rose to her feet, she held onto Professor Clover's shoulder for support.

"We need to get you two out of these woods," Clover said. "You need to go back home. What are you doing?!" she shouted at Nandini as she picked up their phones and her mother's bag from the pile of belongings on the table Boudreau had confiscated from them.

"Just... just grabbing my stuff."

"Fine. Don't use your phone until you're out of the woods. It's connected to the internet. It's not worth the risk. Seeing any ad on any website is a risk. Any pop-up window. You never know."

Aruna was forcing herself to try to flex her trembling hands. It was clumsy.

There was a thumping sound outside that startled them all. It was getting louder as it neared the tent, it was only seconds away. How many seconds had it been since the sounds of the fighting had become inaudible? Clover cursed herself for not keeping track.

Too late.

But it was Boudreau who appeared at the entrance of the tent, not Sally Pencilneck. Where his left arm had been was now a ragged stump with the bone exposed, a makeshift tourniquet at the elbow. His pants and underwear were torn off too, and only one cuff, bunched up around his boot, and the ragged ends of the waistbands held up by his belt remained, like something a caveman might wear. His little penis dangled exposed and vulnerable like a terrified civilian bystander.

He was panting, bleeding from gashes everywhere including the dismembered arm, but he managed a smile. "Well, who's this?" he chuckled. "Doesn't matter," he interrupted himself. "Saved me the trouble of untying you myself. Ha ha."

"Run," he said, that implacable smile still plastered across his face.

The three women stood frozen, stupefied. "Run!" he barked. There was a thump. The smile flipped into a grimace, and the big man thudded face first into the dirt. Behind him was Sally Pencilneck: the Groucho mask, the hypno eyes, pencils, penis necklace, the fetid smell. She was looking down at her prey, her red nunchaku still spinning. She struck him with the weapon again and there was another sick thud. There was something atavistic about her, primitive, that was somehow more frightening than all the accoutrements, like she was here before anyone else ever crossed the land bridge to North America. Ancient. It registered on a subconscious level.

How Sally had appeared behind Boudreau without being seen was impossible, but Professor Clover had witnessed her do similar a dozen times before. She didn't waste time thinking about it. The instant she heard the swishing of the nunchaku, she slashed a gash in the back canvas of the tent with her bowie knife. "Go!" Professor Clover cried and practically forced Aruna out. In a moment of clarity, Aruna fumbled with her phone for an instant trying to get a photo, but Clover forcibly turned her around and kicked her rear end, and the older woman stumbled through the rough opening.

Nandini, though, was transfixed, frozen to the spot, as she watched the nunchaku come down again and again. Sally flipped the big man over with preternatural ease and started whacking his junk. Yet Nandini made no move to help him *or* to flee. She wasn't even really watching Sally Pencilneck. She was instead distracted by what seemed to be happening around the freak killer. She saw something like a heat haze shimmering in the air. No, it was a *warping*, and the fabric of space itself was unfolding, like a shifting fractal *kōlam* design, elaborate and bursting with colors, but one that folded a million times, in impossible directions, giving Sally extra arms and heads. And somehow through that window she glimpsed a landscape, a desert of red and gray dust, populated by emaciated skull-faced beings being trampled to powder by strange diseased leviathans, their bodies covered in sickly growths that were actually miniature conjoined twins, dead, limp, and decaying. As the leviathans passed, a feeble trickle of black ichor leaked from the smashed, empty eye sockets of the peons that were crushed under their feet. In the distance, the soaring spires of a castle that was more like a termite mound the size of a metropolis than any fortress in any dream. There were creatures with humanoid features, but had too many limbs, or no heads. The leviathans crossed cliff faces seemingly made from obese varicose flesh, pulsing pink and bruised. It was a world that stunk of insects and gore.

And then just as suddenly, the "window" closed, space folding back out to normalcy, and Nandini came out of the hallucination and returned to her senses. There was Sally again, in this grimy tent, in the darkening forest, whaling on the French horse-butt sniper. She was real. *She was real.*

Professor Clover, a few paces away from the tent, finally realized Nandini wasn't with them, and for a split second argued with herself about whether or not to go back for a girl so stupid she wouldn't listen to her orders.

"What are you doing?!" Professor Clover hissed, sticking her head in the gap.

Finally, Nandini turned and saw the Professor, but she was still stunned by the vision, feeling she too was drawn to march towards that distant castle. She felt someone was there, a being to be worshipped. That was just a hallucination caused by stress and fear and horror though, she told herself. Sally Pencilneck was real though. It was the sound of the blows that brought it home as much as the sight of her. Nandini had to be careful now. Her grip on her sanity was slipping. This episode was the first evidence of it.

The Professor hissed again, but this time she didn't wait any longer. She bolted, and Nandini finally started running too. Running for her life.

Chapter 13
Epstein Didn't Kill Himself

President Ruby was there waiting when Ferrari Epstein's helicopter landed in the landing field a few kilometers away from the lodge. He tried to stand with his back straight, but he had a tendency to slouch, and he caught himself doing it again and again. It was especially difficult with the helicopter's rotor blowing his hair plugs around like crazy, so his hands were almost constantly on his head trying to smooth them down. Behind him was the black stretch Hummer that brought him up through the woods on a very bumpy gravel road. The driver was still inside, and Rocky, the girl he'd hired for the weekend. That was everyone. As a conscious demonstration of self-confidence, he didn't bring a security detail with him, but as he watched the helicopter's rotor blades slow to stop, he began to wonder if that was a mistake. Ferrari could pull out a gun and shoot him on the spot and there'd be nothing he could do about it. It'd be his duty to accept death, like one of those samurai. *Samurai*, he repeated to himself. *What a weird word. Samurai.* They had some word for killing themselves too, but he couldn't remember it. He repeated the word "samurai" over and over again in his head, until without realizing it he'd slouched into a half crouch like he was trying to take a shit in the woods, with both hands on his head trying to keep his hair from flying away as the helicopter blades blew it everywhere. He also didn't realize that he'd started saying it out loud, and by staring at the ground in a daze he'd failed to notice that Ferrari was already standing in front of him, a $3,500 Brioni blazer bundled around one arm. Standing just behind his right shoulder was his romantic and business partner, the impeccably debonair socialite Foufou Reservoir. He had made her a millionaire too. She was smoking a cigarette and her Omega watch glinted in the diminishing sunlight. Together, they had sex trafficked over one thousand girls. Ruby's thirty-four felony counts hardly even compared.

"Samurai, samurai, samurai, samurai…"

"Donald, what the fuck are you doing?" Epstein asked in genuine disbelief. Reservoir smirked.

"Oh, sorry, Ferrari, I didn't know you were here." The President straightened his back, his hair, and his suit, and smiled a wide orange grin. He couldn't wait to impress Ferrari with how awesome he was and his awesome stuff and the awesome things he could give him. Epstein glanced back at the helicopter, angrily wondering how the President could not have known he was there – had it disappeared? – but, no, the helicopter was still there.

"Don't call me 'Ferrari.' How many times do I have to tell you?"

The smile faded. "Sorry, Mr. Epstein. You're a bit late," he added both politely and rudely.

"We had to dodge the Canadian Air Force. Fortunately, I have an excellent pilot. And we're carrying a bazooka." Epstein smiled.

Donald couldn't tell if that last part, or any of it, was a joke or actually true. It could be true. He gave a little laugh anyway. "Please," he said, indicating the stretch Hummer with a magnanimous wave.

"What the fuck is this? Why is this Hummer covered in neon?" Epstein asked. Reservoir smirked again.

"It's classy," was the only answer. Reservoir laughed.

"And you drive this thing through the woods?"

"Oh, yes. No, not exactly. As you know the lodge is practically a secret and very exclusive. But there are well-maintained private roads that go down there. They're built for vehicles like this. The kinds of cars and trucks that people like you and me have that you don't want to get scratched up and whatnot or have to go four-wheel driving. Though this is the best there is of course."

"You didn't tell anybody else about this place, did you?"

"No." In fact, Ruby had revealed the location to numerous dignitaries from Saudi Arabia, Israel, Oman, the UAE, Iran, North Korea, China, and other countries that had visited him at his Florida estate.

"Anyway, this is nothing," he continued. "Prince Alfred, good friend of mine, you know, he came by helicopter! It's parked down by the lake."

"What the fuck?!"

"And he's got a scepter, you know, a royal scepter. It's covered in Indian rubies that the British found in India, like, hundreds of years ago," Donald said with a smile that revealed his sincere admiration of the prince's taste. "Those kinds of people in those countries, they don't understand the beauty of these things, you know, these beautiful things, rubies, emeralds, the blue ones, what are they called again? It's wasted on them. They're better off in first world hands. Like in that book by Ella Fitzgerald, where the rich man has a box of rubies. You remember that? Ella Fitzgerald was a singer too. Did you know that? That's a fact. A black lady. The greatest black lady that ever lived. I had dinner with her once. She was a sensational eater. Eater and singer too." Donald paused, expecting Epstein to be impressed by his erudite knowledge of books, but the gray-haired man only shook his head. Foufou guffawed.

"Can we get in the fucking car, Donald, or whatever it is you call this fucking monstrosity."

"Of course, of course." Donald pulled on the door handle, but it didn't open. He tried again. "It's locked!" he barked, sending flecks of spittle flying everywhere, lit by the twilight. The driver appeared and opened the door for him. It wasn't locked, but

Donald had been pulling it from the wrong side, because in truth he'd hardly ever touched it before himself. That was the driver's job.

The inside of the Hummer was tricked out in various colors of neon and flashing LEDs as well. There was also a bubbling gold-plated hot tub that took up most of the back, occupied by the woman Donald had hired for the weekend. She was scrolling on her phone, a glass of wine in her other hand, and never looked up at them. Epstein had one foot in the door before he took in the scene and stopped mid-stride. This time he gave Donald a look but said nothing. They took facing seats across from each other, on opposite sides of the hot tub, with Foufou beside Ferrari. The driver closed the door and the Hummer set off.

"This is my girlfriend Rockford," Donald said with a grin. "You won't find better tits on the entire eastern seaboard. Barring my daughter's, of course." He beamed, even more orange than usual under the neon lights.

"Rocky," the woman corrected without looking up from her phone.

Donald winced. He had wanted to impress Ferrari and Foufou with the fact that he made no secret of having a girlfriend even though the whole world knew he was also married. Rocky's correction somewhat deflated the effect. Noticing that Epstein was looking at her dubiously, Donald said, "It's okay. She won't say anything."

There was an odd smell that was bothering Reservoir. Familiar. She crinkled her nose at it but didn't say anything, turning her mind instead to more important matters and pulling a small black leather-bound notebook from her inside blazer pocket.

"I'll give Prince Alfred a talking to about that helicopter when we get to the lodge," Epstein said. "He ought to know he needs to be discreet if he wants me to start helping to facilitate his *habits* again."

"Oh, he's not there," Donald cut in. Foufou had been flipping through the black book but froze.

"What?"

"He went hunting. Took Corky with him, I believe."

Epstein's face went red, but the President was oblivious in the neon-lit interior of the Hummer.

Epstein made an exasperated sigh, and finally said, "Fine. Who's at the lodge?"

"Everyone. Well, they're... here." Donald answered.

"Which ones?"

Donald started naming them from memory. Al Garfield, Corky Phillips, Cardinal Mell, the rest. As he did, Reservoir checked them against the list in her book. When Donald was done, she said something quietly to Epstein that the President couldn't hear over the sound of the spa jets.

"What about the others?" Epstein asked. "There are dozens and dozens more."

Donald nodded, smiling. "Yes. I told them they wouldn't want to miss this, and they all came. Or they're coming. They'll be... here by later tonight. They need me. I'm an important person. I can grant them pardons. I could grant them pardons if I wanted too. But I choose not to. That's the first rule of business. Maintaining demand. That's how I built my empire. Nobody knows supply and demand better than me. I invited Uncle Plush, the rapper. You know, 'U Plush', 'Plushy'. These rappers got a lot of names. Heh. But he's in jail for sex trafficking, not for long, but he doesn't need a pardon really. I'm very hip with young people like rappers."

The smell was bothering Foufou again, but there was a new distraction. She said, "Why do you keep saying it like that? 'Here'?"

"Well, some of them, it's funny, you know, they're not at the lodge."

"What?!"

Rocky continued scrolling, oblivious, despite Epstein's outburst.

The president, too, seemed unaware of Epstein's anger. "I mean, a bunch of them went out walking and whatnot. Woes, Biermug, Mell. I guess they couldn't sleep because of the time zones or whatever. Important to keep healthy. I'm in peak physical condition myself. Garfield is still there though."

"What? You mean they went walking in the woods?"

"Yes. They'll be back though. It's totally safe. Safest place in the world for them to be right now. Nobody will see them. The woods are all cordoned off because of the bear attacks."

"Bear attacks?!"

"Yeah, somebody got killed by a bear or bobcat or lynx. Happens all the time up here. That's what makes it so perfect."

Epstein moved with such speed that even Foufou was stunned. In a blur he was on the other side of the hot tub, and in the next he had Donald's head under the foaming, roiling water. Ruby's arms flailed, he kicked, his feet scraping the ground. Finally, Ferrari let him up and the President gasped wildly. His face was dripping, his hair plugs shooting in every direction like crazy orange mangrove roots.

"Listen to me, you fat fuck," said Epstein, putting his face right into Donald's, the orange hair still in his vice-like grip. "*I'm* the one trying to rebuild an empire here! Do you have any idea how much it costs to buy an island, to set up the kind of network we used to have! The kind of money *you'd* never see in a *hundred* bankruptcies! We need those men, and we need their wallets. We need them feeding their addictions, and we need the threat of Foufou's little black book hanging over their heads. Just like it's hanging over yours. You think any of that can happen with them walking... in the fucking... *woods*?! I could destroy you in seconds. *Seconds.*"

The rage overcame him again, and he shoved Donald's head back into the water, for longer this time. The flailing was even more violent. Finally, it was Reservoir that said, "Ferrari, let him up. We need him alive."

Ferrari relented and let Ruby up, but before letting go of his grip on him, he told him, "I don't care if you have to go out into those woods yourself, you will find them and you will bring them back." He shoved Ruby away and flopped back into his seat, spent. Ruby did likewise, soaking wet and gasping. The plush seats and flashing lights gave him none of their usual pleasure. His eyes flashed up to Foufou's little black book, and Epstein saw the look.

"What? You think if you just had this book you'd have us over a barrel? You'd be safe? You think this is the only copy? What are we? Idiots?!"

Ruby didn't answer, just sat with that dejected dog look frozen on his face, the same look he had whenever he had to wear a tuxedo. The Hummer drove on in silence for a time.

"What's that smell?" Reservoir asked at last.

"Gwyneth Paltrow snatch candles," Donald said, pointing and putting on his game face again. They were placed at corners of the hot tub. "I find they put me in the mood." He pushed his dripping hair back, tried to shape it.

"Yes, of course!" Reservoir cried, elated. She had done "health tests" on dozens of teen girls, and that was it. She recognized it instantly now. "Just imagine," she said to Epstein, "if I had gotten to Paltrow when she was sixteen, fifteen, fourteen, thirteen." Her voice trailed off wistfully.

Epstein said something back to her, but Ruby wasn't listening. He was saying *samurai, samurai, samurai, samurai*, to himself over and over in his head.

***

Earlier, Yorgotha Axegorer had thought she had heard gunshots in different directions. Hunters violating the police cordon, she assumed, but they were far off. They didn't bother her. Yorgotha had a good knowledge of the woods around Killarney Lake. She had brought the other members of the band out here many times to shoot covers for the CDs she burned of their music to sell at gigs. The covers looked best – spookiest – when shot in the winter or fall. What's more, now, even at the end of summer, the heat was so sticky as to be almost intolerable and was especially bad since they always did the shoots in their full, studded leather gear. However, Yorgotha was wise and insisted the band members always bought the best quality corpse paint: it never ran no matter how bad they were sweating.

But there was another reason Yorgotha felt so comfortable in these woods. In what seemed a different life, a life she never spoke about anymore to anyone, she had been here many times as a Girl Guide. She knew, for instance, that on the other side of the lake, to the east, were the camp cabins they stayed in as childlings. Up to the north was the lodge of the wealthy, securely fenced off far from the actual building, but she'd snuck onto the grounds a few times, even after the Girl Guide days, but before she became Yorgotha when she was merely an unruly child.

And now here she was in these woods again. The police had released her from the Fredericton dungeons this morning with nary a word. She had to assume the shopkeeps at the fiber farm had not pressed charges. She did not know why. The police had even returned her grimoire. But the truth was, she was not sure she could have slain that alpaca anyway. Her darkest secret, darker than the secret of her having been a Girl Guide, was that she had lied about sacrificing a raccoon. She had actually sacrificed a cockroach. It was a ritual sacrifice, and she read from the tome as she squashed it, but nevertheless it was only a cockroach. Yet she even felt bad about that: the insect had an eldritch H.R. Giger-esque quality about it. Thinking on her own weakness, Yorgotha disgusted herself. Wasn't her sole ambition to make every person in the world understand the artistic import of Funereal Devastation? How could she achieve that when she couldn't muster up the courage to do any more than stomp a cockroach? All day every day she was surrounded by the direst pabulum. Taylor Swift, Adele, Ed Sheeran… CanCon requirements made it even worse: Avril Lavigne, Justin Bieber. Celine Dion and Bryan Adams! How were those old fuckers even still alive?! Even when they'd been broken up for decades or even dead – every day in malls, on the radio, Loverboy, Men Without Hats, and Glass Tiger. And all these fucking sheep just walked around accepting their programming, thinking that absolute diarrhea they called "music" was good, that it was somehow "art" because it made them "feel good". It was "nice". They could "hum along with it". Anyone who could like such music was eating in a cultural vomitorium. What good were they to the world? They had no understanding of art! Yorgotha wished they would just kill themselves. It made her apoplectic with rage. She was trembling. A furious tear streamed from her eye, dripped off her chin, and splashed off her Doc Martens. Her corpse paint remained perfect.

But maybe, just maybe, they could be converted. Was that the power of the book? Would it change people? She could sense its energy, like something vibrating inside of her. There was something in the book itself, the physical object. It wasn't just the phonetic transcription, otherwise her uncle could have left her just that. Although, she thought, what kind of a legacy would that have been? Maybe that's why he sent the book too. But, no, the power of the grimoire was real. It was palpable, intensely palpable. What form would it take though? She had definitely felt something when she slayed the cockroach, even though, she admitted to herself, she had been distracted at the time. She had once had a boyfriend nicknamed Cockroach. Again, this was in the pre-

Yorgotha days. He had ordered her to go down on him if she wouldn't sleep with him. She refused, and she never saw him again. She hardly ever thought about him these days, but she thought about him when she stomped that bug. How could she allow herself to become so unfocused at such an important moment? She was supposed to be an artist. She condemned herself, but this time would be different. It would be raw. She didn't even bring her Bluetooth speakers to blare out Funereal Devastation's music this time. She would just recite the words to the universe. Then she would find a mammal, a squirrel even, and make an offering of it. The note didn't say a sacrifice was required, but it was hard to imagine it working without one.

She walked up a hill, distancing herself from the walking trail she'd come in on, until she felt she was a fair distance from it. She opened the book to the marked page. It had been a minute since she'd last heard any gunshots. Now there were only the sounds of the leaves around her, some birds chirping, some frogs.

She held the transcription up against the facing page and began to recite. Overhead, a weak breeze tried to move the tops of the trees. Yorgotha looked up at those treetops and beyond, into the firmament, into the universe, as she started. The last of the sunlight was just a pink and orange line on the horizon. It filled her with awe. The sounds of the words came out of her almost unbidden, in a swelling drone. There was something ancient about the cadence, like sounds coming from a distant, forgotten temple. *Stop thinking about Cockroach, clear your mind*, she kept telling herself. Down the slope from her, on the walking path there were approaching voices, footsteps. *Ignore them, don't let it distract you, they won't even notice you up here, just go further up the slope.* She turned in circles as she chanted, the blackening trees were her audience, reverent and occult.

She froze.

From a higher vantage point, someone seemed to be watching her, someone who was only a small black silhouette from this distance.

But the next instant her attention was drawn away in the opposite direction. Two old men had come up the path, one chattering loudly, but stopped in their tracks when they saw Yorgotha up the slope, and they were staring at her. One of them was carrying a rifle. An infuriating distraction. Weirdos. Something about them alerted her danger sense too, but she risked turning away from them to look at the silhouette again.

It was gone. Strange. She tried to visualize it again. Had it just been a tree? The figure had been perfectly still. It could have maybe been ragged twigs jutting out around neck level, and what was perhaps a broken branch, dangling in a strange way from what would have been the right arm. But how could a tree have walked away?

***

A few minutes earlier, Prince Alfred had been marching through the woods at a brisk pace, loading his rifle as he went. He had already tried to kill a fox and a woodchuck but missed. The light would run out soon. A gloomy pall was falling over the woods, like in a short story by renowned writer and hebephile Edgar Allan Poe, who married his thirteen-year-old cousin when he was twenty-seven.

Prince Alfred's rifle was a breechloader that he rested cracked open over one arm as he loaded it with bullets kept in his breast pocket. The stock was inlaid with intricate designs in eighteen-karat gold, ivory, and diamonds that had been mined in the late 1800s. The rifle was a gift to one of Alfred's ancestors from King Leopold II of Belgium, who had overseen the deaths of ten million Congolese to collect rubber. Millions more who failed to meet the rubber quotas were dismembered. A whole generation missing a hand. War, famine, disease, abductions, cannibalism. Alfred wondered if some of that rubber was used in construction of this rifle. Did rubber survive that long? He wasn't exactly sure what rubber was though, or all the parts of a rifle. Nevertheless, he did know that it was a piece of such exquisite craftsmanship that it had to be possible at least. However, even so, the rifle was a mere bauble. His real pride and joy was the jewel-encrusted scepter, an object which he kept with him always, even now on a hook on his belt. At this point, the reader might be speculating that the scepter will get rammed up the Prince's asshole but can rest assured that it will not. The scepter was even older than the rifle. It made Alfred's chest swell up to think back on a line of kings going back to antiquity. The name Alfred itself meant "elf counsel". A time of elves and fairies. He was no fairy though. He was a hot, red-blooded male. *Blue-blooded actually*, he mused to himself, and the thought made him chuckle.

Corky Phillips, who was keeping pace beside him and had been talking incessantly since they left the lodge, thought maybe the Prince was laughing at something he had said. They looked at each other, and Prince Alfred's joviality vanished, and his confident stride through the woods became hesitant. But only for a moment. He recovered quickly, like a royal should. Phillips never stopped talking through the whole moment.

"So, as I was saying, Mr. Phillips," Alfred interrupted, loading a second shell into the rifle without even having to look down at it, "What I need is what you Americans might call 'damage control'. My reputation is tarnished, but why? You understand. A moving picture about my life story is just the thing. For the good of England. The British people need royalty, they need the symbol we provide to them, or they falter. They falter like lost babes, Mr. Phillips. It cannot stand that one such as I should be treated like common rabble when I have done nothing wrong. *You* understand, Mr. Phillips." He locked the rifle, and the sound was so loud birds fled from trees.

"Oh, I understand, b-but, you know, I've never

made a documentary. A documentary is too phony. Now fiction, that's real. And if you want a real dose of reality, you should've met my mother."

"I wasn't talking about a documentary, Mr. Phillips. I meant a story that will uplift the spirit, a story that will make people love me the way they loved that Negro in the Ray Charles movie."

"You want to be played by a Negro?"

"No, no," Alfred protested in disgust. "I meant the general idea of the thing."

A rabbit darted out of a bush and Alfred fired two shots at it as it bolted across the path, but he missed. He shook a fist in frustration then cracked open his rifle again to reload. It was getting dark, like the darkness in a poem by renowned poet and ephebophile Lord Byron, who lusted after his fifteen-year-old pageboy.

Corky was shaken by the blasts, but he managed to recover and pick up the conversation where they left off. "I see. Y-you know, I don't know if I've ever worked with a Negro before. In fact all the blacks I've ever known have been marks on my record. An uplifting comedy is an oxymoron though. Comedy is tragic and vice versa. Just ask my accountant."

"Mr. Phillips, I don't think we're understanding each other." Alfred sighed. "To be honest, I was hoping your contemporary Parisian Kransky would be here this weekend. Wasn't he going to be? It was him I had hoped to talk to."

Corky stumbled and almost fell as he walked. "P-Parisian Kransky? What would you want him for? He's got a name straight out of Mad Magazine!"

Prince Alfred looked at Corky with a look of pity. "Mr. Phillips, you married yours, didn't you?"

Corky knew exactly what he meant, and for once didn't say anything but only nodded. He was the wrong man for the job, and Kransky was the right one.

Alfred shook his head. Corky's wife had practically been his foster daughter. Corky had been in his fifties, she might have been twenty. Now they'd been married so long she was in *her* fifties and they had children. And what's worse she was a slit-eye! Every aspect of it repulsed Alfred in every way. It made him sick to his stomach (even though Corky had dated other sixteen- and seventeen-year-olds while he was in his forties before settling down). Parisian, on the other hand, had simply drugged and slept with a thirteen-year-old and didn't even have to pay twelve million pounds for it. He only had to live in France where they accepted sexual appetites. Alfred accepted them too. The girl was white, and Parisian didn't marry her. Corky Phillips, on the other hand, was incomprehensible. What was he even doing here? Plus, Parisian had a tragic backstory: he had avoided the Holocaust, and his wife had been savagely murdered. Well, Alfred had a tragic story now too. None of Mummy's money, and no respect despite being a royal. A royal! He felt so disgusted he couldn't bear to think of it anymore. He walked on mute for several minutes. Corky never stopped talking. There were no more rabbits.

After another kilometer or so on the trail, all at once, he stopped walking. Corky, confused, stopped too, and followed the prince's line of sight. There was a girl up the hill from them, up among the trees. She was strangely dressed in tight leather and platform boots, and her face was painted like a... panda?

"Well, hello, there," said Corky. "Gee, it's getting kind of dark out here. Are you sure you should be out here all by yourself? Who am I to tell you what to do though if you're an adult? You *are* an adult, aren't you...?"

Yorgotha didn't answer, only glared at them.

Both men took that to mean that she was under eighteen, which encouraged Phillips to prattle even faster. "That's an awful lot of makeup you've got on there. I guess you're insecure. That's nothing to be ashamed of, you know? My analyst once told me I was more insecure than an unlocked bicycle in Amsterdam." It was as if he was doing a set, like renowned comedian and ephebophile Jerry Seinfeld, who dated a seventeen-year-old when he was thirty-nine.

"Are you from a record label?" Yorgotha finally said. "Are you record producers? Managers? Booking agents? Do you have anything to do with the music industry?" There was something familiar about them.

While he was talking, Prince Alfred turned his back

to them, took a Viagra out of his left breast pocket, and Cialis out of his right, and dry swallowed both of them. The girl was a strange one, but she would cost him less than twelve million pounds, that was for sure.

Thanks to the double hit, the blood surged to his penis instantaneously, and he spun around comically, like renowned actor and ephebophile Charlie Chaplin, who had a habit of dating and marrying sixteen-year-olds.

He interrupted Corky's routine and pointed at the girl. "Young woman, do you know who I am?!" His finger quivered at her, mimicking the erection straining against his trousers. "I am Prince Alfred! Without me, this country would be nothing! *You* would be nothing! When Mummy –" he choked, "When Mummy, Mummy, Mummy became queen, no African country was independent! Daddy is older than most countries' independence! Show some gratitude! It is only through Our grace that you enjoy your precious 'independence'! We gave that to you! We've earned and deserved our privilege and wealth! How else could the world function?!"

After a pause, Yorgotha finally spoke. "Fuck off."

"A-Alfred, what's come over you?!" Corky asked, trying to push his arm down.

Corky's words came to him as if from a distance. Even Alfred didn't know what was wrong with him, Perhaps he had overdosed. His great balls were on fire, like in that song by renowned pianist and hebephile Jerry Lee Lewis, who married his thirteen-year-old cousin when he was twenty-seven. Still, he couldn't stop himself. "You will serve me! You are a subject of the empire! My Mummy's face is on all your money!" he shouted. The spittle flying from his lips sparkled orange in the setting sun.

Yorgotha's eyes flashed down to the rifle trembling in his other hand. Then something else caught her eye: a rippling movement in the waters of the lake several meters beyond the two men, behind them. Corky grabbed Prince Alfred by the shoulders, trying to shake some sense into him or placate him, "I saw her first, Alfred!"

"No, you didn't!"

"I talked to her first!"

Yorgotha backed up without taking her eyes from the scene, tricky going backwards up an incline. The movement in the lake was widening. Something was going to come up out of the water. Yorgotha tried to hide behind a tree that wasn't big enough.

The thing that stepped out of the water was a woman, dripping wet, with black hair and Groucho glasses, one hypno spiral eye, and pencils through her neck. A necklace of desiccated dongs that looked like dried figs. Sally Pencilneck. Yorgotha had heard the stories, heard them told in these very woods back in her Girl Guide days. She wanted to look away but she was frozen to the spot, peeking around the birch tree that barely covered her. With Sally was a monstrous toad, too big to be believed, and a scattering of normal-sized frogs that followed them out of the water.

Corky saw Sally, and Alfred knew something had happened behind him, but it was too late. She wrenched the scepter off his back and kicked him in the nuts from behind. Next came the nunchaku to the back of the head, and all he could see were lights and stars, like in a science fiction movie by renowned filmmaker and ephebophile Luc Besson, who married a fifteen-year-old when he was thirty-two. "Owooh!" he cried like a rock star, like renowned musicians, hebephiles, and ephebophiles Chuck Berry, Jimmy Page, Iggy Pop, Marvin Gaye, Steven Tyler, Ted Nugent, Don Henley, Bill Wyman, Anthony Kiedis, Prince, David Bowie, Elvis Presley, MC Ren, and Mick Jagger, among many others, who all slept with, and/or drugged, and/or plied with alcohol, and/or married, and/or purchased the guardianship of, and/or crossed state lines with, thirteen- to seventeen-year-olds when they were all grown men.

Alfred went down groaning and clutching his head. "Wait, wait!" he cried! "I can pay you!" He pulled a wad of £50 notes from a pocket and held it in a trembling hand towards Sally. But in the next instant, the Coleman Frog pounced on him, and he was fighting it off as valiantly as he could.

Sally turned on Corky Phillips.

"P-please, I can't stand pain," Corky begged. "In fact, my doctor said I was on so many painkillers I shouldn't be surprised if a bunch of Afghani farmers showed up in April to start harvesting me."

Sally stowed the scepter and nunchaku in loops on each side of her hip. She grabbed Corky's arms akimbo then put one foot on his chest for leverage. He grunted. She pulled. The arms came off followed by volcanos of blood. He shrieked and ran in looping circles, forming a spirograph blood pattern on the ground and trees. Eventually he dropped dead, face first into the gravel walking trail.

Sally pulled out the scepter, jammed the stumps of Corky's dismembered arms onto each end of it to form a kind of "arm" staff. Then, as if motivated by some vestigial memory, she began spinning it in elaborate arcs like a baton twirler at the head of a marching band.

The insanity of the scene overcame Yorgotha. Her mind tried to flee. She chuckled. It reminded her of that song from the olden days, "Girls Just Wanna Have Fun". That thought provoked a guffaw. But thinking of Cyndi Lauper made her then think of "She Bop", a song that was on the PMRC's "Filthy Fifteen" list along with songs by Judas Priest, Mötley Crüe, AC/DC, Twisted Sister, W.A.S.P., Merciful Fate, Black Sabbath, and Venom, and she thought of its lyrics, and then suddenly Sally tossed her meat baton aside and spun with malevolence in Yorgotha's direction. Yorgotha abandoned her pathetic hiding spot, stumbling as fast as she could over the hilly terrain as she went, clutching the arcane tome to her chest.

But before Sally could take a step towards Yorgotha,

she found herself lassoed from behind. Prince Alfred had managed to fling the Coleman Frog off himself, knocking it out, but he was badly battered in the struggle. Now, though, he had caught her with the hunting rope he had brought along to tie up any game. The rope, like his rifle, was of the finest quality. Sally strained against it, grunting, but Alfred had tied an expert knot in it. He worked his way up the rope to her, and when he reached the trail, he saw Corky's armless corpse face down in the gravel. "My god," he said. "What have you done to my scepter?"

"What *are* you?" he asked now that he could see her up close. The pencils, the strange necklace. She tried to turn her head, but he looped the rope around her neck and pulled it tight. "Whatever you are," he said, "you're an ingrate, and I can see you're some kind of darkie. Do you know how we deal with darkies?" He shoved the barrel of the rifle into her back and began to knot the rope around it one-handed. She was pulled too tight to move, and he kicked her in the back of the knees, so she went down. "Of course you don't. You have no respect for the people who've brought you civilization. It's called 'blowing from a gun'. It's a means of execution, you see? A prisoner is tied to the mouth of a cannon, and when it's fired he's blown apart completely, head and limbs in all different directions hundreds of yards away. The Portuguese developed it in Ceylon. But it was the British East India Company that perfected it in the 1800s. That's how we put down the Indian Rebellion of 1857. That's British ingenuity for you. Far better than starving them to death if you ask me. Although I must admit that was more efficient – 35 million dead. As Churchill said, it was their own fault for breeding like rabbits. An orderly society must be maintained. 'India is to be bled,' said the Marquess of Salisbury, and so shall you be!"

He pulled the trigger. It blew open a hole in Sally's chest, the knots tore, and she pitched to the earth. She wasn't blown apart in every direction for hundreds of yards, which was disappointing, but somehow it made Alfred's raging erection even harder, painfully, like it was going to burst through his pants. He looked over at Corky's body. "Now who's going to make the movie of my life?" he asked aloud.

Sally began to stand up. Now, finally, Prince Alfred began to realize she was more than just a darkie. When she turned around to face him, he realized he could see right through the hole he'd put in her, a hole that was somehow closing up as he watched.

He turned and bolted. The Coleman Frog, recovered again, pounced on him from out of nowhere. His little frog brethren were shrieking with delight. He managed to hurl the thing off again.

The helicopter he'd hired was around here somewhere. The pilot would be there waiting as she was paid to do. He retrieved his gold inlaid compass from the same pocket that held his Cialis. He was headed in the right direction. He risked a look back over his shoulder. Sally was still standing on the track, healing. No. She was starting to run after him. Trembling, he tried to reload his rifle as he ran, spilling bullets everywhere. His head was still aching, throbbing from the blow she'd struck with whatever it was. Finally he managed to get two rounds in and turned and fired. The silhouette of Sally in the distance went down. Then she got up again.

Alfred reloaded again while he ran. The helicopter couldn't be far. He was an expert orienteer. Through the haze of terror his brain told him to call the pilot. He found the pocket with his phone, dialed the pilot, barked: "Get the helicopter ready", and hung up without waiting for a response.

Surprising himself, the next moment, he found himself in the clearing by the water where the helicopter was parked. The pilot was standing beside it, still holding her phone and with a slightly bewildered expression on her face. *How long was I running?* Prince Alfred wondered. "Get the helicopter ready!" he shouted again.

The pilot didn't ask any questions. She got into the chopper and began prepping for takeoff. It was the most lavish form of transport Prince Alfred could find from the airport in this yokel corner of the Empire. And yet, as he stopped and looked at it now, he was compelled to ask out loud, "Don't you think it would look better if it were covered in amethysts?"

The pilot turned to see what he was talking about

but was met with a sight so terrifying she fled out the opposite side door of the helicopter, jumped into the lake, and swam for her life.

Baffled, Alfred looked back over his shoulder to see what had spooked her, and in the same instant Sally Pencilneck's hand was around his throat. With her in front of him and not tied up, he had no leverage. She was strong, so strong. He could feel his windpipe collapsing millimeter by millimeter. She started pushing him backwards, towards the helicopter. His feet were almost off the ground, only his toes or heels ever in contact with it. With her free hand, she ripped his pants and Union Jack underwear off. He tried to squeeze out a word, perhaps "What?", but only emitted a choked noise. She dragged him up the side of the helicopter. He kicked and flailed to no avail. Still holding him with one hand, with the other she wrenched out the retaining nut from the main rotor with her immense strength. Alfred found himself being flipped over for some reason, but his confusion turned to a shriek when Sally shoved his penis into the rotor in place of the retaining nut. She left him and he tried to pry himself free, but it was no use. The meds were too effective. He was well and truly stuck.

Sally went down into the cockpit and continued the launch sequence where the pilot had left off. The rotors began to spin and Alfred with them as if he were on a fun park ride. A perverse, demented fun park ride. "Mummy, Mummy, Mummy," he blubbered, the tears flowing in torrents down his cheeks as he started to revolve faster and faster.

The amethyst-less helicopter lifted into the air. The Prince was screaming uncontrollably now, but Sally focused on the controls. She maneuvered the cyclic stick with expert control and the chopper arced out over the lake and into the setting sun. No more than a multicolored blur, Alfred's body couldn't take any more, and it tore loose from his member. He went flying out over the lake spinning at a full 500 RPMs like a runaway pinwheel, until he crashed into the water screaming "Wooo!" like Gary Glitter.

Chapter 14
Finally, The Long-Awaited Exposition Dump

You had one job! Nandini screamed at herself in her mind. *Your job was to keep her safe, and you blew it out of spite. Now your job is to keep her alive and get her out of these woods.*

Meanwhile, Professor Clover was doing just that. Yet as she guided them through the woods, her only utterances were occasional grunts as she hacked through the underbrush and low branches with her knife. There were clear paths through the forest, but she was determined to move in a straight line. She was on constant alert, her eyes darting in every direction. When Nandini managed to catch a look at her face she saw only a kind of grim annoyance at having to lead these two kindergarteners through the trees. A hint of mania too. And there was a kind of satisfaction present in the chopping grunts as well. She handled her knife with muscular ease.

And yet, despite Professor Clover's silence, Aruna hadn't shut up once. "Tell us. Tell us. Tell us," she kept asking. "Don't you think you'd better tell us? You must know very much. You seem to know. Tell us everything. You can tell us. We can keep it a secret."

That was a lie. Nandini knew her mother only wanted to know so she could post the information in her WhatsApp and Facebook groups. After that she'd show Nandini all the Likes she was getting and comments of praise and interest, most surely made only out of politeness. It would be infuriating. It was already making her blood boil.

"Mrs. Rajan, this isn't like one of your monster stories."

"Mother, please don't be thinking about the *otte molechi*."

"What's an *otte molechi*?" the Professor asked.

Nandini answered, "It's a spirit in the shape of a human woman with a single huge breast. When she comes across a man in the forest, she pretends to drop some betel-nuts, and when he bends over to pick them up for her, she whips out her giant boob and hits him on the head with it."

"What the fuck?!"

"No!" said Aruna. "That is the *hemmalati* of Karnataka. The *otte molechi* is from Kerala. She appears on the highway and looks like a beautiful topless woman. She asks a man passing by for betel-nuts, and as he looks for some, he realizes she only has one breast, which grows bigger and bigger until it almost touches the ground, then she spins around and whacks him in the head with it which shatters him out of existence."

The Professor was befuddled. "Okay, I'll tell you about Sally Pencilneck," she said, but her voice was bitter. "You can't kill her. No. Scratch that. You can kill her, but she'll only come back, somehow, some way. One time she came back when her corpse got struck by lightning. One time a beaver took a shit on a Ouija board that just happened to end up where her body had last been buried. One time it was just a copycat killer but never mind that one. Sometimes, she dies and comes back the next day, sometimes it's ten months later like she's in a rush, sometimes it's ten years. She can appear anywhere…"

"Anywhere?" Aruna asked. "Even outside these woods?"

"Not often, but it's happened. But more often she'll be resurrected here and then end up somewhere else. One time she ended up on the Pioneer Princess III, that river boat the kids have their junior prom on, and she ended up in Washington, D.C."

"How?!" Nandini had to interject. "There's no way Killarney Lake is connected to Washington in any way."

"I don't know. Sometimes with Sally, these things just don't make sense. They must have had a hell of a time explaining away that one. That's nothing though. One time she hitched a ride on the Canadarm and ended up on the goddamn International Space Station and killed everyone on board."

"But how could they cover that up?"

"Tell me: who's on the ISS right now?"

Nandini shrugged. "I don't know."

"Exactly! Nobody fucking knows! And whenever Sally's around, for some reason, there's so much light you can see almost everything, even when you're in the woods at night. Put your phone away!" she barked at Aruna. "Do you know the story about Pablo Escobar's plane crashing here loaded with 500 kilos of cocaine?" she asked Nandini.

Nandini shook her head.

"Escobar wanted to use New Brunswick as a waypoint to smuggle cocaine into North America. In 1989, he sent some of his men up here in a small plane with the cargo. The plane crashed in Burtts Corner. Two of Escobar's men survived. That's an odd thing in itself, actually. Then there was the trial, right here in Fredericton, and the attempted prison break. But that's another story. The point is there were more than two on the plane. Sally killed the rest before they crashed. In a sealed deposition, according to one of the men, the plane went down because the pilot was reading a skin mag, maybe even had his zipper undone, and was 'distracted'.

"That's as much as you need to know. If you stay here you're signing your own death warrant. I'm going to get you out of these woods, and that's it. The less you know, the better."

Nandini for her part didn't want to know any

more. Professor Clover was a voice of authority. She was inclined to trust her.

But Aruna persisted. "But why would she kill us?"

Clover sighed. The old woman wasn't going to let up. Clover looked her in the eye, hard, and said, "Because there are three of us." Clover turned her attention back to the path and kept them moving. She didn't look at them as she continued to answer. "Almost every time Sally Pencilneck manifests, everybody in the area dies except for one. And now there are three of us. If you don't get out of these woods, you two are dead meat. If you know too much, that could lessen your chances."

That prompted Nandini to speak. "But why does that have to be? Maybe we could all survive, or two of us, or you could be one of the ones that…"

Now Nandini got the hard stare.

Clover turned back to her work. "It's just the way it's always been," she said. "Some of these things are hard to explain. Maybe they *can't* be explained. At least, not completely."

"Maybe you should try," Nandini said, despite herself. "Maybe knowing more could *help* us survive." It was so humid, she was sweating. She didn't know how Professor Clover could stand it in that outfit. The professor was *off*. Everything about her was *off*. She was a completely different person from the charming woman Nandini had grown up knowing. She was different even from the warm, kind woman who'd been her ally at the temple only… a night ago? It felt more like weeks.

"Okay," Clover said, "let's do it this way. You tell me what you know first. Or, at least, what you think you know."

Nandini had to think for a second. "Well, the story I always heard was that Sally was a little Indian girl. And she was playing in the art room at camp by herself, and a camp counselor was supposed to be watching her, but he was… busy elsewhere, doing you-know-what, and there was a freak accident. She tried to get some colored pencils down off a shelf and she fell and they went through her neck, and she died. But she comes back when people are… distracted around the lake. For revenge."

"She wasn't Indian."

"Yes, she was. That's why the counselor didn't care. Especially back in the eighties."

"And how many Indian girls did you know named 'Sally' back in the eighties? Tell me something. How did your cop friend tell the story?"

Nandini had forgotten about that. She hadn't thought about it in years, but now she remembered. "She said Sally was Chinese. We laughed at her and told her it wasn't true."

"'We'?"

"Me and the other… Brown kids."

Clover scoffed. "Naw. The way I heard it, Sally was Black. The counselor was Indian. Think about it.

Black perverts are rare. Every Indian man's a goddamn pervert."

Aruna couldn't contain her outrage. "*Chee*! No! Only these people are so disgusting! Men and women!"

"Hah! What about that poor woman gang raped and murdered on a bus by everyone including the driver? That girl kept in a pit on a farm in 2016. Need I go on? Mahatma Gandhi himself making his teenage grandnieces sleep with him *in the nude* to 'test' his 'virtue'."

"That was *Brahmacharya*!" Aruna protested through clenched teeth. "Celibate self-control!" Aruna was so furious her head was trembling like a skull.

"Think about it," the Professor said. "That's the scenario that makes more sense. Asians are complicit. You don't care what happens to anyone else as long as you stay middle-class, living in some kinda 'this-country-isn't-racist' fantasy. Get good grades, good jobs, believe you can assimilate into the White structure. Everything's fine. White cop puts his knee on a Black man's neck in the street in broad daylight until he dies, Asian cop just stands there and makes sure no one interferes. It's worse with Indians. You had the caste system to begin with. Then the British came in and exacerbated it by preaching the Whiter the better. And they didn't want Black civil rights activists traveling to India and giving the natives ideas, so they made it almost impossible for them to get visas. That didn't help. Your man Gandhi lived in South Africa for twenty years and thought Africans were savages. Little Black girl playing by herself in an art room, you think an Indian man wants to be in there with her? In fact, this whole fucking mess was started by an Indian man. An Indian physicist. Double whammy. The only worse pervert than an Indian man is a physicist. Apologies to your father," she said without looking at either woman. "How many jokes about Schrödinger's Cat do you hear every day? Erwin Shrödinger was a serial sexual abuser of girls as young as fourteen, and he kept a *journal* about all his rapes. According to him, the innocence of teenage girls was the ideal match for his 'natural genius'. Wittgenstein said he was thinking about math while he was masturbating at the front in WWI. Richard Feynman: Nobel prize for his work in quantum electrodynamics, self-professed sexual predator. There's a picture of goddamn Stephen Hawking at the Epstein island. But I'm getting ahead of myself."

"Sometimes," Nandini said, though she didn't want to, but she couldn't stop herself, "right-wing creationists cook up accusations to try to discredit physicists."

"Did your dad tell you that?"

Nandini didn't need to answer.

"Hell, nobody ever accused me of raping a fourteen-year-old boy. But, then, maybe I'm not famous enough, and I didn't keep a diary about it either." She sighed. "We want to believe that scientists and artists are people who are trying to understand us from the inside out, and therefore they're going to be more understanding, compassionate, empathetic. No. If evil can find its way into a person, you'll find it there, thriving. Look up. At the stars. 'Milky Way Galaxy'. From the Greek 'galaxias' meaning 'Milky Vault'. These astronomers got titties on the brain so bad, they named the motherfucking galaxy after milk *twice*. Don't think about it!" she barked.

"Should we be talking about any of these things? Won't it attract her attention?"

Professor Clover nodded. "She can know people's thoughts, but, based on my experience, she needs to be within a certain range to begin with. Of course, this hasn't been consistent over the years, and sometimes she's popped up when I thought she was on the other side of the lake." Despite her answer, the Professor's eyes never stopped probing in every direction.

Nandini thought for a second. "But what's the mechanism? How can she possibly know our thoughts? Does that mean every thought we have is sending out some kind of subatomic particles or waves that she can detect? And *interpret*?"

To her own surprise, Professor Clover was getting used to talking. She'd needed to unburden herself of these theories she'd built up for years, things she hadn't even dared to keep logs about, so she continued, testing the waters, almost prodding. "That's an astute question. What if, instead of 'know' or 'hear', I told you that Sally *sees* our thoughts?" She looked at Nandini hopefully.

Nandini had to think about it for a moment. "You mean she's somehow higher-dimensional? So she can see inside us the way we would be able to see the insides of two-dimensional beings."

"Well done," Professor Clover said.

"That would explain how she seems to just appear out of nowhere too."

Professor Clover finally allowed a smile. "I knew you would get it. If a two-dimensional being – having left and right, but no up and down – actually lived in a *three*-dimensional universe, but lacked the sense organs to be aware of the existence of that third dimension, then if a three-dimensional being was also in that universe, the two-dimensional beings would only be able to see it as a line when it was on their level. If the three-dimensional being went *up or down*, it would disappear from sight completely, and when it came into sight again, it could be somewhere else completely, appearing out of nowhere, and the two-dimensional beings would be baffled by how it happened."

"Then why can't she see through walls as well?"

"I think she's something analogous to four-dimensionality but not actually that. Or maybe it's because she's still ultimately *of* our world."

It became dark enough that Professor Clover had to turn on a high beam flashlight. Aruna seemed to have withdrawn into herself. She followed mechanically, lagging behind them a little now. Nandini was absorbing everything the Professor said. For a few moments, there was only the sound of the brush underfoot, and Clover's hacking, the flashlight beam careening wildly whenever she needed to use both hands.

Nandini looked back at her mother. Aruna was huffing and puffing up the hill behind them, but she was keeping up. Her weekly curling sessions had improved her fitness level.

"There's also the possibility of warping reality," Professor Clover said in a darker tone. "Say an amoeba-shaped two-dimensional being is in front of a mirror. It sees only a line. But we, from above, see it and its reversed image in the mirror. We could pick up that being, flip it over, and put it back down so it's now its own mirror reverse. Sally could, maybe, change things in our reality."

"That might explain some of the stories about wish granting," Nandini said.

"Maybe," the Professor agreed. "That said, I don't think we're talking strictly about a fourth spatial dimension here. I believe Sally is a kind of manifestation in our universe of forces and energies from an alternate… you can call it a plane, or realm. Some scientists would call it a membrane or brane for short. But it's an entirely separate universe. One with its own physical laws, such that when a being from that realm enters our universe, for all intents and purposes, it's like a four-dimensional being, or an avatar of that being, operating in a universe whose inhabitants are only capable of perceiving three dimensions. That's us."

Aruna's ears pricked up at the word "avatar".

"But how do you know this? And if there are no points of contact between the two universes, how is she getting over here? *Why?*"

"The answer to those questions is connected. It goes back to the four known forces of physics: electromagnetism, the strong nuclear force, the weak nuclear force, and gravity. The first three are strong…"

"Gravity is weak."

"Correct. When you lift a coffee cup off a table, you're defying the gravity of the entire planet. If the other three forces are so strong, why is gravity so weak?"

"My dad told me once that some scientists think most of the gravity is seeping away through a tiny unseen dimension to somewhere else. You think the brane Sally is from is that somewhere else?"

"No, not exactly. But the principle is analogous. Something from our universe seeped through into hers. In this case: sounds. The person who figured this out was a man named Chandrasekhar Bose. Bose was a physicist at the Bhabha Atomic Research Centre in Bombay…"

… Where Nandini's own father had once worked…

"I'll get back to him, but back in the early seventies Bose found some records carved in stone. No. Wait. Let me back up a minute. You have to understand,

Sally's history is a tangled mess. It seems like every time she pops up some new information about her past comes to light. But sometimes that information contradicts previous information that was assumed to be correct. Then in the early 2000s for a few years it seemed like all that had been erased, and she was back to just being a kind of zombie that was revenge killing wankers in the woods, and there was no more to it than that.

"Anyway, what Bose found was records of Sanskrit chants, hymns, thousands of years old. Proto-Vedas, if you like, chanted by Indian priests. Try to imagine a worse variety of pervert. Worse than the physicists even. Except for Bose, but I'm getting ahead of myself again."

"No, no, no!" Aruna cried, no longer able to maintain her silence. She had trouble understanding the physics even by analogy, but she could accept that it was true that the theoretical principles had to be sound. Her husband had insisted so for years, but this she could brook no longer. She stopped in her tracks and spat. "*Chee*! Disgusting! I told you! It's *these* people that are the perverts, not *our* people! Not our priests!"

Professor Clover stopped too and looked back at her. "You think all those carvings on the temple walls of dancing girls with the giant exposed bolt-on mammaries are devotional? That's straight-up p-o-r-n. Just like the Greeks and their anasyrmata-induced tumescences."

Neither Aruna nor Nandini knew what that meant, but they both knew it was probably better not to ask. In that moment it didn't matter anyway. "No, no, no," Aruna repeated, and veered off to the left. "I'll find my own way home!" she declared.

"Mother," Nandini pleaded.

A rabbit darted out of a bush. Aruna veered back to the right and picked up the trail again.

Nandini was relieved that the Professor had not tried to bring up the Kama Sutra, which was only partly about sex, but that was the part the hypocritically prudish Victorian-era British isolated and mistranslated. Still, the sexy part was sexy, though her mother would probably try to talk her way out of that too. A population of one billion people. Where did she think they all came from?

Professor Clover started walking and chopping again. "At any rate," she said, "according to the records, those priests then began to have frequent visions of frightening beings, beings with shapes that folded in on themselves, or unfolded, and could not be rationally understood. Beings with multiple arms and heads."

"I think..." Nandini said, "I think I saw something like that. Back in the tent, when Sally appeared."

Professor Clover nodded. It was a moment before she spoke, and when she did, she sounded both sympathetic and haunted. "So did I once, that first time I encountered Sally back in 1990. I was the only one that survived that time..." Her voice became wistful. She thought about Grant. She could barely remember his face, but he didn't deserve to die that way.

"But for the priests the visions continued," The Professor went on, "because whatever those beings were on the other side, they were able to feed on human thoughts. The human thoughts leaking into their universe, like gravity leaking away from ours through subquantum gaps joining our worlds, were a kind of sustenance for them, particularly sexual thoughts. How does that work? Who knows. Maybe the sounds get converted into an energy that exists in their atmosphere and can just be breathed in?"

"The universe was created with the sound 'om', and that sound contains all of existence, past, present, and future, within it," Aruna said. "Reciting mantras strengthens the fabric of reality. And this other world sounds like Naraka. Our hell." The Professor's speech was slotting into Aruna's own mythology. Vikram himself, despite his vehement anti-religious sentiments, had been very proud of the fact that there was a Nataraja statue at the CERN campus in Geneva.

The Professor went on. "I mean, every religion has some germs that are later discovered to have scientific parallels, but that is just coincidence. In this case, though, maybe it fits. It's just one idea. I have no clue. No one does, and I don't think we ever will. But *why* does it work? That's the purely random way the laws of physics came to be formed in that universe. And it happened to be in contact with ours. And those chants happened to be ones that could make it through. Like a million monkeys at a million typewriters. Maybe we're in contact with other universes too, but we haven't 'seeped through' into them yet, or maybe if we have, then what gets through has no effect like it does in this case. Or maybe other planes are out there that are connected to each other but have nothing to do with us. It's just a fluke."

"This sounds like it supports the cosmological multiverse theory."

"Right. We know that one universe exists for sure: our universe. What about countless universes formed in the fraction of an instant of the inflation after the Big Bang, each with its own random physical laws? I could buy that too. But just two? That seems unlikely to me, though a bunch of people on Earth would tell you there are three: here, and then heaven and hell, or some variant thereof. I mean, if you spill a drink on the floor, are there just two drops? Though maybe such an analogy shouldn't apply to whole universes.

"I know you're thinking about what Mr. Vishwanathan said last night. But infinite universes means that there *isn't* a god, not that there is one. Imagine a die with a million sides. What are the chances you'll roll a million? Not good. But if you roll it a trillion times, it'll probably come up. And you didn't have to 'make' it happen. It just did. It was almost inevitable. Another fluke. You don't have to create life or a universe with laws of physics which allow life. It was just going to happen eventually. Even if there's only one universe, and it keeps expanding and contracting over and over again, with a new set of laws each time, given eternity, or the lack of the existence of time at all, eventually the right conditions will arise.

"That said," she continued, "we don't know that the constants of nature in our universe, like, say, the value of the Higgs field, are unlikely in the first place, because we've never observed them anywhere else. Maybe it's not a million-sided die, maybe it can only be one way. We'd need data from that other universe to at least begin looking at that. Imagine what we could learn…

"Anyway, back to Bose. He wasn't a religious man, but he had eccentricities. For instance, apparently he refused to completely dismiss the idea of some sort of Indian Atlantis."

"That's Kumari Kandam," Aruna said. "But only Tamil nationalists believe about that."

"In any case, for some reason Bose recited these proto-Vedas. *Anti*-Vedas. I suppose he might have just been reading them aloud, because that's how they were taught to read back then. And he made contact with the other side."

Nandini interrupted. "But how did *he* find out about any of it? Why did it matter to him?"

"Like I said, some of these things don't add up. But there was a combination of things we know from different sources. He kept a diary for one. Some of these men can't help themselves. They're like serial killers. Some people say he was in a career slump, or at least he believed he was. He was a genius and knew it, but he had stalled. He was grasping at straws looking for a discovery of any kind. He started drinking. He was heading for the bottom. But back in university he had made a friend who went on to become a professor of archaeology at the University of Bombay. It was that friend who told Bose about the site after he and his team had recently discovered it himself themselves. My guess is that based on what his friend told him, Bose speculated that maybe the priests had been in contact with another world. It was ridiculous, but he was desperate. Shortly after Bose returned from the site, it was reduced to ruins by explosives by persons unknown. Bose's friend from university was also found dead three days later."

"Let me guess: murdered."

"Heart attack, supposedly."

"But wouldn't the archeological team have recited the hymns too?" The question had come from Aruna. This part of the story had drawn her in.

"Maybe they did, but there was no effect, or it was subtle, like a migraine. Enough for them to realize they'd found something even more important than the site itself, enough for Bose's friend to boast to Bose about it. A key thing to remember is that lifeforms from that side can 'see' our thoughts, so I think intent and belief matter. You can't just say the words, you have to sincerely believe them.

"There's another factor here," Professor Clover continued. "Bose's marriage to his wife Manjula was in trouble. It was India in the seventies of course, so there would never be a divorce, but things were unhappy, to say the least. See, Bose had been overseas to North America and more importantly to Europe for conferences. He'd been to 'adult' cinemas. When he got back he wanted to do 'foreign things' with his wife. She was outraged, of course, and wanted nothing more to do with him. She couldn't even stand to be touched by him anymore. We know all this from loud arguments between them overheard by the house staff.

"So Bose makes contact, but unlike the priests or the archaeologists, if *they* were successful, his perversions are so strong that not only does he see the other side, not only do they feed on his thoughts, one of them, an unusually powerful one, notices him. In his diaries, he sometimes described this being as female, at other times as genderless. He calls her the Devi."

"'Goddess,'" Aruna said.

"If they have gender, do they have sex? Why do they need us then?"

"I think saying it was female was just his attempt to make sense of his own impression of it. I don't think the being was necessarily female. Who's to say how things work at all in another world?

"As he describes it, she claims him for herself, and he's her willing victim. The strength of interaction between them forces the seam between universes even wider. But she wants even more, she wants more access into our world to feed on more of our thoughts. So Bose finally had finally found an outlet worthy of his prodigious intelligence. Around 1970, under the guise of another project, he secures funds from his place of employment, the Bhabha Atomic Research Centre, and, with the Devi's guidance, he begins work on the ultimate 'marital aid', a room-sized device which is somehow based on principles he gleaned from the anti-Vedas. The project consumed him. Those close to him knew whatever he was working on was somehow… unseemly. Manjula took their kids and moved back in with her parents. Finally, he completes the project and on September 30, 1971…"

Aruna interrupted. "*Pitru Paksha*. That period, end of September, early October. An inauspicious time."

Clover nodded at her. Yes, that factoid slotted nicely into the puzzle too. As Nandini saw it, now they were enabling each other and pinging each other's cognitive biases, but she didn't interrupt. The Professor continued, "On September 30, 1971, Bose engages in congress with the custom designed entry port on the machine."

"During *Pitru Paksha* one must maintain celibacy," Aruna said.

"Well, Bose decided to fuck the universe. There were lights, sounds, the works. And then he never heard another peep from his interdimensional lover ever again. This ruined him. Reciting the anti-Vedas produces only the vaguest sensation of being in contact with another world. That's not nearly enough for a man who had communed with a being in a parallel universe. Dissatisfied, he became a drunk and an addict. He lost his job and died unloved and alone half a year later.

"But that same September night, just as Bose was sticking his business into an interdimensional opening in Bombay, 13,000 kilometers away, here in New Brunswick at the Our Lady of Calvary Convent, a plumber who'd come in to do some repairs – or according to some stories a pizza delivery man, or merely a lost traveler who'd knocked on the convent door – was plied with Spanish fly and raped by the thirteen nuns living there."

"Isn't Spanish fly just some kind of cayenne pepper extract?" Nandini had heard this from a documentary series about comedian Al Garfield's many rapes.

"Doesn't matter. This is the story that we have. One of the nuns became pregnant and murdered the other twelve that same night, but that's more of a prelude and not as important as the fact that the child she gave birth to was the avatar of Bose's Devi here on earth: Sally. The man escaped. At some stage, he even went back and claimed the child. He told at least some of his tale, and that's all we have, however distorted it's become. If any of it's true, and if we knew his race or the nun's, we'd know Sally's."

"But," Nandini ventured, "strictly speaking, there's no connection between Bose and the nuns. It's just coincidence. And the location doesn't make sense. If Bose entered into congress with his machine in Bombay, why would all this happen way over here?"

By now, Professor Clover was only a silhouette, and Nandini couldn't see her face, but she could sense a kind of defensive alertness around her shoulders. Whatever this narrative was, however, much she ostensibly protested that it was sometimes incomplete or contradictory, in Professor Clover's mind actually it was complete and cohesive and not open to question. She must have put a lot of mental energy into piecing it together. When she finally answered, it sounded almost through gritted teeth.

"The timing is too good. Think about it. And what difference does location make to someone on another plane? If you shot an arrow at the moon, would you care which crater it hit? But, actually, I think the Devi hit exactly the crater she wanted to. She was using Bose. He admitted that himself in his journals after she severed contact with him. She wanted a more direct way to feed on nasty human thoughts, and I figure whatever was going on with those nuns was the brightest beacon for her attention at that moment, that moment she managed to push a piece of herself through thanks to the machine she instructed Bose to build. It was a small piece but bigger than anything that had gotten through before.

"I have a hypothesis that if enough nasty Earth mojo got through to her, that portal you sometimes see around Sally could stay open." Her voice became wistful. "Think about it. A portal into another world would be the greatest discovery in the history of physics and cosmology. Everything would start to fall into place. The problem is maybe it could even become big enough for the Devi to come through into our world. It's like those priests were throwing coins at her. Sally is like a coin magnet, channeling coins from this world to her. If she came through herself, she'd be like Scrooge McDuck swimming around in his money vault. The reality warping would be a lot worse than an amoeba looking in a mirror."

"Even *Pralaya*," Aruna said.

"What's that?"

"The destruction of the universe. In cycles."

The look on the Professor's face, even in the dark, expressed that she didn't like the sound of that. She changed the subject. "I'll tell you something else. I don't think it was just the nuns. This place is a nexus for bad shit, all those bad energies. Construction on the Point Lepreau Nuclear Generating Station started in 1975. There's probably been bad runoff into the water ever since. The pulp and paper mill in Saint John for decades before that. Did you know there was a leper colony in New Brunswick? It was a hospital with armed guards and six-foot-high fences. The inmates burned it down. What about the WWII internment camp for German and

Austrian Jews? How about the goddamn Coleman Frog? That must've come from this place's bad energies too." She looked up and around, squinting as if she was hoping to catch sight of these energies.

"I'm pretty sure the Frog's just papier-mâché. No one believes it's real," Nandini said.

"The Coleman Frog is real," Professor Clover said. "Haven't you been hearing the frogs around here going crazy all the time?"

"Sure, but that's just frogs."

The silhouette of Professor Clover shook her head. "Weird frogs. You saw into another universe just a little while ago, and you can't believe New Brunswick has weird frogs?"

"There's no connection."

Clover sighed. "Maybe not. Actually, I'll be honest. I don't think Sally was Black. My guess is she was maybe Mi'kmaq or Maliseet. Maybe she was half Black, half Native. I think she manifested here, around this lake, because this is a bad place. People here like to talk with pride about the Underground Railroad, coming up through Nova Scotia, some freed slaves settling in New Brunswick. Willie O'Ree, first black hockey player in the NHL is from Fredericton. His grandparents escaped and came up that way. But there were slave owners here, plenty of them, especially after the American Revolution. They were Loyalists who migrated here. The Klan was in New Brunswick too, in the 1920s and 30s. Mostly they hated French

Acadians though. New Brunswick refused to give Doctor King a visa to vacation here in 1960. Anyway, you know how bad it was for the First Nations. All the residential schools, surrounded by the bodies of children dumped in the ground. Across the country, *six thousand dead children.*"

"There was no residential school in New Brunswick though," Nandini said.

"That hardly matters," Professor Clover said. "New Brunswick has Indian day schools in Sussex Vale and elsewhere. Practically the same thing. Assimilation, no education, kids forced into unpaid labor. And think of all those missing and murdered Indigenous women. How many? Four thousand now? And no one doing anything about it but their grieving families.

"Or, hell, I don't know. Maybe she *was* an Indian girl named Sally. Maybe there's been more than one Sally and she's been all of them."

"Then, how do you stop her for good?" Aruna asked. "That's what you're here trying to do, right?"

For a moment there was only the sound of leaves crunching underfoot as they marched. When the Professor finally answered, her voice was pensive. "I don't know that she can be stopped for good. I don't even know that she should be."

Nandini opened her mouth to speak, but barely a sound came out before Professor Clover put up a hand to interrupt her. "The best we can do is observe. The best *I* can do. You two are going home."

The images of the butchered bodies she'd seen that night swam through Nandini's mind again, refusing to be flushed out. After another moment, she said, "You're just here to observe? Look, I'm no hero, but isn't there anything we can do? I mean, we can't even report any of this? Shouldn't we try to stop something so evil? It doesn't feel right to just walk away."

"Yes," Aruna added. "I thought you said she was a demon from some hell dimension?"

"Who said anything about evil, or a hell dimension?" Clover said. "Maybe there's no sex perverts over there, and to *them* the Earth is hell." She preemptively put up her hand again. "What is evil?" she asked, as if she had a third eye on her palm that glowed and radiated in the darkness.

"When one does harm to others." The answer came from Aruna.

Clover: "What if it's by accident?"

Nandini: "To deliberately cause harm to others."

Clover: "What if the other wants to be harmed, for reasons, say, that I cannot detail in these woods because Sally might appear, or other reasons?"

Aruna (now understood the rules of the "game" and was getting into it): "To deliberately cause harm to others who do not wish to be harmed."

Clover: "What if the action was deliberate but the actor didn't know it would harm others?"

Aruna: "To deliberately act in a way that will knowingly cause harm to others who do not wish to be harmed."

Clover: "What if a parent takes away a child's toy to discipline them, something which could be construed as harm to the child?"

Aruna: "Or what about a man who beats his wife and *thinks* it's for her own good?"

Nandini, after thinking for a second, said: "To deliberately act in a way that will knowingly cause harm to others who do not wish to be harmed for one's own pleasure or benefit."

Aruna: "Self-defense or defense of others is a 'benefit', isn't it?"

Clover: "Okay. To deliberately act in a way that will knowingly cause harm to others who do not wish to be harmed for one's own pleasure, satiation, or greed."

Aruna: "What if a poor person steals from a rich person?"

The Professor thought for a second. "I guess it depends how much they steal. Up to a certain amount, it's not going to cause any harm to that person."

Nandini: "What if a poor person hurts a rich person's feelings, on purpose?"

Professor Clover thought again. "I suppose that could be a minor evil. A wrong at least." She exhaled. "But the point is: what is the definition of a demon? Is it a monster? What evil acts did that monster commit, according to our definition of evil? If a thing has come 'from hell', why does that mean it is evil? Does Sally fit the definition? Does an earthquake?" She paused. "I wonder if any of her victims over the years felt any guilt. I doubt it, but if they did, maybe on some level, they wanted to be killed in an earthquake," the Professor replied.

"What if she's seeking revenge?" Nandini asked. "Revenge, even generations later, on people who weren't the ones that caused her death by negligence? Isn't the edification or satisfaction she feels through revenge a form of pleasure?"

"Who knows what she feels?" Professor Clover mumbled.

Is she really going to get them out of these woods alive? Nandini wondered.

"Anyway," the Professor continued, "you won't just be 'walking away', as you put it. You'll be working through the trauma of this night for the rest of your lives. And there's something else…"

"What?"

"I need to know that… you've got a clear head. Given that we've got looking into heads and reality shaping combined going on here, given certain circumstances things could go very wrong."

"What do you mean?"

"I mean about… the death of your father."

"He died eight years ago."

"Of an aneurysm," the Professor offered.

"What are you trying to say?"

"And it… can't be passed down?" For a moment, it was the compassionate voice of the Professor from the night before again, from all the years before, not this stranger.

Nandini didn't answer, and the Professor didn't say anymore. They emerged from the woods into a moon-frosted scene: a semicircle of camp cabins that formed a crescent around a placid, lapping beach. This was their destination, a waypoint and place of fragile safety before they tried to get home.

In front of them was a humanoid creature dressed in obsidian black, with a face like a corpse. She made a chthonic droning sound that sounded like "Another one!", then fired a rifle at the ghillie monster that was between the two Indian ladies, sending the leafy creature flying into the dirt.

Chapter 15
Porno Pilot 1989

The pilot was looking at porn mags.

His name was Gary Pavlovich. He had locks like spun gold that cascaded over his buff exposed shoulders, and he looked like he should be fronting a glam metal band called Totul Attitood on the Sunset Strip.

Actually, he was a Canadian and a black belt in karate. When he was seventeen, he won a second-place trophy in a citywide tournament in Regina, Saskatchewan. He'd even competed in regionals and once went to the States. He was supposed to be somebody, like Don Corleone in that movie about the docks that he didn't really understand. Piloting was a thing his dad had pushed him into, because that old hard-ass had been a pilot. What Gary really wanted to be was a karate man.

But instead now he was flying short hauls for a Columbian scumbag, and his life had turned into a living hell over the past six years. It was an art heist that went bad, a heist in which he was supposed to be the getaway driver, or "pilot" to be more precise, but the RCMP had been tipped off and the whole deal went south. Gary fled to Colombia, where he'd been living for the past six years.

He was an open-minded guy, or at least he tried to be, but the politest way he could put it is that Colombia was all culture shock. The food, the heat, the bugs, the living, the everything. Even after his piloting skills earned him a position of trust in Pablo Escobar's crew and the privileges that came with that, Bogota just didn't compare to Regina.

What he missed most of all was those Canadian women. Hell, Regina even rhymed with vagina!

And second to that, he missed his favorite skin mags: VIP and VIP Confidential. Down in Colombia the best he could get would be some battered playing cards with naked ladies from the seventies on them, if he was lucky, and not even a complete set of fifty-two. VIP Magazine, on the other hand, was so glossy it almost sparkled. There was something pristine, almost futuristic about it.

So now, irony of ironies, he was the one that had turned informant and was ratting out Escobar to the feds in Canada. The RCMP had offered him amnesty and a lifetime horde of pornographic magazines if he flipped. They had given him a box with some sample issues. He looked at the covers, cherished them, but he did not dare to open them and waste them. They were precious. He felt he needed to exercise self-control, even if there really would be a lifetime supply waiting for him on the other side.

How did the feds know it would be enough to tempt him? It didn't matter. It worked.

He had gotten close enough to Escobar, had even been his "air chauffeur" a few times, and felt he had earned enough of the drug lord's trust. One night, in his compound, when Gary "happened" to encounter him and walk in the same direction, he risked slipping into conversation the casual fact that he had learned many useful things in his long years as a pilot, including the tidbit that he knew of a discreet landing strip in New Brunswick. More of a clearing in the forest actually. He didn't need to say more. Escobar had taken the bait. He could use the strip to get cocaine into North America. Gary could almost see the wheels turning in Escobar's mind. "Come with me," Escobar had said. "I do my best thinking in the hot tub."

At the hot tub, Escobar stripped nude. He remained semi-erect the entire time despite no source of arousal that was evident to Gary, not even himself. Escobar was surprisingly fit for a man that lived a life of every indulgence anyone could desire. Gary kept his thong Speedo on, keeping his package nicely contained but prominent. His buttocks were like two perfectly shaped buns from a Montreal bakery, and they shimmered in the dim lighting of the hot tub room. The heat brought on an instant sweat, and their taut muscles glowed. His golden tresses flowed down over his back like a waterfall. By god, Gary wanted to look at those magazines! But he pushed the thought out of his head at once and focused on the conversation at hand.

Escobar didn't waste any time. He fired question after question at Gary about the landing strip: how safe was it, how many times had he used it, who else knew about it. Gary's answers were all both feasible and enticing. The landing strip was real. The RCMP had only coached him on how exactly to parcel out the information to Escobar. As with Gary and the porno mags, they knew exactly what they were doing. Escobar was an easy mark.

And so here he was, finally flying back to his home country after all these years, with amnesty and pornography awaiting him in equal measure. It was just New Brunswick though, not the big smoke yet, but he wasn't going to complain. Finish the mission and he'd be back under the bright lights of Vagina Regina. He'd get back into fighting shape, maybe even register to compete in a Provincial tournament if he could get good enough again.

Seven of Escobar's people were on the plane with him, back in the cargo cabin with all the crates of narcotics – five men and two women, all dressed in army fatigues, like professionals. Tough customers, all of them. *Distributors, actually*, he thought to himself, *hardly "customers"*. They got as much nose candy as they wanted for free when they weren't on assignment.

The women especially unnerved him. They were all hard angles and gritted teeth, without a Saskatchewan curve in sight. Unconsciously, as he thought about this, he arced the plane around in the shape of a woman's hip.

He was alone in the cockpit. On the ground next to him was a steel lockbox with the sampling of mint condition VIP magazines the RCMP had given him, the ones he had resisted even a peek at for months. Now he was breaking out in a thin sweat. He was only wearing a tank top, but beads formed on his forehead and exposed shoulders. They weren't even in the heat of Colombia anymore. His eyes kept darting away from the instrument panel and down to the lockbox.

He ventured a look behind him into the cabin. It was an old WWII-era Douglas C-47 Skytrain, used in those days for transporting paratroopers. Now it was full of crates, and those crates were full of cocaine. There was a narrow "aisle" between the crates, and Escobar's people were at the very back. They were using some of the boxes as a table and seats to play cards. Pablo was that stingy: every available space was there for the crates, not for the comfort of his people. There had been benches along each wall for the paratroopers back in the day, but Escobar had even had those taken out. There were two parachutes on board. Gary wondered if they were from WWII as well.

One of the men (Andreas was his name, as Gary recalled) seemingly lost a hand and threw his cards down, got up and announced he was going to the toilet. At least that's what Gary thought he said. Even after six years, Colombian Spanish was inscrutable to him. Actually, any version of Spanish was inscrutable to him. He also couldn't figure out why they made him learn French at school. He'd found it so useless, it was surely one of the factors in his quitting school in Grade 10. He liked those French chicks though.

He peeked again. The guy was gone to the toilet at the back. The toilet too, was just a seat with a hole, worse than an outhouse – Escobar didn't waste time with a septic tank either when the weight could be allocated to another crate of cocaine – so the crew were pissing and shitting all over the eastern seaboard from on high. The others were distracted by the next hand of cards. Gary glanced at the instrument panel – they would be over Fredericton before too long. He pulled the box up onto his lap, and clumsily entered the combination with his moist, slipping fingers. The latches opened with a satisfying snap. When he lifted the cover, he was bathed in light. The gloss of the pages was so shiny that one could barely see the parts that were supposed to be the most obscene.

Something thumped the fuselage. On the outside. Too abrupt and isolated to be turbulence. Gary slammed the box shut. At the rear of the cabin, at the toilet, there was a scream, and the bathroom door flew open. Andreas stumbled out of it backwards, pants around his ankles, babbling and pointing a shaking finger at the toilet door.

None of the others were paying any attention to the direction he was pointing though.

Instead they were aghast at Andreas's rear end, which had been torn off.

"A-Andreas…," someone managed. This was a hardened crew, they had seen and done some of the worst that can be done to a person, but one of the other men passed out, and two more cowered in a corner. One of the women, Luciana, now noticed the toilet.

Sally Pencilneck was climbing up out of it.

Luciana, always the superstitious one, immediately assumed they were being punished. They had made fun of Andreas's bony ass, and now they could actually see the bones of his ass. She crossed herself. Sally fully emerged from the shitter swinging her nunchaku, and she started more in Ferdinand's direction than Luciana's. Luciana and Ferdinand finally got their machine guns out and blasted away with no regard for Andreas, whom they cut to flesh confetti.

The bullets punched holes in some of the crates too, causing an eruption of white powder haze in the air.

Gary went from horny to frenzied in an instant. "What the fuck's going on back there?!" he shrieked.

The crew ignored him. Sally lay on the ground, unmoving, but Escobar's crew weren't stupid. Whatever crawled up through the toilet of a plane mid-flight was no ordinary person. Luciana and Ferdinand edged forward, stepping gingerly through the mounds of Andreas's meat. Beatrice, the other woman on the crew, and far more collected and calculating than her comrade Luciana, rose off her crate and prepped her Kalashnikov without ever taking her eyes from Sally's prone body.

"Hey! Hey!" Gary cried again over his shoulder. "What the hell are you shooting at? You don't shoot guns inside a plane! That's, like, fucking basic." He shook his head. These fucking savages. Without a copilot he wasn't sure that he should trust the autopilot, but he couldn't see what other choice he had. He flicked it on, ventured a glance at his precious lockbox, then made his way into the cabin, and worked his way past the stacks of crates towards the back where the others were. The "aisle" was so narrow he had to turn half sideways to get through it.

Sally's body was splayed on the floor in an awkward, twisted position. Ferdinand stood over her and prodded her "corpse" with the muzzle of his machine gun.

"What is it?" Luciana asked.

"I don't know," he answered. It looked like a woman, but she was wearing a strange mask, and a necklace with desiccated trophies on it. Ferdinand had seen similar in his jungle fighting days. An evil omen, to be sure. But he was just as guilty of his own crimes from those days. What was worse, maybe it was all the cocaine he was inhaling, but looking back at those days now as he stood over Sally's body, he felt not remorse, but longing. Especially that one village, those village girls, their houses on fire…

One of Sally's arms was draped across her face. He moved it out of the way with the machine gun. Sally reached up with her other hand, ripped his nuts off and jabbed them into his ears, pushing them through into his brain. As he keeled over backwards, he unleashed a spray of bullets that opened up another perfect row of holes in the plane's roof.

"What the hell's going on back here?!" Gary tried to yell over the noise of Beatrice and Luciana unloading their clips at Sally. Luciana screamed as she fired, her lips curled in a sneer. Beatrice stayed cool. She timed her bursts so that she reloaded while Luciana was still firing.

"Hey! Hey!" Gary cried as he grabbed Luciana's shoulder. She turned the gun on him, and he put his hands up in instant terror. Beatrice stopped too.

He felt weird. There was the smoke from the guns, the white haze, and air was being sucked out through the bullet holes in the fuselage. And yet, he felt ready to party. Even with these joyless hard-asses. He felt high is what it was. Beatrice stopped firing too.

As the smoke cleared, Sally was nowhere to be seen.

"What the fuck are you even shooting at? Christ, the crates!" he moaned. Now he knew why he felt high. But he needed this mission to go smoothly. He wanted the hoard of porn promised to him by the feds, he wanted to go back to a civilized life, get back to karate again, and maybe quit flying for good. Quit flying these kinds of missions anyway. Then he saw the body of the man with his balls ripped off, and the other man shot to pieces. His first thought was to wonder if the RCMP would turn a blind eye to the dead men as long as they still nabbed Escobar. "Why... why'd you kill these guys?"

The women ignored him. Luciana was pouring with sweat and speaking too quickly for Gary to understand any of it. Beatrice too ignored his pleas and carefully swept her machine gun around the cabin in full, slow arcs.

The man who'd fallen unconscious earlier groaned. Luciana hissed at him, grabbed the shoulder of his uniform, and clumsily tried to help him up while also swinging her gun in every direction while her teeth threatened to grind each other down to the gums.

"What's... what's happening?" the man mumbled. Miguel was his name.

There was a thump on the roof, just like before. How?

Beatrice had been to the toilet just a few minutes before Andreas and nothing had happened. And it occurred to her that when that creature emerged, it was Ferdinand it had started going towards.

She grabbed Miguel away from Luciana and held the dazed man in front of her like a shield.

Gary could sense his trip going bad. He thought he could handle all of this. He was a somebody. But now it was getting to be too much. It was the one thing he never wanted to admit. He could feel the weight of it all closing in, Colombia, the drugs, the cartel, even the bungled art heist from way back when. Plus, with all of the cocaine in the air and the guns and the air roaring around in crazy ways through the bullet holes and the mutilated bodies, it was a bad scene.

The words of his sensei at the strip mall in Regina came into his head unbidden: "Refocus". Yes. He closed his eyes and refocused, zeroed in on his training song, Toto's "Hold the Line". He was sweating, he stripped off his tank top and threw it away, ran his hands over his slick buff chest, his nipples like hard sensors guiding his inner spirit. Once he was grounded, so to speak, his center told him to go back to the cockpit and pilot the fucking plane. He did an about face and strode back to his place, doing karate chops in the air along the way in time to Jeff Porcaro's drumming. *I am special*, he told himself. *I am a karate champion. I am the Buddha.*

Back in the cockpit, he whipped off his pants and sat down in the pilot's seat. He was already fully erect. He whistled with cocaine confidence as he opened his precious lockbox and began jerking off to the first magazine he pulled out of it, latching the box closed again with his free hand.

"This is the life!" he exulted aloud, when the window shattered, and Sally Pencilneck launched into the cockpit feet first, directly into Gary's chest.

He flew backwards, but rolled when he hit the ground, just like he'd practiced. It was amazing, but he actually did it, even though it had been years. He leaped up and assumed an opening stance. "*Hiya!*" he cried as he instinctively chopped at his attacker, but he missed and hit the control panel. The plane veered. He turned and finally took a good look at the thing which had attacked him. It seemed to be a woman, but wearing a Groucho mask with swirly hypno eyes, and she had pencils jabbed through her neck.

"*Wata!*" he cried, but he could barely even hear himself over the air rushing through the broken window. Gary kicked her in the face, his veiny tumescent penis flailing wildly as he did so. Amazingly, again, he made contact, and broke one of the "lenses" of her comedy glasses. If it was possible at all to understand any of Sally's emotions, the eye behind the lens looked genuinely surprised.

She nodded in approval. A worthy opponent. She began to circle, left then right, spinning her nunchaku.

He punched her in the stomach and she buckled, creating the opportunity to launch another strike that connected with her clavicle. He risked another high kick, but she swung her nunchaku and hit him in the side. The pain was searing. He went down on one knee but managed to punch her in the thigh. It wasn't much, but with the plane veering wildly it was enough to send her off balance and tumbling into the wall behind her.

Three of Escobar's surviving crew members lurched into the cockpit, the two women and Miguel, weapons raised. "No!" Gary commanded, putting up a hand to stop them. "This is between me and her! This is my moment!"

Beatrice yelled at him, using the muzzle of her machine gun to point back and forth between him and the control panel. He couldn't understand much of what she was saying except the words "fly" and "plane". Luciana, meanwhile, had noticed his nakedness, and though her English was limited she knew this was called the "cockpit" and she could see his "cock". How strange.

But in the same instant the creature was right in front of her. Sally put the nunchaku over Luciana's head so the chain was behind her neck, then crossed the batons in front and yanked them so hard the poor woman's head popped off. Blood gushed out of her neck like it was the Chorro de Quevedo fountain for a full two seconds before the body slumped to the floor. Miguel tried to avoid the gore, lost his balance, fell into the control panel, and sent the plane veering in another new direction. The two men still in the cabin grabbed the only parachutes and jumped.

Beatrice opened fire on Sally, but there was no hope of hitting her with the plane veering the way it was and the air belting them at breakneck speeds. She perforated Miguel instead, and his body whipped out the window like it had been sucked into a black hole. She missed Sally completely. Gary dodged her fire.

Beatrice stumbled and started to go out the window too, but she clutched at the control panel, mashing every button, every lever, hoping to find some purchase to save herself. No use. Even with cocaine-enhanced strength, her sweaty fingers slipped, slipped, slipped, millimeter-by-millimeter, until finally she was gone with a cry too.

The C-47 dove and did a full barrel roll, a final gift from Beatrice's final random button presses, and something which according to the laws of physics it should not be able to do.

Sally went out the window too, but the plane leveled out in the same instant, and she face-planted onto the plane's nose. Her rotten nails clenched the steel plates, and with great effort she struggled back to her feet, only to get jump kicked in the face by a naked Saskatchewan.

High kick, punch, punch, low kick, block. Gary was landing his blows and knew to watch out for the nunchaku this time. He was on a roll, but it was too good to last. The plane decided to go vertical. Gary and Sally were launched into the air, still grappling as they fell. Gary was in a state of perfect Zen, his naked body automatically performing the *kata* he had practiced over and over again even in midair. At some point, the lockbox full of VIP magazines flew past him, latched, but not locked, and he felt a pang at its loss, but he was too focused to ever come out of the zone again.

KILLARNEY LAKE MASSACRE

I'm a somebody, he told himself. *I am the Buddha. Regina Vagina.* He went ass-first into the top of a pine tree that shot through his whole body and blasted his flesh in every direction as he descended it.

Unfortunately for him, Gary Pavlovich was not a somebody. The RCMP and CSIS covered up the whole thing, of course, even changing the name of the pilot to make the story coherent. They even made up a story that they themselves had forgotten to chop down the trees in the landing field that were in the flight path because government incompetence made the story more believable.

But, worse than any of this erasure, Gary was no different than dozens of other drug mule pilots that the CIA and CSIS seduced with the promise of pornography in the 1980s. Due to the natural and unnatural hazards of the trade, or as a result of these inevitably "distracted" pilots, many of their flights crashed, scattering glossy printed smut across forests all over North America. And this is why, throughout the 1980s, when underage boys sought pornography, they somehow knew to go looking in the woods, where they were able to find pages or whole magazines under rocks or in the hollows of trees. Gary was forgotten. His legacy endured.

Chapter 16
There Are Communists in The Funhouse

Aruna dressed Yorgotha's wounds with a first aid kit they found in the rudimentary camp counselors' office where they were now sitting. They sat at one of the four desks in the room, all were practically buried under half used office supplies. Behind a door on one side was a small kitchenette, and on the opposite side the cabin had its own toilet.

Aruna went to wipe off the black and white makeup around the injuries on Yorgotha's face before disinfecting the area, but the girl caught her arm in an iron grip before she could, and said, "Leave the makeup on."

Aruna shook her head in that Indian way that could have been "yes" or "no" but in this case was "c'est la vie". She had the soaked cotton wad in her hand but paused. "Do your parents know you dress like this?" she asked.

Yorgotha replied by looking at her through narrowed eyes.

Another head wobble, this one definitely more disapproving. "*Chee*," she said almost under her breath, and then got to work. "What's your name?"

"Yorgotha."

"How can I tell if your head got hurt or not if you don't tell me your real name?"

"It's my name. My *true* name." The antiseptic stung, but she accepted the pain as any worthy practitioner of Black Metal should.

"I see. Okay. What day of the week is it?"

This took a second. She had to think, longer than she wanted to. "Saturday?" she asked.

Aruna gave an approving head wobble and applied a bandage. "Do you remember what happened?"

"Yes. I shot… I shot that monster outside." For an instant, Yorgotha had been frozen in terror, a kind of terror that seemed inappropriate for one who advocated the ways of Black Metal. She'd just shot someone dead. She had thought it was a *thing*, something like the thing that killed those two men, but when she shot it, it made an all too human grunt. After that, she was embarrassed to admit to herself that what came next was almost a relief. "Then you and your… daughter, did you say?" Aruna nodded. Yorgotha tried to commit it to memory that the other woman was her daughter, and that today was… Saturday. She had almost forgotten again. Her wounds pulsed as Aruna applied the antiseptic. "You and your daughter screamed and ran away. And I wanted to run too, but shooting the rifle made me fall, and the monster suddenly sat straight up, and the next thing I knew, she was flying through the air at me like a leafy bat. After that, I don't know. She was on me, striking me, and none of the dark forces could protect me."

"*We* are the dark forces that protected you," Aruna said as she opened another bandage.

"Are you a nurse?"

"No. But I worked in a nursing home once, a long, long time ago. It's lucky for you, my daughter heard the commotion and stopped and brought me back, and we dragged Professor Clover off of you."

"You said that before… 'Professor'. In any case… thank you." The words sounded incongruous coming from that gothic face, but the bandages mitigated it.

"Follow my finger," Aruna said. She moved a finger back and forth in front of Yorgotha's face, and the young woman's eyeballs tracked it.

"Anything else?" Aruna asked.

"I need to change my tampon."

"Okay. Do you have extras?"

Yorgotha nodded, but she didn't get up to go to the bathroom.

Her shoulders sank. There was something worse, something much worse than the brief guilt of mistakenly thinking she'd murdered someone. "This is all my fault," she said with a quivering lip.

The leaf monster herself burst into the office, unhooded and carrying Yorgotha's "borrowed" rifle. Nandini was behind her.

Aruna looked up at them and asked, "How are you, Professor?"

"A cracked rib or two. I'll live, thanks to my Kevlar vest." Despite the cracked ribs, she thumped herself on the chest, and it made a knocking sound. There was a hole in her disguise from the rifle blast, and it had destroyed the zipper as well, ruining the suit. "I wear it 24-7. You should both start too. How is she?"

"She'll be all right."

"Good," said the Professor as she put the rifle down on a desk. She pulled out other firearms from under her foliage and set them down too. Then she pounced on the seated girl with an animal growl.

"Professor!" They struggled to pry her off again, but finally she relented and shook Nandini off her arm.

"Stupid girl!" she cried. "Now three of us will die!"

Even through the makeup, Yorgotha's distress was visible.

"The area seems safe. For now," the Professor said, wiping the spittle from her lip. "As for you, young woman, if I didn't have my wits about me out there, I could have killed you. The woods are cordoned off. You shouldn't be here, and certainly not dressed like that."

"I know," Yorgotha answered, "There's a *thing* in these woods."

Professor Clover sighed. "So you've seen her?"

Yorgotha nodded. "It... She? Killed two men. I saw it. I saw her... do it!" Again, she felt like an imposter. She should have reveled in that carnage.

As she spoke, Professor Clover started to peel off

her ruined ghillie suit. Underneath she was wearing the same pantsuit she had worn the previous night at Dr. Jayakrishnan's retirement party. So she probably never went home that night, Nandini figured.

"When?"

"Just a... I don't know. Just a few minutes ago?"

"That's two more then," Nandini said.

"They looked familiar," Yorgotha added.

"They were people you knew?"

"No. I mean, like, I'd seen them on TV or on a cover of something or something like that."

"Wait," Nandini interrupted. She'd been trying all night not to think about the first body they saw, but now she forced herself. "There was something familiar about the man we saw too. Wasn't there, Mother? His face..."

Aruna shuddered, shook her head, waved a trembling hand, looked away.

"Why are all these people in the woods anyway?" Nandini continued. "What about the police cordon?"

"Who cares?" Professor Clover said. "Why are *you* in the woods? Nobody cares about the cordon. In fact, the police were probably ordered to make it porous so people could get through, and the government could observe via spy satellite! Are you from Fredericton?"

The question was so mundane under the circumstances, it confused Yorgotha for an instant, but finally she nodded.

"Have you heard of Sally Pencilneck?"

Her eyes widened.

"Think pure thoughts," the Professor told her.

Yorgotha started to panic, her breathing was becoming labored. "Are you all right?" Aruna asked her.

"What are *you* doing here?" the Professor asked Yorgotha, homing in on her distress like a missile and looming over her.

"Professor Clover," Nandini said. "Maybe go easy on her."

"Get your hands off me!" the Professor barked.

"It was me!" Yorgotha cried.

All motion stopped.

"What was you?" Nandini whispered.

"I brought it… her. Here. To the world."

"How?" Nandini asked.

"It was a book. An ancient book. My uncle left it to me in his will. He was an antique book dealer. I never met him, never even heard of him, but when he died last month, I got this book in the mail. A spell book in some language I couldn't read. I can't even recognize the script. But there were phonetic transcriptions of some of the text. And there was a letter explaining about the will and that my uncle knew me and wanted me to have the book."

Through all of this, the Professor had her back turned to them and appeared to be fuming. Her hands gripped the edge of a desk, and her knuckles stood out like steel.

Nandini looked back at Yorgotha. "And what

information did your parents have about this uncle?"

"I don't speak to my progenitors. And then I read some of the pages and now all this has happened. It was all my fault!"

"Wait. What were you expecting to happen?" Nandini asked.

"I wanted to change people's opinion about music."

A part of Nandini empathized, but the only word she said was: "Christ."

"Do you like… heavy music?" Yorgotha asked Nandini.

"I like Hüsker Dü," she offered.

"What's that?"

Nandini chuckled, and it was actually good-natured.

Yorgotha said, "The book and letter made it sound like… it could change the way things are. I thought I could control it."

"That's vague," Nandini said.

"No, maybe she's right!" exclaimed Aruna.

"Mother! Professor Clover, didn't you say something about the intent of the chanting? That it had to be sincere?"

Professor Clover spun and grabbed Yorgotha's shoulders in a violent grip. This time Nandini and Aruna didn't try to pull her off. "Where's the book?"

"In my backpack."

Professor Clover went over to the desk with the backpack on it and opened it, aggressively, but she kept looking back at the young woman.

The bag was full of audio cables, makeup, and other paraphernalia, but the book was large, practically a ledger. There was no mistaking it.

"You call this ancient? I can tell you exactly when this was written. 1971. It's one of Bose's notebooks."

"Who... who's Bose?"

"A scientist who opened a glory hole to another dimension and got us into this mess."

"What's a —"

"Mother, don't ask."

"Let me try to read it," Aruna said, wanting to participate in some way. "Maybe it will say some way to close the hole. There's always some way."

There was a brief tug-of-war for the book. "By what logic?! Is there always 'some way' to reverse the flow of a river?"

"A river isn't magic!"

"*This* isn't 'magic'! You're not going to be able to understand these mathematical formulas anyway," the Professor hissed.

"I can read Sanskrit!"

"*You* can read Sanskrit?"

"I studied it in school! Did *you* study Sanskrit?" There was no arguing with that. Professor Clover let her have the book.

Aruna flipped through it, flipped through it, flipped through it, stopped, and pored over some pages slowly, made noises of approval, of disapproval, wobbled her head in admiration at certain passages, held her fingers over her lips and chin in thought. "I can't read this," she said finally.

The Professor yanked the book back from her and slammed it down on a desk.

"Let me look at it again," Aruna said. "I just need another minute."

But Professor Clover blocked her way. "No. Forget it. You three need to keep heading west, away from the woods. Eventually you'll reach the highway. Flag down a ride and go home. Never think about what happened here ever again. Do it, or die. Something always goes wrong, or someone does something stupid. Don't go north. Do you know where the supposedly secret executive lodge is? Sally's nexus of power seems to be around there. That's where the old campgrounds were. That's where she's most active. Don't go there."

In a move that would have stunned Kevin Martin, the greatest curler of all time, Aruna did a duck-and-weave around the Professor, snatched up the tome, and dashed out the flimsy wooden door. It banged and bounced behind her. For a split second, Clover was stunned but then gave chase. By the time she got to the front porch and steps and looked out across the moon-frosted grass and to the lapping waters of the lake, Aruna was nowhere to be seen. An instant later, Nandini and Yorgotha appeared behind her.

The Professor spun on them. "Nandini, wait here in case she comes back. You! Grab one of the weapons I left on the desk in there and go look for her. Sweep the west and the north," she said, tilting her chin in each direction. But the two younger women were frozen. Nandini's eyes were wet. "Move it!" They dashed back inside.

Professor Clover descended to the grass, turned east, and entered the woods. She heard Yorgotha come out of the cabin behind her.

"Aruna!"

"Lady!"

"Aruna!"

"Lady!"

***

Yorgotha didn't imagine she would ever have to pick up the rifle again. The first and only time she'd fired it before, the recoil had knocked her on her ass. Also, it felt incongruous. She wanted a scythe. That would be appropriate, and she could just swing it in an arc without having to worry about aiming or the recoil. She could keep Sally at bay. For a second or two. Maybe. She remembered all those campfire stories. Funereal Devastation's drummer, Nemesis Decapitator, once even suggested she write a song about her, but the idea of Sally was so childish and preposterous, something she associated with Girl Guides, that she dismissed the suggestion without another thought. It would have been like writing a song about Mr. Snuffleupagus. Sally wasn't Black Metal enough, she thought. Now she knew differently. Maybe Mr. Snuffleupagus was Black Metal too.

She was thinking all these stupid things to try to distract herself, to settle her ragged breathing, to slow down her heart, the very thing which gave her life, and now felt like it was trying to kill her by bursting from her chest.

"Lady!" she croaked. Even if she were nearby, would that nice lady actually have heard that? "Lady!" she tried again, but it was even worse this time. She sounded like that man that had tried to make a movie about a clown in the concentration camp. Now that was Black Metal.

Don't think any impure thoughts. That part was easy. Yorgotha hardly ever thought impure thoughts. Everyone else seemed to talk about their impure thoughts all the time, so much so she sometimes wondered if there was something wrong with her. And yet now, for once, in this situation, it was like armor against Sally. In fact, Yorgotha thought, she might be the one that actually beats the monster tonight.

She had a little pen light that she held against the rifle barrel. It was one of many useful little items she always had attached to her chain belt, especially since she was out in the dark so much. It wasn't great, but it was something. About twenty meters in front of her, there was an oak tree with an especially thick trunk, one big enough for a person to hide behind. What really attracted her attention to it though, was that something had moved, maybe an elbow in and out. It was very brief. She crept up on it. "Lady," she whispered, then summoned all her courage and spun on the other side of the trunk, baring her teeth and making a face in case her visage would be enough to scare off anything she didn't want to meet.

Nothing there. Leaves. Leaves all over this place. Every one of them, moving in slow motion in the breeze, every one of them easily mistaken for an elbow or a knee.

A sound to her left. Perhaps a footstep in the underbrush. Maybe just a scurrying animal. There were some more large oaks in that direction. Gingerly she stepped towards them. "Lady," she whispered again. Her own steps might have been louder than that initial sound, but it was already gone from memory. There was a rushing and pounding of blood in her ears. That and her tinnitus. The crickets and the frogs too. Maybe she *hadn't* heard anything. She made the face again and leapt to the other side of the trunk. There was nobody there anyway. She zigzagged back and forth between the larger trees like this. She knew how ridiculous it must look. This was not the music video she had envisioned for Funereal Devastation, but, she supposed, perhaps in some ways it was.

She jumped around a trunk and made her evil hissing face. But this time she tripped on a tree root and stumbled. She turned back and stomped the root in anger. It wasn't a root. It was something that had a straight edge and made a dull clank when her boot struck it. She shone her light on it. It was the corner of a metal box, just barely sticking out of the ground, and even what was exposed was so rusted and brown that it almost disappeared against the earth around it. Only the faintest glinting reflections of her flashlight revealed that it was steel. It might have been the size of a briefcase, but she couldn't know without digging it out. It was curious, but there was no time for that now. She had to find the nice lady. She had to get out of these woods. Sally Fucking Pencilneck was out here somewhere. A campfire boogeyman. How was that even possible? She started to walk away.

There was no way to know which way the nice lady had gone. She turned in circles yelling, "Lady! Lady!" When she stopped, she was facing in the direction of the box in the ground. Sweat was running down over her makeup. Curiosity got the better of her. She went back for it.

She pulled at it. There was a little bit of give, but not enough. She cleared a bit of the dirt away from each edge. She pulled at it again, and this time it budged a little bit more. She pulled harder, summoning all her strength and grunting brutally. The case flew out of the ground and Yorgotha fell backwards. The case had been latch side down, and the latch was not locked, so when the case arced out of the ground, all of the contents in it burst out of it spinning, fluttering, and flapping to the ground.

Yorgotha staggered to her feet. That was the second time that damn box had beaten her. And when she shone her light on the ground, and the beam pawed the glossy magazine pages like a tech bro, in that one moment, she saw more eighties' tits, ass, and spread beaver than she thought they even *had* in the eighties. "Aw, fuck," she rasped. The tears came down, stinging and hot, and she knew that the box had beaten her a third time. She did not even need to turn around to know that Sally Pencilneck was already standing right behind her.

***

Inside the camp counselor office, Nandini looked at a chair and considered sitting down to wait, thought it would be the right-thinking thing to do, but then suddenly the idea made her sick. She paced instead. She looked at the weapons Professor Clover had left on the table. Her hands were trembling even after everything else that had happened tonight. She wanted to run out and join the search for her mother. Why should she listen to the Professor? Did she really know what she was talking about? Signs even pointed to the woman being mentally ill.

The voices outside calling for her mother had receded into inaudibility, but there were the shrieking crickets, the croaking frogs. The fucking frogs. Why wouldn't they shut up?! She looked up and squeezed her eyes shut as hard as she could, as if they were her ears, and the tears dripped out. She wanted to be a tiny little girl again. She wanted her father to suddenly appear and scoop her up and carry her home, the rough bristles of his moustache scraping and tickling her cheek.

The cabin door opened behind her and Nandini spun in terror, but it was her mother carrying the book.

"Mother! What –"

"Shh!" Aruna hissed with a finger to her lips. "I just went in a circle!"

"What?!" If Nandini could have shot fire out of her eyes, she would have flame broiled the woman. She went to the door, pulled it open, and called out to Professor Clover.

Her mother grabbed her arm. "Forget about them. Let's get out of here."

"You just want to abandon them?!"

"Professor Clover can take care of herself."

"What about that girl…"

"Yorgotha."

"Yorgotha."

"I don't know," said Aruna. "Maybe we can find her on the way. Just let me go to the toilet."

"What?!"

Aruna went into the toilet. Nandini was still holding the cabin door open and was wondering if she should call out to Professor Clover again. Eventually she let it fall shut and crossed to the bathroom door.

She knocked. "Mother! Hurry it up in there!" she called through the door.

"Just give me ten secs!"

Nandini waited. She knocked again.

As she knocked, a noise came from the closed kitchenette door behind her.

Or at least she thought there was a noise.

Maybe she imagined it.

She froze.

"Mother... What did you say?"

"I said give me ten secs!" Aruna became curiously silent in the bathroom. The toilet flushed. She came out. "Ten secs," she said again, slowly, rolling the words around in her mind.

Again, there was a sound from the kitchenette.

This time they both heard it and looked at each other and the closed door. "Ten secs... Ten sex," said Aruna, wobbling her head apologetically. "I'm sorry, *chinna kutti*..."

Nandini looked at her wide-eyed, then gingerly crossed to the kitchenette door and pushed it with the lightest touch. It drifted open in complete silence. Even the crickets and frogs stopped for it.

Inside, Sally Pencilneck sat at the little dining table for two with her feet up on it, eating beans out of a can with a fork. The Coleman Frog sat on the ground beside her, its whole body pulsing like a heart as it breathed. When the door had swung fully open, Sally plonked the fork into the can and set the can down on the table without looking up at the two women standing frozen in the doorway. Then she stood up and picked up her nunchaku off the table. When the frog bared its fangs, Nandini and Aruna regained enough self-possession to slam the door shut and bolt away at speeds neither of them thought they were capable of. Nandini managed to grab the Professor's backpack before they fled.

Chapter 17
So Disgusting! Truly Disgusting!

Which way *was* west anyway? They had been going kind of north to get to the camp cabins. That meant if they turned sort of left, they should reach the highway. They ran for a while, but then Aruna begged for relief. Nandini had little choice but to allow it. They couldn't really run quickly through the spruces and firs anyway. They slowed to a determined stroll.

Professor Clover was out there somewhere but based on what Nandini thought she heard her say, she would have gone east. When they switched to walking, Nandini asked her mother if they should look for her, but the question was hardly sincere. The Professor could take care of herself, Aruna had said. Given the circumstances, however, there was the much worse unspoken possibility that she was already dead.

"It's very strange though, isn't it? Who knew Professor Clover was someone like that," Aruna said.

Now that was a good question, even if it was only meant to be rhetorical. Who *did* know? Maybe her husband. Was that why her husband and daughter had left her?

When they got to the pines, though the moonlight was faint, it was cruel, and some distance away from them, maybe twenty meters, they could make out shapes on the ground, not boulders or roots, but *clumps*. They both knew even at this distance that those clumps were Yorgotha cut apart into clean pieces as if with a scythe. Nandini even thought she could see her torso cut into two halves. It would have been from bottom to top. Each woman wanted to cover up the other one's eyes. Neither did. Instead they both just looked away and kept walking. Aruna clenched her teeth and clutched Bose's book like it was a security blanket to protect her from what she had just seen. Would there ever be an end to it?

Around them were the birchbark trees, like the arms of skeletons reaching out of the ground. Nandini looked up at the black, black canopy overhead. The maples in the dark. Now, even in the middle of the night, it was sweltering, but in four or five weeks it would be cold. "Autumn with her sun-burnt caravan." That was a Bliss Carman poem. And that canopy would be shrieking reds, purples, and oranges, a cold fire in the sky. *Compartmentalize, compartmentalize, compartmentalize*, she had kept telling herself the whole night, her whole life, in fact. Maybe that even made her especially suited to survive this night. Yet now, for a brief moment, she let herself imagine that cold fire coming down and consuming her, washing over the whole world, everything gone in an instant.

Out of the corner of her eye, the glint of her mother's glasses brought her out of her reverie.

Without Professor Clover dominating their party, Nandini's mind wandered into the cold calculations. Now one of them was dead, just like Professor Clover said would happen. If the Professor herself was also already dead, then that meant Nandini or Aruna would be left alone. Nandini couldn't bear the idea of her mother suffering another loss and being left all by herself. But the idea of her mother dying was unthinkable. There would be nothing left to tether her. A dark cloud at the back of her mind wondered if the best outcome would be if Professor Clover was the one that survived. She dare not let that thought come to the fore though. This could be the one time they broke the precedent. This could be the time more than one survived. *This could be the time.* She had to believe that.

She glanced over at her mother. She was still clutching Bose's book to her chest. She was so skinny. Almost like a skeleton with a bouffant, and in her blue and white curling outfit she looked like a native bird that had originated in this forest to begin with. Nandini loved that silver and gray hair. It was evidence of a life lived, a real life. There were a million things she didn't know about her mother, could never know. What was really going on behind those glasses? Even if the toil of village life meant those days and years all melted into each other, even if the toil of her marriage meant those days and years all melted into each other,

Nandini refused to believe that all of Aruna's experiences and thoughts were obliterated by the facades put up by life, her own shields, even Nandini herself. Nandini certainly couldn't let this night obliterate the woman.

And the instant after she cleared her mind, as if by some miracle, they emerged from the trees and the highway was before them, and the shift was so jarring that it blurred Nandini's vision. Her mother, who a moment ago had seemed like a bird that belonged in the woods, now appeared distressed, like a bird stuck in a food court. Nandini looked up and down the road. There were no vehicles in sight. The sweat was pouring down her face.

"Nandini," Aruna said. Her words were far away and slow, almost like they were spoken underwater. "Did I ever tell you about a *maltong*? It's a creature —"

"Shut up, Mother." Nandini's eyes hadn't left the highway. She thought she heard a noise, maybe an engine, but it seemed too much to hope for. Then the faint glow of headlights appeared. Through the stinging sweat in her eyes and the tears welling up, the lights became pieces of shifting gray stained glass as they approached. She started to walk out into the middle of the road. Aruna grabbed her hand. "*Chinna kutti*, wait," she said. Some corner of Nandini's awareness was aware that her mother was being insane, but she ignored her and pulled her hand free and waved her arms at the car.

Red and blue panels of light joined the white and gray ones as the car pulled up and slowed. It was a patrol car. It came to a stop, the spinning carnival lights stayed on as Michelle Chow got out of the vehicle. Nandini finally let the tears fall. Out of the woods, a car, a police car, and it was Michelle. It was almost like the universe was paying back all its debts to them at once for the night it had just put them through.

"Nandini? Oh, my god!"

"Please, Michelle! Listen to me. It's nuts, but it's all true," she pleaded. "The stories about Sally Pencilneck. It's not a bear."

"Nandini, I need to tell you something," Aruna said, pawing at her.

Nandini ignored her and continued speaking to Michelle. Michelle spared a split-second glance at Aruna. "There are bodies in there, in the woods. It sounds crazy, but you have to call it in."

"Nandini..."

"Mother, shut up!"

"Okay, okay," Michelle said calmly. "Just wait here. I'll call an ambulance. Why don't you just, maybe, sit in the grass?"

"I don't want to sit!"

"Okay, okay. You don't have to sit. Just wait here one minute."

Michelle went back to the car. Through the windows, Nandini could see her on the radio.

"Nandini, I need to tell you something," said Aruna. "Listen to me."

"What?!" she barked.

"We need to go back in the woods."

The night mist, dimly lit by the halogen headlights of the patrol car, swirled around Nandini's glistening demonic face. She said nothing, only stared in disbelief, shook her head, almost laughed.

"I looked in the book, this book," Aruna went on. "It's true, Bose says the Devi's avatar can give wishes to devotees. It says the Devi herself can change reality for her devotees, like Shiva."

"So? So what? What are you talking about?!"

"It's just like Michelle said. She let her boyfriend die, then she became police."

"Have you lost your mind?! That wasn't Michelle! That was some urban legend about some stranger's supposed cousin who never existed! What is the matter with you?!"

"What about that poor girl? That kabuki girl? Her wish?"

"What about it?!"

"Suddenly, I... I hate rap music!"

"You always hated rap music!"

"Everybody thinks they have good taste in music. No one thinks they have bad taste in music. So in a way her wish came true."

"Think about what you're saying! That doesn't mean her wish came true! Things were already that way!"

"The *pugri naad* grants wishes when you make sacrifices to it. Sally is another thing like those things!"

Nandini wanted to be rescued. She wanted this conversation, this whole night to just be over. She wondered what was taking Michelle so long.

"Nandini, listen to me. Listen to me," Aruna pleaded. "What if your father didn't kill himself?"

Nandini slapped her. The reaction was instantaneous, a reflex, though she had never struck a person in her life. Nandini covered her mouth and gasped, aghast that she had done it.

Aruna soldiered on. "Sally did it. She came to our house and hanged him."

Remorse flipped back to rage, like a light switch. Nandini's eyes bulged out of her head and every vein on her face and neck threatened to burst and spray her mother with blood. She grabbed Aruna by the shoulders and shook her. "What the fuck are you talking about?!"

She briefly looked at the patrol car. Michelle was still on the radio. She had a confused look on her face. Nandini didn't have the capacity to process that now.

"Listen to me," Aruna said. "A-a-about a week before he died, one day, I… I… I went into his office… in our house. Please, *chinna kutti*, you have to understand it's hard for me to talk about this kind of thing. He… he… he was there on his computer, and… on his screen was so disgusting! And *he* was so disgusting! Truly disgusting! Right there what he was doing!" The memory alone seemed to fill her throat with bile. She was shuddering with revulsion as Nandini's fingernails bit into her shoulders. "I... I... I... I wished he was dead!" she spat. "I... I told him so! I never wanted to look at him again! I couldn't speak to him that whole week."

"What the fuck does any of that have to do with Sally Pencilneck?!"

"That's who Sally likes! That's her victims!"

"Sally..." Nandini was apoplectic, could barely form the words. "Sally doesn't go to people's houses!"

"She can! She can go everywhere! Anywhere! Professor Clover said so! She can even go to Washington and outer space! Why not our house?"

"She doesn't hang people!"

"Why not?"

"She just... doesn't! You saw what it was like in there!" Nandini said, tilting her chin at the woods.

"Why not?! Don't you see? I *wished* it! I *wished* he was dead, and then he was dead! Don't you see?! Sally did it! *But what if the Devi can bring him back?!*" She shook the book desperately in her daughter's face. The faint halogen light outlined her tear-streaked, grimacing skull. She was sobbing.

Nandini thought about it. It was deranged but was it any more deranged than any of the other things they'd witnessed tonight. Those things were all real. They had happened. She couldn't even call those events supernatural anymore. Professor Clover had explanations, of sorts, for almost all of it. "How do we do it?" she asked. "I thought there had to be sacrifices. We're not making sacrifices, Mother, not to the *pugri naad* or the Devi."

Aruna sniffed. "That's only one way. Remember, Professor Clover said Sally comes back lots of ways. Maybe we can make wishes lots of ways too then, if I understand the book. As Sally becomes stronger, the portal becomes bigger. We can go to where Sally is strongest, the lodge, the rich lodge, and recite the *mantras* again that Yorgotha was trying to sing. Maybe that will be enough for the Devi to hear us."

For a moment there, Nandini had almost been won over to her mother's side. Now she was flummoxed again. "That's exactly where the Professor told us not to go!"

"Yes, but we'll have the book!" she cried, holding it up again. "If we're empowering Sally, maybe she wouldn't attack us!"

Maybe... Yes, maybe one could make a case that those who enabled Sally and the Devi, like Bose and that cousin of a friend, weren't targeted.

Nandini looked at the patrol car again. Through the window, she saw Michelle, still with a quizzical expression on her face. She was frowning and running a hand over her cheeks and forehead as she listened to whatever the station was telling her on the radio. Then she checked her sidearm, re-holstered it, and made moves to get out of the car.

Professor Clover had warned them about trying to contact the police.

"Go! Go! Go!" Nandini said, as she turned her mother around and ushered her back across the ditch.

"Really?" Aruna asked, looking back over her shoulder.

"Shut up! Just go!" Nandini whispered.

And by the time Michelle got to the spot where they had been standing, they were nowhere to be seen, swallowed up again by a hell forest, of their own volition.

Chapter 18
Sugarfoot Has Flown the Coop

President Ruby trudged out onto the porch of the lodge, scowling, squinting, almost drooling. That loser Epstein, A CRIMINAL WHO WAS CONVICTED, was driving him crazy. Epstein was completely ungrateful. Ruby had let that bastard use his residence in Florida to recruit those juicy young girls, but now *he* was trying to make demands of Ruby, and Ruby was the goddamn President of the greatest country in the world, so sad ruined by Sleepy Joe and Crooked Kamala, the United States of America, so sad. There was a word for his type. "Ungrate", "Ungrote"? No, "Degrate", that was it. He was a SICK and CORRUPT degrate who was NOT EVEN HANDSOME ANYMORE! *Well, that son of a bitch will get what's coming to him soon enough*, he thought.

The porch's pillars were flanked by two secret servicemen. When the President stomped down onto the first step, the agent on his right interrupted him. "Mister President, sir, I don't recommend you go too far. Several of our men have already gone missing tonight."

"Fake news!" the President said to him.

The man was taken aback. His partner on the other side of the President tried to ignore the exchange.

"But, sir…"

"You're fired!"

"What?!"

"You heard me. Go pack your bags, your little bags. A ladies purse, I bet." Ruby snickered at his own joke.

The fired agent's lips flapped. He looked to his fellow secret serviceman for support, but the other man maintained his air of obliviousness. Finally, he had no choice but to turn and go inside, his head sunk like a beaten dog.

The president whipped out his phone and began typing a social media post. "Just fired a secret service agent WHO WAS HIRED BY SLEEPY JOE and would not have been so incompetent if not for the RIGGED ELECTION which I won by a lot and would have hired competent people, only the BEST people. OBAMA BIN LADEN should be prosecuted for this! Where is the Supreme Court?! CROOKED MUCH?!!!" He relied almost entirely on autocomplete suggestions, which even knew what words he liked capitalized.

Ruby pressed the SEND button and stepped down onto the grass. The other secret service agent knew not to stop him, but he spoke into his wrist microphone, saying: "Sugarfoot has flown the coop."

On the grass, the President pulled a small Ziploc

bag from his inside breast pocket. It was full of little pills. Fentanyl. The best fentanyl in the world came from Canada. As soon as they arrived, Ruby had sent out an agent, the one he had just fired in fact, and who he himself had hired a few months earlier, to buy enough to fill two suitcases worth to take back to the White House with him. He popped two of them now. Immediately he felt much better. He did his little dance, the dance where he extended and retracted his arms like a Rock 'Em Sock 'Em Robot. As he did a little whirl, he saw the remaining secret service agent standing stone-faced on the steps.

"You want one?" the President asked, holding up a pill.

The man held out his hand and accepted it.

President Ruby got out his phone again. "I am the most generous president of all time. Sleepy Joe, WHAT A LOSER!!!" *Send.*

The lawn was a semicircle, maybe 200 meters in diameter, with the forest beyond that. There was a huge driveway to his left. How great it would be, he thought, to clear all those trees. This whole forest could be a golf course. That amazing driveway would have to be moved though, a beautiful driveway, goes all the way up to the lodge, a beautiful, curved line, never seen a curve so beautiful except on his daughter Ivana. People would say to him, "You know, why did you name your daughter 'Ivana'? Don't you know they're going to call her 'Ivana Humpalot'?" And he would say to them, "I don't know, maybe she does want to hump a lot. She's a beautiful girl." He snickered at the memory of his joke. It was a professor at Yale that had told that to him.

***

At the edge of the woods Nandini was lying on her belly, struggling to figure out the controls on the infrared binoculars they'd found in the backpack they'd stolen from Professor Clover. There was a lot of other weird gear in there, like electronic gauges and meters.

When she finally got the binoculars working and in focus, her immediate response was: "What the fuck?" Even through the infrared haze there was no doubt it was him. Who else could it be? He was leaning forward at that odd twenty-degree angle.

"Why do you have to use that language!" her mother whisper-growled. She was crouched behind her. "Let me see," she said. She got down on her belly too and took the binoculars. "Donald Ruby?"

"But what's he doing here?"

"Did you know Roosevelt had a summer cottage in New Brunswick?" Aruna said, looking away from the binoculars.

"You think he's on vacation? At the same time Sally's reappeared? It's too much of a coincidence." Nandini took the binoculars back. "And where is she anyway? If this is her habitat like Professor Clover said, and he's just hanging out here, then how is he even still alive?"

There were lights on in some of the rooms of the lodge. Nandini scanned across them and had to adjust the binoculars for the light. In one of the windows she saw Al Garfield. For a split second she was starstruck, until she remembered his crimes. There was someone else in another window, but she couldn't make him out. She was struck by the crazy memory that the first corpse they had seen that night had been familiar. Suddenly it hit her: it was the frat boy rapist turned Supreme Court judge. She realized then that they must have been two of the barely incognito men she saw in the diner the day before. Now, she was even more confused.

"Maybe Professor Clover was wrong," Aruna said.

"Or maybe she lied."

"What do you mean?"

"I don't know yet," Nandini answered, her voice trailing off. She rolled over onto her back and let her frizzy hair be her pillow in the dirt so she could gaze up and ponder.

"Nandini, would Sally ever go into a house full of people and attack them?"

"Who knows?" Nandini wasn't paying much attention.

"Maybe she has enough sense to not attack twenty people at once, not indoors anyway. She waits for them to come out. Maybe she just hasn't had a chance to find and get him yet. But what if we could keep him here long enough for her to arrive."

Nandini swung up from the waist like a drawbridge. "Keep him here how?"

"There's lots of rope in Professor Clover's bag."

A day ago, Nandini would have been aghast, but the Nandini of this day only hesitated for a second before saying, "Mother, give me your *thaali kodi*."

Even in the dark, her mother was visibly struck. "I couldn't…"

"You'll get it back."

Ever so reluctantly, the elderly woman reached under her collars and pulled up the chain she had worn from the day of her wedding to the present, never taking it off except twice for surgical procedures. She stalled again before lifting it off over her head completely. When Nandini accepted it, it was still warm with Aruna's body heat. The links and ornaments were so thick and detailed and elaborate it looked like it could have been designed in the days of the maharajas. It was said that eleven percent of the world's gold was owned by housewives in India, and as she held the chain Nandini didn't doubt it. Its weight made her think it was more like a bullock harness than a necklace.

"Now go find a branch, Mother, a nice big one. The heaviest one you can manage."

While Aruna set about her task, Nandini found a fishing line in Professor Clover's backpack. She tied one end of it to the necklace, walked to the very edge of the tree line, and then tossed the chain out onto the grass as far as she was able. Aruna had come back and gasped when she saw this. Then Nandini shone a flashlight at the necklace so it sparkled like the poster for *Xanadu*.

The desired effect occurred almost immediately. President Ruby saw the golden shimmering in the grass and rotated towards it. He took a lumbering step towards it, and it moved. He took another tentative step. It moved again. Away from him, towards the woods. He took four dainty rapid steps, it moved just as fast away from him. He ran at it and it disappeared into the woods. Then he did too. The secret service agent on the porch did nothing: behind his sunglasses he was asleep while still standing, leaning against the column. The fentanyl had knocked him out. If the President had been paying attention, he would have accused him of being an amateur and a loser.

As Ruby tramped into the trees after the necklace, Aruna came up behind him and conked him on the back of the head with such force that for a moment she worried that she might have killed him. Alas, he was still alive.

They propped him up against the trunk of a tree that was small enough for Aruna to tie his arms together behind him on the other side of it. He was plopped on his butt with his legs splayed out straight like an infant playing on a kitchen floor. They set their flashlights on the ground so they had a little bit of light to work in but avoid drawing attention.

Nandini was getting another length of rope out of the backpack to tie his legs. "Now what?" she asked

"I'll recite the mantra for Sally. When she comes, we simply stand aside and act like we're giving him to her. Just stand and gesture, 'Here you go, this is for you, you can have him'."

"What? That's it?! That's ridiculous! She could kill us first!"

"She reads thoughts, remember! Intentions!" Aruna shout-whispered as she cinched a knot.

That was true, but… were they really going to do this? President Ruby hadn't been a part of the plan. Still, Sally would have killed him eventually anyway. They were basically "summoning" her though. They were making it happen. And their offering was the President of the United States! That was its own tiffin carrier of craziness. If they didn't get away with it, deportation to a gulag in El Salvador would be a dream compared to what they'd really have coming to them. Of course, she didn't care if he died, in fact she welcomed it, he deserved worse than Sally even. But she was sure the Nandini of a day ago would have had pangs of conscience, might have even tried to talk her mother out of it. They had spent just a few hours with Professor Clover, incredibly intense hours, but Nandini began to wonder if they hadn't started thinking like her.

"What have you done, you fucking idiots?!" the

Professor's voice said.

It was not in her head. They looked up and Professor Clover was there. Pointing a machine gun at them. They put up their trembling hands.

"Elizabeth, what are you –"

"You stupid imbeciles! I told you to go home! To stay away from the lodge! Why are you still here?! Everything was going perfectly!"

Nandini spoke up. "But Sally's nowhere near. If she were, *he'd* be dead," she said, daring to tremulously tilt her head at President Ruby just enough that it wouldn't trigger the Professor. "He's the President. He's a rapist, pedophile, and human trafficker. She wouldn't be able to resist!"

"I know who he is! Do *you* realize who he is?! You've abducted a goddamn president!"

"So you were wrong about Sally being here, or… Wait. What do you mean 'everything was going perfectly'?"

The President moaned. He was coming to. Suddenly he realized his predicament. His arms tied, the women, the woman with the machine gun, and all three women were colored. "Jean Claude! JCVD, save me!" he cried. He tried to scream but all he could manage was a plaintive moan. He kicked his legs, and they flailed like two inflatable tube men at a car dealership.

"We're going to use the book to draw Sally here and offer him to her," Aruna said.

"The fuck you are!"

Here, it seemed to Nandini, that President Ruby made a noise when Sally's name was said, but it could have been a sigh, or the wind in the leaves, or all the madness of the past night taking its toll on her imagination. In any case, he stopped struggling again.

"That's insane!" the Professor continued. "Why?! To make a stupid wish?! This is bigger than that! Shit! They'll all be here any minute! This living toilet brush is supposed to be there with them like everything's normal, not tied to a fucking tree!"

"Who's going to be here?" Nandini asked. "You mean those men in the house?"

"No! Carloads and carloads of perverts, molesters, rapists! All his pals! Fuck! Fuck!" She stomped and in her rage forgot about keeping her firearm pointed at the two women.

"What do you mean everything was going perfectly?" Nandini repeated.

"I mean I'm Yorgotha Axegorer's 'uncle'! I'm the one that sent her Bose's journal, you ignoramus! I transcribed those pages! It was hard work!"

Nandini's eyes turned into saucers, aghast. Aruna froze too.

The Professor went on. "Bose filled three notebooks about his experiences with the Devi. Those notebooks are currently held by Annamalai University, and anyone can go and ask to see them, but they're all in code or in Sanskrit. However, Bose wrote a note in English in a margin of the third volume which said, '4th floor'. He worked on the fourth floor of the Bhabha Atomic Research Centre. Scholars dismissed it as a doodle, or his mind wandering. But I thought about it and wondered if it meant there was a fourth book hidden under a floor somewhere, a book with all the most dangerous material in it. Turns out, I was right."

"I knew it," Nandini said. "Somehow I knew it. That girl is dead!" Her voice was cracking. "She's dead and it's your fault!" Nandini stepped towards the Professor, no longer caring about the machine gun.

President Ruby was chuckling to himself now, delirious

"It's *not* my fault! She *chose* to read those words! More than once! She came here twice to recite from the book! No one made her! Why'd she come back to the woods? She didn't need to do that! That's on her!"

"Why did you do it? Why?!"

"Because I had the book, and when my sources told me those dozens and dozens of scumbags were going to be here, it was time to put it to use and bring Sally back! Think of the volumes of data from the kills! And never mind the data, besides that –"

"I think I can guess. So much pervert energy would be channeled through Sally at once that it would open an actual portal to the Devi's plane. She could even come through."

"The scientific revelations will be almost too much for the human mind to contain!" The Professor lifted the machine gun again, rattling, and Nandini backed off. "When I found out what was happening here this weekend and crunched Bose's numbers, I realized there might be enough energy to open a portal, literally. It will completely overturn everything we think we know about physics down to the quantum level. This is not a thing to be avoided. It's to be pursued, aggressively."

"Then why didn't you just read the book yourself, Professor?! Why did you have to get Yorgotha killed?!"

Through his fentanyl haze, Ruby laughed again.

"I wasn't about to let myself get turned into another Bose. And, besides, like I said, I think the Devi understands intentions. She wants to be worshipped. And I saw the posters for that band around town, and I knew what had to be done. Yorgotha's sacrifice will benefit science and mankind forever! And, besides, if the experimenter is part of the dataset, it pollutes the data!"

Nandini shook her head.

Clover started talking to herself. "If they discover he's missing, they raise the alarm. If we let him go, *he* raises the alarm. Either way the whole thing is ruined! Shit! Let me think. Maybe there's still a way to salvage this." She trailed off, lost in her own thoughts.

Tentatively, Aruna and Nandini returned to the task at hand. "Nandini, hurry up and tie his legs!" Aruna said. The command from her mother pulled Nandini out of her dismay over Yorgotha and the Professor and back to whatever reality this was. But the instant she grabbed his legs at the ankles, she recoiled with a cry, and her hands flew to her mouth.

The other women stopped what they were doing and looked at her. "*Chinna kutti*, what is it?"

Nandini was gagging. "There's something on his ankle. I felt it through his pant leg. On the... on the inner side."

"What was it, Nandini?"

She gagged again, almost dry-heaved. "I don't know. It felt weird, like... like something out of Cronenberg."

"Maybe he shit himself."

"No, it was... it was more solid, *squishy*. Like a hamster."

"A hamster?!" Aruna cried.

President Ruby himself was saying nothing. But, in fact, in the dim light, Professor Clover even thought he was smirking, that shit-eating grin he had whenever he thought he'd made a joke. She walked up to him, wondered at that odd look on his face for a moment, then used the muzzle of the machine gun to edge up the cuff of his pant leg millimeter by millimeter. "What... the goddamn... fuck..." she croaked as she caught a glimpse of the thing there next to his sock.

"Professor Clover, what is it?" Aruna asked. There was an edge of terror in her voice.

"You're the professor?" the President asked. "They allow negress professors in Canada? I must admit, I'm surprised. I was expecting a Canadian. Very surprising things up here in Canada. Ice. Windmills. Milk in bags like they're actual tits. Poutine. Sounds like Putin, a good friend of mine, very good friend, up there in Russia. I had a good talk with him on the phone for a few hours just yesterday. Powerful man."

Professor Clover raised the machine gun. "If I kill him, then when the others arrive, at least he won't be able to raise the alarm."

"That's worse than kidnapping him!" Nandini said.

"Professor, what *is* it?" Aruna asked again.

"I'm afraid you can't kill me. I can't be killed. Thank you for your attention to this matter."

"It sure feels that way sometimes, but I can goddamn try."

"Professor, what *is* it?!"

"It's his dick." She pulled the trigger. The bullet passed through his head as if it wasn't even there and hit the tree behind him. The only evidence of its passage through his head was a trickle of blood on his forehead, but there was no wound.

The women were wide-eyed but speechless.

"You see, I've been in business for a long time. Longer than anybody, and I made a deal already with Sally before you. That's what makes me a great businessman. I had a friend say to me, it was Margaret Thatcher, she said, 'Sir, how did you get to be such a great businessman?' 'It's not easy,' I told her. It takes business. And I've already been granted boons, a word I use and invented. I use a lot of words. But, you see, those were perfectly proper deals, but some people didn't keep their end of the bargain, so I had to make a bigger deal, a deal that requires a lot of dead bodies, unfortunately, and a certain book. Only, I didn't have the book. Now, you should ask yourself, Professor, and I'm not so sure you really are a professor, maybe somebody should look into that, look into those records. They might be surprised. I won't be surprised. I've never been surprised. You should ask yourself, how did you find out about this big gathering?"

Here he actually stopped talking for a moment and awaited a response. When Professor Clover answered, the wheels were turning in her mind. "I got an anonymous email from someone who said they were on the Sally Pencilneck bulletin board…"

"Uh huh."

"It contained a link to access a Signal chat before a certain date and time when the chat would be automatically deleted."

"Uh huh."

"When I went to the chat, I found the details of the meeting here."

"And just who do you think that anonymous sender was, Professor?"

Professor Clover unloaded a three-second burst into President Ruby's head. There was smoke and noise. The bullets had shredded the trunk of the tree he was tied to, and it keeled over with a boom. The women jumped out of its way. The secret service agent at the house remained asleep. The President remained sitting there unfazed.

"Perhaps it's time you ladies heard a certain story," he said. "Listen closely while I tell you…"

Chapter 19
"The Tale of the Presidential Penis"

To start at the beginning, when I was a young man, a very smart young man, some even said the smartest they had ever seen, I grew up in New York. My parents and my grandparents were all Americans, born and raised. My grandfather made his fortune running a brothel right here in Canada. My father was a brave man, a hero who was once arrested at a Klan rally. My wives and kids are all all-Americans also, by the way. Anyway, back then little boys and girls used to play with a little thing called marbles, maybe you've heard of them, marbles, an old word –

You know, it's very rude to interrupt a person when he's telling you his life story, a man's life story. Quiet, Piggy! These are pertinent details. You're a nasty lady, I'll tell you that. Very nasty. Who are you with? What do you mean, what do I mean who are you with? I mean, which news outlet? You're a university professor? No, you didn't tell me that. No, you didn't and I'm never wrong about these things. University of New Brunswick? Never heard of it. What I do know is it's full of radical leftists, full of anti-Semites. Also coons and pakis apparently.

Anyway, the point I was getting to is, people say, "He's a pervert." Not true. I respect women more than anybody. They call me the fertilization president. Heh. They say, "Oh, he said 'Grab 'em by the pussy.'" Always taken out of context by the woke left loser media. "They let you do it," I said first. That's something I like to call "consent".

When I was a young man we had a butler, those other boys and girls had marbles. And this butler used to read to me from a book called "Animal Sex". Did you know that down there in the deep dark ocean, it's so rare for an anglerfish to find a mate, that the tiny little male will *fuse* onto a female, and they melt into each other so they share the same bloodstream, and then the male's eyes and internal organs atrophy and dissolve until only its gonads are left attached to the female's flesh? Did you know that in spotted hyenas, both males and females have penises, and they have sex by putting one penis into the other, and the baby comes out of the penis? And that the lady penis is actually a giant clitoris? The echidna penis has four heads. Male cane toads get so horny that they'll even hump snakes and mangos. Did you know that female penguins will trade sex for nice rocks from males? Sometimes they'll just take the rocks and run! Ladies, as you can see from the look on your professor friend's face, this is all true. She's heard it all before. Male seahorses shoot out hundreds of babies at a time. The *males*! Do you know about antechinus mice? They only get one mating season, three weeks long. So they lose three hours of sleep every night during it so they can screw as much as possible, then they all disintegrate and die off at once. Some octopi have detachable "penises" which they pull off, and then the penises swim on their own to the female to inseminate herself with. What about slugs? Have you heard about this, ladies? They're hermaphrodites with super long penises. There's an Italian keelback slug that's three inches long, but its penis is almost a yard! They have to lower themselves on ropes made of mucus and then exchange sperm packets in mid-air using their super long penises. Then they lick up all the mucus. Some slugs just shoot "love darts" at each other. Ha ha! Male spiders will wrap prey in silk and gift it to a female in exchange for sex. It's wrapped in silk so she doesn't run off with it without putting out, and sometimes it's just a bit of garbage in there. Flatworms are male *and* female. They've got two-pronged wieners, and when a couple meets up, they fight each other with their penises, trying to stab and inseminate the other. The stab can be anywhere on the mate's body! Male bedbugs also have knife-like penises, and the females have no genitals. The males just cock-stab them! I notice you're not interrupting me now, are you? You know it's all true. There has never been any bedbug found in any Ruby Hotel ever. They say over 1,500 animal species have gays in them. When male honeybees mate, their penises explode and they die. And when male bees get too hot, they ejaculate to death. The "lesser water boatman" is an insect that's two millimeters long but makes a sound of 105 decibels by rubbing its schlong against its belly. Guinness World Records lists the insect under 'Loudest Penis'. Did you know that some female squids wear fake testicles to avoid male advances? Female dragonflies fake sudden death to avoid males! Did you know that ducks have corkscrew-shaped penises, and they're all rapists? A pig orgasm lasts thirty minutes. A lion mates fifty times a day. The split gill mushroom has over 23,000 genders! I mean, what the fuck?! A female mantis will bite off the male's head *while* mating, which *improves* his sexual performance! Elephant seals keep harems and beat the females if they try to leave.

You paki ladies think I'm lying but look at your academic elitist friend over here, and you can see it's all true. And yet people call *me* a pervert! With all those animals out there. People don't understand, I only did good things, not bad things. It was a different time.

So when Sally Pencilneck showed up in Washington, what did I have to worry about? I'm a perfectly moral individual. Anyone who says otherwise is a Grade-A loser! They're the ones who should be investigated for their real estate fraud schemes and election interference!

We were having a huge party at the White House ballroom. Everybody was there, all the most famous people, the richest people. Kid Rock was there. I was dancing. People always say how impressed they were by my dancing. Not as good as my daughter Ivana though. She's a real good dancer. Very sexy dancer. There were champagne fountains, everything. I had all the chandeliers re-done in there. You know, Jackie Onassis had done the chandeliers, but there was no sense of style, it was old-fashioned. So tacky. You know, the head decorator at the New York Museum, she said to me, "Sir, you have better design sense than even me. You should take over the museum." I would have done it. Of course, now the museum has been infiltrated by liberals I'll have to do something about that.

I felt the need to go to the bathroom to not do cocaine. I have my own bathroom attached to the ballroom. It's all been done up in gold, gold everything, toilets, it's incredible. Nobody's supposed to use it but me. One time I left the tap running, you know, I like a good stream. But my son went in there, he's very smart, he went in there, and he just turned off the tap, just like that, I said, "How did you do that?" He said, "I turned the tap." Very smart boy. Nobody's supposed to use it but me, I don't like other people using my toilet. But the door was locked, some crooked Shylock was in there, I'm sure. No respect. So instead I had to go out to the public toilets to not do cocaine. I also needed to change my pants, not for any reason. But should I go to the bathroom first or go to the presidential suite and get changed first? I decided on the bathroom.

Should I go to the toilets on this floor? No, I said to myself, too busy. I looked down the halls, there were people gathered around the elevators waiting for them. I didn't want to go over there and wait, but not because of my pants. It annoyed me very greatly, but I decided to take the stairs. Strange thing, there's usually a guard on each side of the door to the stairwell, but there weren't any. Corrupt Kamala had fired them, American workers, out of jobs. It's a sad day for our country, I'll tell you that.

The stairwell was very quiet, just how I wanted it. I could even hear my footsteps echoing over the sounds of the party I'd left behind. However, it was also quite dark, which it's not supposed to be. It's supposed to be well-lit. But it was dark because of that scum Biden and his windmills which are killing all the birds, the beautiful birds of America and the Bible, which is my favorite book.

When I got to the bathroom, I knew I had made the right choice, I always make the right choice, because there was nobody in there. I could have used the counter, you know, in public bathrooms, they have that long counter, with the long mirror, but I decided to go into a stall anyway. It was strange though, the lights were out in here too, just flickering. But despite the business with my personal bathroom, and the guards, and all the lights, and my pants, which were fine, I still felt good and was doing my dance. So I laid out a few lines on the tank, but then I froze.

I heard voices, shrieking girls' voices, they sounded like teenagers, young teenagers, and they came barging right through the door of the men's bathroom! Trans perverts, for sure, like Obama's transsexual mice, they were everywhere. These were men dressed as women so they could get into men's bathrooms and diddle little kids. It's a terrible world, a terrible world. It's not safe anymore. It takes a President like me to make it more safety again.

But once they got through that door, they shut up real quick, and they locked themselves both in together in the stall right next to mine. They were trying to keep their voices down, but I could hear their voices trembling and kind of sobbing. Very quietly, I climbed up onto the toilet and peeked over the divider. It was hard to see in the bad light, but I was right, they were about thirteen or fourteen years old. Unfortunately, they weren't pissing or kissing each other. They were kind of holding onto each other, trying to – what is it they call it? – "comfort" each other? Other than their uneven breathing, there was no sound. It was like the sound had been sucked out of the whole world, *shoop*, just like that.

The main door burst open. Over the divider I could only see a little. There was a weird person there, very weird person, from what little I managed to catch a glimpse of. Not sure which bathroom this person was supposed to be in. The open door let in a bit more light, but not much. I was startled and fell from the toilet bowl, and crashed through the stall door, and landed on top of the door on the floor, which actually is what I meant to do. Now I could see a bit more of this lady, another trans lady! She was still just a silhouette, but she looked dangerous, I'll tell you that. She was carrying a Bruce Lee thing and twirling it like a key chain. Very unattractive. These trans women are ruining our beautiful women of America.

I leapt up and jump kicked her, delivered two blows to her chin and ear that would have flattened a lesser man. I'm a great fighter. I go to all the UFC fights, and the head guy there, he says, "Sir, you're such a great fighter, we should get you there in the ring." I say, "No, I had my time, let these youngsters have their glory days now." I'm a benevolent man. Then I kicked her in the box and did a kahratee chop to her neck, *hiyaa*! No dice. This was a tough broad, I'm telling you. Reminded me of Margaret Thatcher, who I met once, met many times in fact. She gave me a blowjob. Anyway, this lady tried to defend herself with her Bruce Lee sticks, but I dodged, weaving left, right, left. Then she left an opening, and I lifted her up and did a piledriver, but she just got up again. I mean, what was it going to take to keep her down? Thank you for your attention to this matter!

But then she just stopped and just stared at me with this look on her face like she couldn't believe what she was seeing. Very strange. It's not because I had been wondering about her pussy since I fell on the floor and none of that fighting stuff happened. Actually I did beat her up, then she stopped. Anyone who says otherwise is a liberal scumbag and a LOSER. But I needed to distract her, not so I could run past her, but so I could beat her up again, you see. So I nodded my head real subtle-like sideways at the stall with the two girls in it. I did it again and again.

Finally she got the hint and kicked the door in. The girls screamed, but this chick, she dragged them out by the hair, and she clonked them with her Bruce Lee sticks, and then she did things to them I can't even describe. It was kinda hot actually. Heh. Boy, I saw some things. But it was real nasty. Only a really nasty person could take any kind of pleasure in that sort of thing.

Now here's where things get very strange. This woman with the bird's nest hair, she looks like Lezzie Borden, who, you know, must've done those murders naked so she didn't get any blood on her clothes. Can you imagine that? A nice girl like that walking around naked. I've seen naked girls, you know. Anyway, she looks at me, and I hear this voice, only it's not her voice. I shouldn't even say it's a voice, it's more like a presence that's just there in my head all of a sudden, a lady, but it's also coming from somewhere else, real far away. I get the sense it's the late, great Aileen Wuornos. It's weird, you know, this voice is telling me it's not the first time Lezzie Borden's been in DC. She was there in the eighties one time 'cause Washington's a good place for her for some reason. And she says this is, like, "Back 2 Da District", whatever that means. Anyway, by the presence of this presence, heh, I just have this awareness that I can, I should, ask for something.

So what I demanded was the biggest wee-wee in the world.

Now, I've seen some big doodles in my time, in the locker rooms at golf links around the world. Arnold Palmer. This is a guy that was all man. This man was strong and tough, and when he took showers with the other pros, they came out of there, they said, "Oh, my god. That's unbelievable."

As soon as I made my wish I felt a tingling down there. I can't say it, you know, with political correctness gone mad, they'd lock me up if I said what I wanted to say. Whatever happened to the constitution and freedom of speech in this country? You tell me that. Immediately my dingdong is starting to grow, but there's a funny feeling about it, that my willy, like the voice, is part of me but also part of some faraway place.

Suddenly the bathroom door bursts open and it's a security guard. He says, "Sir, I saw something on the security cameras, but I couldn't believe it, so I came down to see for myself before I call it in." But before he can get out the last word, *splat*, she kills him, stick in the eye, and flings him into a urinal. Now Lezzie Borden walks straight out the door, like I was never even there, and looks up at the ceiling, and I can tell she's sensing all those people upstairs 'cause her shoulders are rising and falling like she's all hot and bothered. She turns to make for the stairwell, but something comes over me, and I grab her arm, can you believe it? But all sorts of stuff is going on in my head as I feel my sausage growing. I'm thinking fast. Cleaning up the bodies in the bathroom was gonna be bad enough, but what if she went crazy up there? And those people were donors! And cabinet members! Uncle Plush was there! Also, my dorkimus maximus was still growing, but I had another idea. A brilliant idea. I have lots of brilliant ideas. People are always so impressed, they say, "Sir, how is it that you have so many great ideas?"

Lezzie looked at me like I was crazy. But I shook my head and indicated with my head that she should follow me. "I'll take you to the massage parlor," I whispered. Amazingly, it worked. My thoughts were all totally correct, so it wasn't that she read my mind. She followed me 'cause she knew a good deal when she saw one, and she could tell I was gonna give her a good deal, the greatest of deals. In any case, she was really impressed by me, kind of stunned actually, it seemed, for some reason, and so she was sort of doing what I told her.

The massage parlor was actually a reception room. It had been designed by Florence Knoll, obviously a DEI hire. So I had it converted so it was entirely gold plated and had spinning and swirling colored lights.

Much better. I have an amazing taste for these things. But I had chosen this room to convert because it was far from the ballroom, so anytime there was a party and a gentleman wanted to relax he could come down and get a "massage" in peace and quiet! Without people making inappropriate accusations! Everything that happened in this room was completely proper!

Well, when I opened the door there were four gentlemen in there and one "masseuse", she was maybe about fourteen years old, a totally appropriate age for giving massages. These guys were senators, governors, powerful men. Tycoons. And they were taking turns getting "massages" from her. A true honor for any young masseuse. Well, this time Lezzie didn't waste any time. She went in there and made short work of these guys. With ninja stars! Meanwhile, I can feel my hooha is still growing, and there's still that otherworldliness about it too that I can't quite describe. The whole time, the masseuse is screaming, but then these two teenagers appear at the door, one boy and one girl, and the girl's got some weird science device in her hands, and the boy chants some foreign-sounding words, and a zap comes out of the science box and hits Lezzie. She's crisped. These teens, they're, like, "We got her, eh!" Nope, she's up again and a second later she was chasing after them. How'd those teenagers get in the White House? I don't know what happened to Lezzie after that, but during my morning briefing the next day the one item that caught my attention was a vague report that someone matching her description had been killed by somehow being dropped on the point of the Washington Monument.

Anyway, this is all besides the point. The point is that while Lezzie was killing those fine men, I was making another wish, a wish to be unkillable, and, as with my still growing winkle dinkle, I could feel it being true.

Boy, now I was feeling excited. And the masseuse was still there. I mean, she was cowering in a corner and covered in blood, so I decided to get a massage from her. I was especially keen to try out my new plus-sized peen. For some reason, she was ungrateful! She even fumbled behind her back for one of Lezzie's ninja stars and tried to slash me with it, but it just kind of went through my neck and came out the other side without doing anything.

I think I had used this particular masseuse before, but somehow she didn't seem too happy about giving me a massage this time. In fact, she cried the whole time. Something about it bothered me. In fact, my new doody, while it performed very well, somehow didn't quite satisfy me the way I thought it would. It was a strange feeling. In fact, I stopped before the massage was finished. As I left the parlor, luckily I wasn't so distracted that I forgot to call in a cleanup crew. Boy, were they in for a surprise! Usually it's the bodies of the masseuses that they have to disappear! Ha ha!

For an hour or more, I wandered the empty halls

on that floor, wondering about my niggling sense of dissatisfaction, which I did not feel! And also… concern. My peepee was still growing, slowly still, but it was growing. It was what I wanted, it was nothing to worry about, but still, at the back of my mind I wondered. By the time I went back upstairs, the party had cleared out.

The next day I had various important meetings, making important deals, which I won all of, and I was awake for all of them. But that evening something came over me, something I hadn't felt in a long time. I decided to visit my wife Carmilla in her bedroom.

"You don't sleep in the same bedroom?" you might ask. That's a very rude question. Carmilla needs a big bedroom. She's an opulent lady, a luxurious lady. The whole room's covered in diamonds and rubies. She's got a big four-poster canopy bed in there that's heart-shaped and rotates. When I went in there, she was sprawled out on it reading her iPad and wearing a long tie-dye t-shirt for a nightgown that said, "LIKE I GIVE A FUCK ABOUT YOU, YOU FUCKING IMMIGRANT," in glitter sequins. The back of the shirt was all slashed up, like with a razor, which is the style these days, Carmilla is a classy lady, you know. She wasn't wearing any underwear! Can you believe it! There was a secret service agent in there too, scooting from one part of the room to the next, just shuffling papers and fiddling with flowers in vases, moving things around. A Negro fellow, a very nervous character, which I thought was odd. But as he scooted out of the room I had to laugh, 'cause the dumb-dumb had his pants on backwards! That's what you get with these DEI hires.

When he was gone, Carmilla said, "What the fuck do you want?" in that kooky Yakov Smirnoff accent of hers.

"My darling dear," I said, "Don't you think we should fulfill our marital duty and make sweet love? I think you'll be much more impressed by the size of my member this time." Carmilla is really old and ugly these days, but her cooch is quite loose, I mean it's like a rubber glove down there, you can hear the ocean, so I knew she'd be able to handle my new jumbo-sized-and-still-growing dinkydink, not like that masseuse that cried like a baby. My daughter, on the other hand, is quite beautiful, you know, when that Paris Hilton sex tape came out, I said to her, "Gee, you should do one of those too, it would be a lot of good publicity." In any case, right now I wanted to pork a lady and not have any niggling doubts about it this time. It had been a while since Carmilla and I had engaged in marital relations. I mean, she wants it every day, sometimes I satisfy her multiple times a day, so I thought I'd give her a break for a while. Now, though, I unzipped my fly and pulled out my wiener to show her.

Well, she must have been reading something very funny on her iPad, probably a YouTube supercut of all my best jokes, because she just laughed and laughed and rolled around and around on her big bed, her box on full display for anybody who walked in and wanted an eyeful.

Well, she was obviously too distracted for making whoopee for once. I laughed a little too. What a funny situation. So I left there to try to find another way to sort out my meat torpedo situation, and when I closed the door behind me I could hear her still laughing in there. What a gal!

But, somehow, now I felt even more unsatisfied. There had to be somebody that could take care of me. And, I will admit, the thing was now growing to a somewhat awkward size. I texted my fixer: "GET ME A COMPANION! NOW!!!" But I guess he was sleeping, which is a thing that happens if you don't do cocaine.

The next day I had more important meetings. I gave them my full attention, but the whole day I was also constantly texting my fixer and expressing my outrage that he ignored my texts of the night before. This country used to be great! He promised there would be a companion waiting for me in my bedroom that night, a new one I hadn't seen before, and he would make sure she had signed the NDAs, etcetera, and they would be delivered to my office. The Oval Office!!! I'm the President!!!

Now, a companion is not like a masseuse. A companion is a nice lady who is there just for that: company. I called these ladies to the White House sometimes. They're very discreet, and, more importantly, professional.

Two nights in a row now I had been let down, and yet my doodeedoo was still growing. But when I got to the room, I was not disappointed. This was a very pretty lady, with an eighties look about her. My fixer knows my taste. She had big hair and shoulder pads and a pencil skirt. She looked like a Duran Duran cover. Immediately I walked over and kissed her. She liked that. I put my hand up her skirt. She liked that even more. They love it. "Would you like a drink?" I asked, being generous. You don't have to offer them drinks though. You've already paid!

I gestured to the drinks caddy and she followed me. I poured each of us a drink, but I had a little move in mind, one that always works. When I handed her drink to her, I also had my flesh hammer in my hand, pressed to the glass. I was able to lift the glass quite high! When she saw it, her eyes went wide. "Oh, no! No!" she said. "I'm not doing it with that thing!"

I pulled the NDA she had signed out of my breast pocket. "You signed an NDA!" I said.

"Sure, I won't tell anybody. But I'm not going through with this with that thing!"

"You have to!" I said. "It says so!" And I shoved the document into her hands.

She uncrinkled it and her brow furrowed. I could tell she was looking at the part at the very bottom which was very proper and not written in a different font or with a sharpie, which said: "I PROMISE TO HAV SEX WITH THE VERY HANDSUM

PREZIDENT." She was shaking her head crazily now, and she threw down the pages and ran for the door. I chased her, but because of the size and weight of my growing Bilbo Baggins I was off balance and tripped, actually falling into the drinks caddy and knocking it over.

Two secret service agents charged in at the noise and helped me up, but I yelled at them. "You idiots! Not me! Her! I'm fine! You were supposed to hold her down! What's the use of you! Let me guess. Obama hires?" My companion was long gone. I shooed the men off me. "You're fired!" I said. And they left.

At this point, the vice president, Jack Daniels, wandered in and looked at the mess. "Gee whiz, what happened in here!" he said. "Nyeh heh heh!" He always laughs like that. "Nyeh heh heh!"

Now, Jack is my best friend. I tell him everything. He fucks sofa cushions, which is weird, but I accept him. I'm the most forgiving person in the world. He's married to a paki though, which is weird. That's got to be one fucked up pussy. The Speaker of the House, Mike Penis was with him. Mike hates the gays, and he and his son check each other's internet histories to keep each other from masturbating. Men like Mike Penis are why this is the greatest country in the world.

I told them everything all about the bathroom and Lezzie Borden, and the voice, and my wish and my big winkle and everything. Jack seemed a little perturbed when I told him about the immortality. That bothered him for some reason. But in the end he laughed. "Nyeh heh heh! Gee, Don, that big ol' dick isn't a blessing! That was a curse! You've ended up with a Faustian bargain, my friend! Nyeh heh heh!"

Mike Penis just pushed up his glasses on his dork face and smiled like an idiot. That's all he ever does.

"A Fausta-what?" I said.

"A Faustian bargain, like in 'Doctor Faustus' by Christopher Marlowe."

"Fuck that noise!" I said. "I only like Shakespeare!" Shakespeare is my favorite book.

"Okay, Don! You're the boss! Maybe this is your fate, buddy. Nyeh heh heh!"

Mike pushed up his glasses again. What was going on in that head of his? They left the room, and I put my penis back in my pants, an act which now took a degree of effort.

By the next day, I was having trouble walking in a straight line. I had developed a permanent lean. It was another day of stupid meetings with stupid people. As the thing dropped past my knees, now even sitting was becoming difficult. So much blood was going down there, I had started to fall asleep during cabinet meetings.

That night I decided to dismiss my secret service detail, and I wandered the streets with a hoodie on over my suit as a disguise. Those dirty, crime-ridden streets of Washington D.C.

What could I do? How could this be a curse? I got

what I wanted. I wanted the biggest hot popsicle in the world. But why was it still growing? I realized then that that was what was bugging me, as the kids say. Do kids still say that? Bugging? Not the size of it, but that it was still growing.

And then something happened that made me realize that Jack was right, that this was my fate, my fuck banana, and my meeting Lezzie, and everything. I was walking past a bookshop and in the window, as if by a miracle, I'm a big Christian you know, there was the book "Animal Sex", the book which my butler had read to me when I was ages six through seventeen, and suddenly it hit me. It all came together, but I had to be sure. I ran into the shop and started gunning through the pages, until I found it. There it was. I had forgotten it, but there it was: the blue whale has a penis three yards long. And here I had asked for the biggest beef hose in the world. I didn't know how long a yard was, but I knew that I was doomed. That sucker's real big.

My whole body started trembling. The book fell from my hands. I ran out of the shop, through the streets, stumbling and tripping because of my mega phallus all the way. I had no idea where I was going, everything was swirly and like pinwheels. I shouted, I screamed. My head was ringing, ringing. In fact, it sounded like music, like my favorite song, "Do You Hear the People Sing?" from *Les Mis*. There was orchestra music coming from nowhere. And so I started singing at the top of the voice, dancing through the streets of that great city:

> *Do you fear the people ding?*
> *Dinging a dong of hungry men?*
> *It is the Busey of the papal*
> *Who will not be a knave of gin!*
>
> *When the melting of your farts*
> *Eggos the heating of the bums,*
> *There is a wife about to shart*
> *When Tom Zorro cums!*

This went on for several hours, until I found myself in a grimy alley. The lights from the street and the neon signs barely reached into it, but I could see the silhouettes of two women in there, working women. They were standing by a shop's back door, I think, not too far from some dumpsters, and they were smoking cigarettes. Filthy habit. But surely a street walker would service my ham rifle, I thought, and here were two of them! I couldn't see them so well though, 'cause it was so dark in there. And smelly, if I'm being honest. But I got somewhat closer to them and I said, "Are you ladies working tonight?" as I held up a roll of bills. Even up close I couldn't see them so well, which frustrated me because I don't fuck ugly ladies. They couldn't really see me either, I guess, which is a good thing since they hadn't signed NDAs.

"Sure, honey," one of them said, stepping forward and taking the roll of bills. She had hair like Edward Scissorhands. I dropped my pants. Her eyes shot open and she screamed. Her friend said, "What is it?" The one that took my money dropped the roll of bills and started to back away. Her friend said, "What is it?" again, but then, I guess with her friend no longer blocking her view, she could see me in silhouette with my full length there between my legs. The Scissorhands one now tried to run, but something came over me, and I whipped my love snake along the ground, so she tripped on it and bashed her head. The other one ran up to try to help her, not a smart move, and I came up behind her and wrapped it around her neck and pulled until she stopped moving. I didn't know what I was doing or how much time I had. Scissorhands was still alive, but I didn't even want to waste time turning her over. So I put my sex missile in her butt, but it would only go a little way, and I tried to work fast. I didn't want to end up fucking a dead person, and she was already bleeding profusely from her Adam's apple, which I have to say was surprisingly prominent. I have limits, I'm a moral person, a very moral person. Only democrats fuck dead people. And mallard ducks, with their corkscrew penises, which are also rapists. I'm very respectful of dead bodies, ask anybody. But to no avail. The next second, she was dead too. In fact, it occurred to me that she'd been dead for a while. I screamed again, like I'd screamed when I ran out of the bookshop. I screamed to the heavens.

And then a jolt went through me. My front snake felt like it was in two places again, and there was that presence inside me again, the presence of the late, great Aileen Wuornos.

"What have you done to me?" I said. "How do I get out of this?! I'm making a deal! You have to accept it!"

"You want to get rid of the immortality too?" she asked. As before, it wasn't like she was talking, more like I could sense what she was saying

"No! I want to keep that."

She said, "Well, you're actually doing a pretty impressive job. I couldn't help but notice. Normally I can't just speak to people in your world, but you're generating a lot of nutritious energy for me over there. It's giving me a tiny window." She says, "I can stop the growth, that's a freebie from me to you. But if you want to reverse it, you're going to have to make a wish again. You'll have to give Sally some victims."

Easy enough, I thought, but then I realized that Sally was Lezzie, and I remembered that Lezzie was dead. "But she's dead," I said.

"Jeepers," says Aileen, "then you'll have to bring her back somehow. There's usually a way."

"How?"

"I don't know. I'm actually trapped in another place. I can only interact with your world sort of indirectly."

I have a lot of respect for Aileen Wuornos, but she was starting to sound like a loser, and I don't like losers.

"I'll tell you what though," she said. "You do some digging into a guy named Chandrasekhar Bose, and I bet you'll be onto something. I perceive time in a sort of non-linear way sometimes, and I can tell this will work for you." (I have no idea what the fuck any of that meant.) "She'll actually even be obedient to you, sort of. I've never encountered any humans with your kind of energy, Don. It's really something else. And, in fact, if you can bring Sally back, and if you can give her enough victims, it'll create a portal big enough for me to come through and I can make *your whole world* into anything you want."

I liked the sound of that, but I didn't know what a portal was. "What's a portal?"

"It's like a magic door, Don."

There was something fishy about this. If she was so powerful, why couldn't she just make her own portal? And why would she want to come over here so bad? It would be like me going to some shithole country like South America. But before I could ask any more questions, she was gone. My pants hotdog was back in a single world, ours, and I could feel that it had stopped growing, which was a relief. I looked down at the dead bodies. I had negotiated the greatest deal that had ever been made. I got many points, all the points were for me. Congratulations.

As soon as I got back to the White House, first I called a meeting and ordered my team to kill every single blue whale still in existence. A GOAL WHICH WE ACHIEVED, THANK YOU VERY MUCH!! "Let's use the nukes," I said. "Where's the suitcase with the button in it?" They said, "We'll take care of it, sir." No more blue whales.

My people did some digging, it's incredible, they use this thing called Google, maybe you've heard of it. They found out all about your little town here and this lake, and that Lezzie maybe started here. Then we looked up this Chandrasekhar Bose fellow. He was long since dead, but I sent a team to his house in India. One of his kids was there, and his old housekeeper. There were some language problems, translation problems, and things had become foggy over time, but what they told me was this: All of Bose's things were taken or destroyed years ago. Some of it was in libraries. But just a few months earlier someone had shown up there, a foreign professor, a lady, and asked to look at his old office. When she left, she had a book, a ledger, that she hadn't been carrying when she showed up. And afterwards, they found that the floorboards in Bose's office had been torn up. We looked at the flight logs, did background checks. A professor from this very town had flown to India and back right around that time. What a coincidence!

In fact it seemed a yuge coincidence also that someone had come for whatever was in the floorboards, the very thing that Aileen had wanted *me* to find, only a few months earlier. There was something about that, like an idea about it that was trying to form in the back of my mind, but it hurt to think about it, and I had made a great deal, so why bother? In any case, this Professor's name is Elizabeth Clover, which seems like a strange name for a man. But now I know he must have the book from the floor. The smart thing to do is confiscate the book and read it. That must be the way to bring Lezzie back. I could do it easily, I'm an excellent reader, I can read better than anybody, and I speak multiple languages, I speak seven languages. But it's better to delegate these things, let other people have a chance. I'm benevolent that way. I had already made the deal with Aileen, Lezzie would obey me no matter who had the book. But Clover didn't know that. What was he waiting for?

Then it hit me. This was a liberal left-wing academic do-gooder type. These people are always looking out for themselves, they don't care about other people. He was waiting to use Lezzie for the right time when he could make a big enough offering to Aileen to make the world however *he* wanted it. VERY SELFISH!!! Well, my IT people, that stands for "internet theory", they knew where she was, and they figured out what her fake name was on the secret forums online where they talk about Lezzie things, and I used that to send her an anonymous message that led her to the Signal chat about the big very important meeting I was having here this weekend, and I made sure our travel arrangements weren't too secret so she could see that it was really happening, and wouldn't you know it, she took the bait. And when I saw the news about the animal attacks in this area, I knew it had worked. If she hadn't done it, well, I would have had to break into her house and use ChatGPT to translate the book, which would have been completely accurate and fine anyway, and the book would have been hidden under her pillow. In any case, this is why I am a genius and the most beloved President in the history of our great United States, THANK YOU FOR YOUR ATTENTION TO THIS MATTER!!!

Chapter 20
Final Girls

Professor Clover opened fire on him again, uselessly.

"Lezzie, come over here and untie me!" President Ruby shouted into the dark. The women ignored him. After a second, there was the sound of footsteps in the dark of the woods, and then Sally emerged from it, the shin-high glistening Coleman Frog by her side, and a thousand other little frogs gleefully bounding in every direction like slimy popcorns. The women recoiled, the Professor fired at Sally too, but she just walked past them and untied the President from the shattered tree stump as she had been ordered to do. There was something about her body language, or the look in her one visible eye, that made Nandini wonder if the ghoul was not completely the President's puppet, but in some part... reluctant. There were split seconds of hesitation, and she looked just as enraged as ever.

President Ruby struggled to his feet, fell down, got up again, and brushed himself off. "You see?" he said. "She does what I say. She knows how to be grateful. Not like you people. I could get her to kill you right now. You've been very nasty to me." He went into a crouch with his fingers out like a witch. He was thinking about giving Sally the order. Sally didn't move, but the Coleman Frog took a step towards the women, and they edged backwards.

But then President Ruby changed his mind. "Don't you think I'm a genius?" he blurted. "Can't you see that?!"

The women ventured looks at each other, bemused, while still keeping a wary eye on Sally and the Frog. They couldn't tell if it was a question or a statement.

"You should say that I'm a genius," he said. They could barely hear him over the sound of the mini frogs croaking and bouncing all over the place.

The women still didn't answer him. He stomped his unencumbered foot. "I'm going to prove it to you! You're going to thank me. You're going to applaud when you see what I make Aileen do. Then you'll be sorry. I love women. And I'm going to fix everything. I'm a very benevolent person. I'm going to fix all the men and women. Once she fixes the submarine full of semen in my pants, I'm going to make Aileen rewrite the entire history of humankind, so the genders are reversed. Think about it! Women will masturbate into potted plants and force men to look at their vaginas! Women construction workers will proposition random men as they walk down the street! There will hardly be any men construction workers! We'll see how those women like it! They won't like it very much, I can tell you that! Construction is hard work! *I* know! A woman boss will force her man employee to eat her pussy if he wants a promotion! Women will pee on men, video tape it, and then they'll be forced to become Russian agents! Then finally women will understand how hard it is for us and that they should be grateful for these things! But I'll still be president, the first man president! You'll learn your lesson, you'll see! I'm going to make a huge portal and she's going to give me everything I want! I deserve the noble prize! And while I'm at it, I'm gonna teach that loser Ferrari Epstein a lesson he'll never forget! Don't you think I'm a genius?!" he repeated.

"I think you're a fucking piece of shit."

"Professor!"

"Kill her."

The Coleman Frog leapt onto Professor Clover's face. Her Bowie knife was up fast enough to at least nick its leg and keep it from sinking its fangs completely into her throat at first, but she fell over, still fighting it, and soon the blood was pulsing out of her neck. As they wrestled, the mini frogs went crazy with delight. Nandini didn't know how to help, but she gingerly approached the combatants.

"Nandini, no!" her mother cried

Nandini kicked at the Coleman Frog, hoping to send it flying, but the move was pathetic at best. The thing only turned and leapt at her and clamped its jaw on her arm. She screamed and bashed it against a tree, and it flew loose. Aruna ran to the Professor and tried to stop the blood gushing out of her neck.

"Why are you just standing there?" President Ruby shouted at Sally. "She's woke! She's a pedophile! Kill her!"

Sally gripped her nunchaku, but there was a sound from the direction of the lodge, a vehicle coming up the driveway. Sally spun towards it. The Coleman Frog had been furiously scampering towards Nandini again, but it too stopped in its tracks to look towards the noise.

The SUV pulled to a stop. As the passengers got out, even at this distance, Nandini could tell who it was. A pro-life US senator who had raped a fifteen-year-old girl and then paid for her abortion, and a TV evangelist who blamed homosexuals for 9/11 and had posted a picture of himself and his wife's secretary on social media with their pants unzipped. Another car pulled up and US Attorney General Pam Cronulla, a woman who had watched videos of powerful men raping twelve-year-old girls and then publicly claimed the tapes didn't exist, got out. Those who did not make child pornography at least kept a cache of it, like a sixty-eight-year-old judge from Charleston who had given bond to a killer who murdered nine Black people while they were in church in 2015. Ruby smirked and chuckled. Even Nandini almost laughed, both at the audacity of his plan and at her self-realization of a kind of amusement that they were going to get what was coming to them and had no idea what they were in for. The world was only worse with them in it.

But then even more cars and vans and trucks started to pull up. Sally was breathing in such slow, heavy breaths that even in the dark her chest was visibly rising and falling. There were dozens of them. Sometimes the cars even bumped into each other and the passengers got out and yelled at each other or laughed about it. Mayors, governors, senators; movie directors; religious leaders; founders of groups promoting family values; cult leaders; podcasters who called for the extermination of everyone on the LGBTQ spectrum; royalty; diplomats; a French man that drugged his wife and invited fifty-one men to rape her; magicians; so many youth pastors; musicians; an author of gothic comic books and novels who claimed to be a feminist and then spent decades raping, humiliating, and degrading women; an heiress to a liquor empire that lured female victims into a sex cult that literally branded them and then raped them; an entire Canadian band that shot to fame on Canadian Idol, then all sexually assaulted fourteen-year-olds; newscasters; titans of industry; athletes who were rapists but still actively employed because they were grown men who were able to throw a ball back and forth; comedians; a nineteen-year-old white man who raped a woman and served only three months lest his "twenty minutes of action" ruin his life. They all sexually assaulted women (and other men), fornicated with prostitutes, trafficked humans for sex, raped children, and were rich. The entire power structure of the United States and beyond seemed to be here, governmental, financial (billionaires), and media (propaganda). More cars pulled up. There were some women, but very few. Still, they too should have been in jail. There was a Canadian woman who, along with her husband, had raped and murdered three minors, the first being her own sister, had served ten years in prison, and was now living free.

Nandini's brief glee faded. "No," she said. Though it repulsed her to do so, she grabbed Ruby's arm, trying to get him to listen to her. "It's too many. The portal will be huge. The Devi will come through!" she shouted.

The door of the lodge opened, and Epstein came out onto the porch to greet the new arrivals.

"Holy fucking shit," Nandini said when she saw him.

Sally must have thought the same thing because her eyes shot wide at the sight of him. She rotated her neck, rotated her shoulders. Then she started swinging her nunchaku around her shoulders and waist, switching hands back and forth almost too fast for the eye to see, like a tenth-dan martial artist. She took a step towards the lawn, then stopped herself. She looked at the trees around her, then pulled off a branch and examined it, as if to see what size orifices she could fit it into and then skipped out of the woods and across the grass, twirling her nunchaku in her other hand like she was eight years old again. The Coleman Frog leapt alongside her, and all the little frogs followed too, like a chaotic Chola army.

Nandini, on the other hand, stepped backwards, receding towards the foliage where her mother was still nursing Professor Clover.

The carnage was immediate and spectacular. The first victim had no idea what he was looking at or what was coming. Sally was spinning her nunchaku like a lawnmower blade, and he was blown to pieces, spraying everyone in the immediate vicinity with a downpour of sludgy viscera. The next instant, the security teams had their machine guns out, but too late. The frogs swarmed over them, and they were firing blindly in the air as the security men were ripped apart screaming and flailing. The frogs returned to Sally with their testicles. She swapped her nunchaku for a souped-up ping pong ball gun she'd had strapped on her back, loaded the testicles into it, and fired at the people who were fleeing. There were a few who seemed like they might get away, but the Coleman Frog leapt at them from distances that boggled the mind, ripped them apart into red clumps, and then leapt at its next victim.

Al Garfield stood off to one side of the lawn, watching the scene with delight as he smoked a cigar. As soon as the cars started pulling up, he'd come outside to say hello, but this was even better. Boy, it reminded him of the neighborhood rock fights they would have as kids, when all the kids would split into two gangs, and then one gang would bring in somebody's six-foot tall gorilla of a brother, and he'd be running around whipping boulders like a maniac, until somebody's momma came out and started whupping kids with a rolling pin. *Back in those days, there was no swearing*, he reminisced as a boulder struck his head and exploded it.

In terror, Epstein ran back into the lodge. Sally spun and gave chase. He slammed the front door closed behind him, and she smashed straight through it. The frogs devoured their screaming prey on the lawn, the Coleman Frog bounced back and forth across its entire length claiming victims, and a moment later Epstein's body came crashing out through an upstairs window, sailed over the balcony, and thudded onto the lawn, naked and folded completely in half, sucking his own dick. A line of frogs marched into his asshole, a delightful game, not stopping until he exploded. Sally stood on the balcony for a moment admiring the view, then leapt down onto the grass and got back to work.

***

"I can see the light," muttered the Professor. She was repeating herself. The first time she'd tried to say it, it had only come out as a moan and a liquid mumble.

"Don't speak," Aruna said, her own voice shaking. She had used bandages from the backpack to attempt to staunch the bleeding from the Professor's throat, but her prospects weren't good. Even in the darkness, she could see the blood glistening black everywhere.

Nandini knelt to the other side of her and held one of her hands. In the Professor's other hand, she still clutched her precious Bowie knife.

Nandini tried to make a joke. "Don't go all religious on me now, Professor. It's not like you." She forced a chuckle. She was trying not to look at the massacre happening on the lawn, but in fact was also aware that it wasn't as hard to look at as it should have been, that in just one night she was becoming desensitized to it, as if she'd been working in an abattoir for years.

"No," whispered the Professor, "I see the light." And she limply raised her free hand. It sank, she raised it again, pointed vaguely at a spot in the sky above the lawn. She found a reserve of strength and got back on her feet to start limping out of the forest and into the bloodbath happening on the lawn.

Aruna and Nandini would have stopped her, but when they looked up into the sky at what the Professor had been pointing at, they were mesmerized. It wasn't a light. It was a patch of complete blackness in the sky where the stars and clouds should have been. It seemed to be hovering over the lawn, but it could have been ten meters overhead or billions of light years away. It was sometimes circular, "cutting" a scoop out of the sky, or a perfect square, or a triangle, or a rotating cube with no edges. There was no visible transition between these forms. From one instant to the next it just suddenly seemed to be one or another as if it had not been the one before it.

Lightning struck the black object in the sky. No, not lightning. It was a rope of pink energy that had shot out from the bodies of those being slaughtered on the lawn of the lodge. Then there was another, and another. An unnatural wind came up, localized underneath it. As Sally and the frogs continued pulling apart the lodge's visitors like string cheese, more energy bolts shot out from the corpses and into the object. With each energy strike the object seemed to be getting bigger. The Professor stood under it, lurching, barely able to maintain her balance.

"Another world," said the Professor. No one heard her. "Oh, my daughter," she said. She collapsed in a heap.

Aruna dashed out of the forest and towards the Professor's body.

"Mother!" Nandini followed her out onto the grass, but she was still transfixed by the thing in the sky.

Donald Ruby gave chase too, though he had no hope of outracing them.

When Nandini got to her, Aruna was on her knees beside the Professor again. But when Nandini looked at her enquiringly, she shook her head. Professor Clover was dead.

The wind was picking up leaves now, even snapping twigs.

Aruna looked up at the object worshipfully. Ruby was sneering into it.

All around them the visitors were screaming and being shredded to bits, but none of them were in any position to pay any attention to the phenomenon happening above them. The machine gun fire was constant. As before, the fabric of space was folding, but on a much larger scale. Three-dimensional "sections" of space were shifting around each other and through each other in impossible configurations. On the other side of it, through the portal, she glimpsed that red and ashen realm, full of cyclopean bluffs and cathedrals, creatures that were all organs, inside out, vaguely humanoid shapes that seemed to be formed of root structures that had fossilized eons earlier, skeletal vermin that skittered across the dusty land, graveyards so full of tombstones that new corpses were left piled on the ground, their faces all crying with no sound, everything dry and crumbling. Nandini put up her hand and saw her own back in front of her holding up her hand, like a trick mirror, and that image in front of the same and the same and the same as far as the resolution of her eyes could see. She looked behind her and could see a million copies of herself melting into each other, until she was back in the woods kneeling over the Professor's body beside her mother, the moment when the black thing in the sky had appeared. In front of her, her hand waved, then she decided to move it, and it was the wave which she had already seen. "Mother?" she said, and her voice came from outside herself. She could see her mother there, still looking into the portal. Nandini shifted her head slightly and her mother folded in half like a piece of paper then unfolded again. The older woman still had a look of reverence on her face, her eyes closed, but there was an expression of disgust too, like when she had tried to summon Sally when they had first arrived in the woods. "Mother, don't."

The portal was being continuously zapped by energy bolts from the lawn. A flying twig cut Nandini's cheek. Her hair was out of control. The weird wind was actually more like a gravity, she realized, pulling things towards the object. The object itself descended out of the sky to hover facing them like a mirror. To the three standing in front of it, its shape didn't appear to change as it descended, which implied that it was a sphere, but anyone looking at it from the side would see it as a flat plane.

A tremulous, fuzzy black form appeared in the middle of the portal. Its shape was maybe vaguely spherical, but when Nandini tried to look at its edges, she felt the thing was inside herself and she couldn't see it anymore. If anything, it was like she was outside herself and looking at herself from every angle, as if her eyes were a fish eye camera.

"Ha ha! Ha ha!" laughed Ruby. He was rubbing his hands all over his crotch ecstatically, feeling his diaper through his pants. "It's working! It's working!" he cried. "It's back to normal! Now, let's do the rest of the deal! You owe me! Come on! Come on, Aileen! Ha ha!" He started doing his arm pumping dance.

Nandini looked away from him. Her mother was still seemingly praying in revulsion.

The black thing began to cross the threshold of the portal, but as it emerged what came out was a series of hundreds of almost invisible lines hovering down through the air. These lines then rotated and merged as they floated down to reveal they were flat rectangles, completely flat, just surfaces without objects, impossible. These surfaces then rotated into three-dimensional forms which seemed to swell larger in space, and then into one three-dimensional form which settled on the ground in front of Aruna.

"Aileen!" Ruby called. *Gosh, she's beautiful*, he thought, *just like Charlize Theron. And she's topless!*

But as he stepped closer, the thing that had come through the portal stopped being Aileen somehow, like it was only the shadows that made her look that way...

To him, I am now some hideous squat creature. I have a single huge breast and with each passing moment it is growing bigger and bigger, drooping to the ground like it is made of molasses.

"Mother? Is that...?"

"*Otte Molechi*," Aruna said.

"What? What have you done?! You stupid fucking paki loser! That isn't Aileen! What the fuck is that?! Fuck off! Go back! I made a deal with Aileen!"

I look at him, and then start to turn on the spot, slowly, like a dancer. But then I start to accelerate to what is obviously going to be an incredible speed.

"Get down!" Aruna said.

I speed to a blur, my freakish breast extending out like a helicopter blade. It whacks Ruby on the head, and he goes flying backwards, hitting the ground with an ugly thud. Nandini saw him wipe a streak of blood from his cheek and look at his hand in bafflement and alarm.

I stop spinning and look down at Aruna.

"Please, please," Aruna said to me, her fingers interlocked together in supplication. "Please. My husband." Her eyes were wet. I look at the woman with something that Nandini might have taken for pity or kindness. The lightning bolts from the lawn were now blasting me directly, and with each strike, that gray and red world seemed to be turning into vibrant purples and yellows and blues, what seemed to be the colors of life in that world. There were the beginnings of movement in branches and leaves that had been dead for billions of years.

Nandini wondered: Were there other worlds in that universe? Worlds like the Earth? Were there planets like that one in *this* universe, too far away to ever be accessible? And yet here was one so close. Frozen by the scene, Nandini did not see Donald Ruby dive behind her with speed driven by fury and grab Professor Clover's Bowie knife.

"Please," Aruna said to me, and it was the last word she ever spoke. Ruby stabbed her in the back twice.

"No!" screamed Nandini.

She shoved him away. He managed to maintain his balance and not fall over again. He pointed the trembling knife at her, mumbling "Don't" as she stormed towards him, but she easily grabbed the knife out of his weak, puny little hands and stabbed him six times. His disgusting, corrupt blood was all over her hands. He was still standing. Teetering, but standing, looking at his own blood in disbelief. Sally appeared next to her, and Nandini stepped back in fear, but Sally only ignored her and gave Ruby a little shove and he was sucked into the portal completely with a flash of purple and pink.

Nandini went over to her mother, her mother who lay bleeding on the grass, a wet sound coming from her throat.

Aruna reached up and touched Nandini's face. She remembered the stirring of her in her belly so clearly she could feel it even now, a part of her own being for nine months, a part of the same system, indivisible and glorious, and her awe-struck husband reverentially massaging her sore feet and back, but even in his wonderment he would never really understand, only venerate at a remove. And then the birthing and hours and hours of punishing pain, the sensation of which somehow she had never been able to bring back to the front of her mind again. And that beautiful little mouth that drew milk from her breast, her miniature hands opening and closing, and the little thing took to it so easily. And then, as if only moments later, she was a naughty girl just like Aruna herself had been, and then she was this magnificent young woman with her own mother's blood now on her cheek, and she reflected with a pang of remorse that she could have done more for her.

And she remembered her village, her house with its thatched roof and open courtyard in the middle, and all the visitors that would come there and seemingly do nothing but gossip all day, and running through the house with her sisters as her father yelled at them, and the torrential rain pouring in through the open roof, or outdoors the heat coming off the sand and the smells of the animals and the dung and the sewage, and taking the bus into town, an absolutely pummeling ride since it had no shock absorbers, to see a movie seated on folding chairs set up on the dirt ground under a tarp in case it rained, and walking to the well every day barefoot for kilometers, or to the one-room mudbrick school with the stained walls where she liked math the best so she was happy to keep going, and she stayed in school longer than most of the other girls in the village who were done at Grade 4 or 6 to go home and learn to be dutiful wives, and her family almost pulled her out in Grade 8, but she stayed all the way to graduation at the insistence of her arranged future husband when he was astoundingly only eighteen years old and he himself defying the wishes of his family by insisting on further education. He was amazingly defiant and headstrong, even as a teenager. And then she was married, and she was seventeen and knew what was going to happen that night and she was frightened but she endured it, got used to it even, and then suddenly she was in a whole other land, to the dismay of their families again, and whom they would now only see every few years for the rest of their lives, and in those days before the internet it was hard to even get them on the phone, and now she was in a place where she couldn't even speak the language despite all her schooling and knew no one, was dropped into a world that was alien in every way, culturally, functionally, technologically, even morally, nothing even like any of those fantastical movies she saw under the tarp or the year they had lived in Bombay, and the displacement was even more frightening than her wedding night. But she could send money home to their parents and her sisters and that's why they were here, and she endured it again, though the homesickness threatened to crush her into powder, and sometimes she prayed, in secret because she knew her husband would disapprove of prayer, and she worked at the nursing home and the grocery store and the library, and then after so long, after the miscarriages, there was the child, an absolute miracle, and there were her own transformations as there always are in life, a life she could never have imagined, and the village girl was sometimes completely unrecognizable to her and sometimes her entire being.

And then she was gone.

Chapter 21
Pralaya

Nandini screamed. She rose off her knees into a hunched position, compressed, and screamed. Then she held her arms and legs out as far as she could and screamed until she went hoarse, and she pulled her arms into her torso as tight as she could and fell to her knees again and sobbed. And she keeled over and covered her face with her hands, her body shuddering as she lay beside her dead mother. Her ears were ringing, everything happening around her sounded much further away. For a time, there was only the sobbing, and she was incapable of thought.

When she started to come out of the red and black darkness, she was conscious that she had become insane. She begged the universe for her mother to not be dead. *Maybe she's not dead*, she forced herself to think. Pathetic. She had seen so many dead bodies tonight, she'd become an expert. *It's a dream.* It was so obviously false. She had even consciously thought, *I'll lie to myself and tell myself it's a dream, maybe it will be true.* She was insane and this whole night had never happened. How could any of it have happened? Somewhere inside her, a brutal rage was building. Surely she was in a padded cell. No, that was too far-fetched. Maybe she really was here at Killarney Lake, but she was hallucinating. Her eyes and ears were not to be trusted. Her mother was alive beside her, it was only a trick of her mind telling her she was dead. She turned to look at her. Her mother said, "It's okay." This is what she forced herself to try to imagine her mother saying. In fact, the body was unmoving and silent, the face still turned away from her.

Come back, come back, come back to me, she begged.

And she sobbed and screamed again and kicked her feet like when she was a newborn infant in bed beside her mother and wouldn't go to sleep.

Nandini had brought Aruna here out of meanness. Her awareness of her own selfishness invaded her mind and was trying to blow it apart. If it wasn't for her petty literary delusions, her mother would be at home watching her shows right now or listening to music or reading her stories, alive. She wailed. She wanted a rewind, a reset. Then, again she felt the fury welling up in her. Suddenly she shifted the blame to the man who had killed her, to all these people here, these subhuman parasites, and the storm churning in her gut pulled her onto her feet, and she shouted to the skies again and she wanted the whole world to end. And somewhere in the back of her mind was her awareness of all the innocents and all the survivors and her friends and whatever decency and beauty there was in the world, all the people who were already victims, and those who had been all their lives, and those whose ancestors had been for generations, and art, and the innocent, and the blameless. And somehow her mother had spared the entire universe from falling prey to Ruby's ludicrous fantasies, and that meant it had deserved or at least earned a second chance, didn't it? Nandini knew even through her blinding mental agony that she had to focus on those things so she did not lose herself completely to both grief and rage at the same time in that moment. But she couldn't, she couldn't. And she wailed at the universe from a depth that abandoned all rational thought.

A single calcium atom in her brain entered a certain synaptic junction in her prefrontal cortex and caused a certain neuron to fire which caused other neurons to activate. In sum total, a decision was made. According to the laws of quantum mechanics, if that first atom was in two different places at the same time, then, some physicists would argue, that means each would have to branch into its own universe. Yet even if that was the case, the fate of *this* universe was sealed.

Something touched her back and she whirled.

It's me, tugging on her shirt. Sally stands beside me, docile and holding my other hand like she's a pet orangutan. And so I give Nandini an Indian head wobble which meant yes or no or "What can you do?" or "It was a fun party". And I raise a hand to the sky, close it, and then Sally and I turn around and step into the portal together. The Coleman Frog clumsily scampers in to join us, apparently coming back to the place where it really belonged all along. Light is pouring into me in constant undulating waves now from all around, a deluge of every visible color. And the world into which I step is now full of lush luxuriant hues, and creatures that had been wizened and skeletal, starved and dying, look to the skies with astonishment and newfound vitality. Then the portal vanished.

Nandini never had the chance to understand what had happened. Nor did anyone else.

For billions of years, the value of the Higgs field in the universe had rested at its lowest possible energy state, with the lowest possible potential, and thanks to this a stable vacuum was possible across every point of space in the universe, and matter could exist. Galaxies could form. Stars, planets, life. However, before stepping into the portal, with a thought, and a dramatic wave of the hand (because Aruna had imagined me as a dramatic being and I had manifested as one), I had forced the value of the Higgs field to quantum tunnel from its current vacuum state into an even lower energy state at all points in the universe simultaneously. There was an unstoppable cascade, the end of existence. Vacuum decay. Everywhere at once the universe plunged into the more stable lower vacuum state in the form of vacuum bubbles that formed at each point in the universe where I had lowered the energy value of the Higgs field.

Initially infinitesimal in size, they expanded into each other at the speed of light. Inside these bubbles, the laws of physics were entirely different, the forces that allowed matter to exist were no more, and matter within them ceased to be.

And so, the instant after the portal to Naraka closed, the entire universe simply blinked out of existence like it had never been there.

Chapter 22
The End

The End

Chapter 23
Sultana's Dream

Rokeya had no idea why she, out of anyone in the world, maybe even the universe, had been chosen over anyone else. Her mother would have said that gods are fickle. But fickle really just meant incomprehensible to a human mind. Rokeya herself didn't believe in any deities, although the intellect that touched her mind in the dark could certainly have been mistaken for a god. The mind of a human compared to the mind of an ant might seem godlike, and in the presence of that unfathomable cosmic intellect anyone would shudder and fall to their knees in worship. Rokeya knew that she was an ant, and that the other mind was something bigger, but that was all. Fickle maybe, but not a god.

But she should not have been able to know or think anything. The world had ended, there was only nothingness, a void, so how was she capable of thought? Not so much thought, but just a sort of feeling or awareness, but even that should not have been possible in the absence of any form of matter to possess that awareness. And yet she *was*, she existed in some way, and another mind, vast and unknowable, touched hers, and she knew without thought what was being offered to her.

Rokeya had read a lot of science fiction, so she had some ideas. She really only wanted two changes to the world.

The first was that at some point in humanity's evolutionary development, empathy would become more strongly written into its DNA than it had in the previous world, that circumstances would somehow make it advantageous for survival or breeding or both, and that the genetic change would hopefully stick. "The fittest" in this world effectively meant "the most social". In Philip K. Dick's *Do Androids Dream of Electric Sheep?* people thought you could tell a human apart from a robot because humans had empathy. No, she'd met plenty of humans with no empathy. In fact, they had ruled the world because of it. Now, the scales had tipped towards cooperation rather than competition. Internal conflict and competition within a species or with other species was often a driving factor in evolution, without it many species would not have evolved into what they are in the first place, but at some stage the human race veered away from that path. The result was respect, kindness, and altruism. People understood that to hurt others was to hurt one's own self. She briefly wondered if this wish made her some sort of eugenicist, but she decided that, considering the alternative, she didn't mind the burden of this sin.

"Do as thou wilt but do no harm" became the central tenet of human life.

The other thing she wanted was a world without money, so she was conscious about that too. It occurred to her that in a world of innate compassion and empathy, money might never come into existence in the first place, but she wanted to be sure. Of course, perhaps she could have just wished the money away and maybe that alone would have tipped all of culture in a more empathetic direction. Well, she wasn't a sociologist, economist, or geneticist, so how could she know?

And then she woke up in a world where people were decent to each other, and where harm to the world in any form was avoided as much as possible because of the hurt it would cause to people, animals, and the world itself. People were free to be true to themselves.

She was a strange outsider here: she had no past, and she was the only one in the world that remembered what the old world was like, as far as she could tell. She woke up in Fredericton (now known as Wolastoq), lying by the lake, and she decided to keep living in that city. Being from Florida, she found the four seasons unique and she liked it.

Quite often, as she did on this day, she borrowed a bike and cycled up to the lake again. She had a favorite spot on the trail where the view of the lake was almost framed by the autumn leaves.

It had been a little more than a year since she awoke in the woods. In terms of world time, it was the equivalent of 2026 in the old world, but now it was called 5132. No one was sure why, though there was a meeting hall built around an obelisk in India that was dated to that many years ago, and some anthropologists argued that there might be a connection, but this link had never been proven, and it remained a mystery. Writing in an ancient language was carved all over the hall, but its meaning was lost.

Everything was free: food, clothing, shelter, education, entertainment, information, experiences, clean water, electricity. Resources were plentiful. There was more than enough for everyone on earth to live in more comfort, even luxury, than they had in the old world. There were enough people in the world to sustainably extract, process, and distribute those resources.

People didn't have to work, but generally they did because they felt their work was enriching to themselves or could be of benefit to others. People went from one job to another as often as they pleased and according to their own interests and strengths, because there was no money and no barriers based on sexism, racism, homophobia, ableism, ageism, or the like. For instance, anyone could pursue medicine or architecture or pearl diving if they pleased and either stay with it or move on to something else. This resulted in some inefficiency since often people were training up for new jobs, but the talent pool was so huge that it was still more efficient than the way things had been in the old world. For bigger jobs, like public works, a sort of guild could be formed, but these too were mostly temporary. For jobs that were considered unpleasant or dangerous in the old world, they were done by everyone, with people being assigned to them in short rotations, and, of course, they were free to refuse it. These jobs were slowly being taken over by robots. But generally people took pride even in mining and grave digging, and the work was respected by their communities and themselves. People exercised their minds and bodies out of kindness to themselves. The more effort they made, the more satisfaction they discovered. She herself had decided to continue with her engineering studies for a while.

The sciences flourished. Thousands of people that would have been obstructed or wholly barred from those fields before, were now free to at least attempt an education in them and often go beyond that to make worthwhile contributions. Because there was no such thing as financial gain, improvements in fields like medicine were never hindered in their discovery or held back when developed.

The arts also thrived. More people than ever at least tried their hand at it. Those who were compelled to make art could make it their entire career for as long as they wished. There was a different quality to it, though, since none of it was born of poverty or strife. It also varied from region to region, as cultures varied, especially in the eras before oceans were crossed, based on what resources were available locally. This also affected clothing, foods, everything. The local nature and wildlife had a shaping effect on poetry and dance and stories.

But in this new world, none of the art had a religious flavor. Down through the millennia, philosophers wondered if the universe might have been created by a conscious being. Since humans, like many species, had evolved to try to detect patterns as a survival mechanism, there may have been an innate pull towards belief in such a being to connect lightning or floods with errors in human judgment. However, none of these ponderings were codified into ritual, because in the old world the motive behind such regulation was exploitation and domination of believers. In this world, that would have been another form of harm. Consciousness was still not understood. Speculating about its nature and the awesome profundity of its emergence was the closest this world got to spirituality.

When cultures did start crossing paths, especially with the dawn of seafaring in the spirit of exploration, they were fair with each other. Resources were plentiful. There was no desire to take more than was rational, and no era of cruelty and destruction. Because of this, Rokeya had expected the population of North America would be maybe sixty percent indigenous, but in fact there had been so much interbreeding and cross-cultural pollination, that many people tended to be more similar than different. Still, the difference had bred richness. She was a pale stranger among them.

When things were taken out of the earth, people tried to pay it back in some way. Foresting was much more limited and managed than it had been in the old world, but it didn't matter because there was more than enough anyway. People cultivated the Earth, they did not exploit it for more than was needed. Almost everything was reused, even more so as new technologies were developed. If something couldn't be reused or recycled, it was generally shunned. As plastics were invented, their exploitation was delayed until ways could be found to make sure they were biodegradable if not at least completely reusable. With all the people working in the sciences, solar, wind, and tidal power were developed and adopted early. Even human waste was used to produce methane gas. People avoided producing waste. There was no island of plastic bottles in the Pacific. There wasn't even litter, and people didn't leave behind messes for others to clean up. People were thinking about other people.

They were thinking about the planet and the other creatures on it too. It was understood that to hurt nature was to hurt other people and oneself. Animals killed and ate other animals, and humans still did too. In the Pleistocene epoch, Neanderthals and early humans had a small amount of meat from hunting, but most of their food came from gathering. In the modern era, there was hunting with modern compound bows and knives, and every part of an animal killed was used down to its bones, but artificial meat was prevalent, a human endeavor even larger than the meat industry had been in the previous world.

Actually, there was a third thing Rokeya had thought to include in this world, something so minor that it slipped her mind most of the time. She had learned from all that science fiction that there was no such thing as a true utopia, there was always a dark side. So she had brought back President Ruby to her Omelas. Like her when she was in the darkness, he had been transported into a universe in which his matter could not exist and had been blown into oblivion. However, now he was chained, naked and immortal, at the bottom of the human waste processing plant of Manna-hata (known as New York in the old world), with his mouth and eyes clamped open.

Her grandmother used to tell her the story of "The Fisherman and the Jinni". This was the story that originated the idea of genies granting three wishes. That was another reason she chose to declare that the cosmic intellect that made contact with her mind was not a god, but a shapeshifting being on the same plane as her.

Without money, there was almost no crime, but there was still some. As ever, not everyone was the same. There was genetic variation. Some people were less compassionate than others. For some, their empathy was overwhelmed by other factors. Or, in some cases, the culprit did not realize that their actions were damaging. In many if not most cases, the perpetrator felt remorse and wanted to take responsibility for the act, and an atonement would be worked out between the culprit, the victim, and an arbitrator. If they didn't mean to do it, then their community would try to heal them. If there was a chemical imbalance, then that could often be treated too. Sometimes there were still people who wanted to exert power over others, to rule over and dominate them. This was considered a mental illness like any other, and there was no stigma attached to it, but it was treated with therapy.

Humanity's violent origins were no secret. The evidence was there in the fossil record, in the gashes found in Neanderthal bones, and one could see the behavior of animals. There was an era in which a tribe coming over a hill that looked or acted different to one's own in any way would have been a threat. But it was a point of pride that they had literally evolved beyond that.

However, some people feared attacks from the animal kingdom. Some people even hypothesized about attacks by space aliens, if such a thing existed. Rokeya wondered: if there was life on other planets, was it all exactly the same as it had been before? Was only Earth affected? In any case, these speculators felt that humankind ought to learn to be more aggressive, like the animals were, or their ancient ancestors. There was some agreement, but most people prioritized their efforts into an asteroid defense system or figuring out how to survive the next ice age.

Government was minimal, it was mostly just administration, but what government there was, was handled by sortition. Public officials and jurors were chosen by random lottery. The jury would listen to an informed debate and then vote on a decision, after which the jury would be disbanded. It was virtually impossible to sway the government beforehand since no one knew who the jurors would be, and they would not vote in special privileges for the institution of the jury itself, since the members were only ever temporary. The jurors would immediately return to their communities as ordinary members, so they voted to benefit the ordinary members of those communities.

Otherwise, people were essentially in charge of governing themselves. They were responsible for their own lives. An individual's judgment was interfered with as sparingly as possible. On an individual level, without a hierarchy to settle into, one had to think for oneself, so it was harder in some sense, but it was better.

One's body was inviolable, subject to one's own will alone.

The children were everyone's children, all of one family.

People could speak to each other without shame or judgment.

Of course, it could not last forever. Nothing ever

did. And out there in the wilds, the skies, the oceans, the mallards were still being rapists, the seals were beating their mates, the anglerfish were parasitically codependent.

She thought about the old world sometimes. *Couldn't those people ever figure out that life is just easier when you're decent to people?* she wondered. There was one odd thing here though. The music everyone seemed to care most about was Scandinavian black metal. It was so weird. *What the fuck is that about?!*

Oh, well, she thought, *that hardly matters.* Life was usually sweet, and it was still sometimes hard. But it was fair.

When she got to her spot, the lake was molten silver and almost blinding in its scintillation between the red and orange leaves. The air was delicious.

Yes, life really is good, she thought as she looked out across the lake.

For everyone.

www.ingramcontent.com/pod-product-compliance
Lightning Source LLC
LaVergne TN
LVHW041619060526
838200LV00040B/1343